W•CLARK
PUBLISHING

A Life For A Life

A Novel By

Mike Jefferies

Wahida Clark Presents Publishing, LLC
60 Evergreen Place
Suite 904
East Orange, New Jersey 07018
973-678-9982
www.wclarkpublishing.com

ISBN 13-digit 978-0-982841457
ISBN 10-digit 0982841450

Library of Congress Catalog Number 2011924181
1. Urban, African-American, Hip-Hop, Atlanta, New Orleans, New York, Music Industry, Street Lit – Fiction

Cover design and layout by Oddball Design
Book interior design by Nuance_Art.*.
Contributing Editors: Linda Wilson, VIP Editing, Intelligent Allah and Rosalind Hamilton

Printed in United States
Green & Company Printing., LLC
www.greenandcompany.biz

Dedication

This jewel, this long effort is dedicated to Paris Love, Lil Mike and Komicia Jefferies. Y'all are the best children God has ever brought into my life. Every day I wake up, y'all are my motivation. My love will always remain unconditional under any circumstance. Never forget that Daddy loves you.

A special "thanks" goes to you, Towanna. For always remembering the things that everyone else forgot. Damn, ma, I never thought it would be you who'd connect all my dots. And you did it from the heart. You didn't owe me a thing! I also know this journey has been long and hard, but look what we discovered! It's like potato chips to me, too (smile). I got your back, baby. I love you, always.

A Word with the Author

First of all I'd like to thank you for your support. I hope you enjoyed *A Life for a Life* as much as I enjoyed writing it. This novel was my first contribution to Hip-Hop Fiction. I categorize it as such because of its strong Hip-Hop underpinnings. It also turned out to be some of my most fun writing yet, and you can look forward to the plot thickening and moving even faster in Part 2: *The Ultimate Reality.*

With every tale I give my best effort to stay fluid with my style of writing. There are so many aspects of urban life, and with my extraordinary experiences and wild imagination, I plan to explore lots of them with you. I choose subject matter that I find relevant and entertaining. I want all of my books to be a different journey, but all within urban life. I hope to capture your imagination in fun ways, for years to come.

Be on the lookout for upcoming Mike Jefferies releases. I look forward to all of your reviews and e-mail. Get at me and get at WCP with your feedback. Until we unite for a word with the author again, stay up. One . . .

To write the author
Send mail to:
C/O Mike Jefferies Fan Club
60 Evergreen Place
Suite 904
East Orange, NJ 07018
Also visit my fan page on Facebook, *Michael Jefferies.*

Chapter One

Toney Domacio

"What the fuck is this all about?" Toney Domacio huffed with urgency in his tone. He sat up straight and fingered the gold-rimmed Armani glasses back over the bridge of his nose as he spotted what could soon be danger nearing. He glanced to his right as his most trustworthy henchman gave a smooth signal to place the other soldiers on alert, then lifted his cup to his mouth and whispered, "It's about to go down . . . The GDs made the call and they're ready to move."

Toney nodded his head and raised his cup to conceal his lips from being read before he spoke, "Is it Damu or Peru they're going after?" His eyes traipsed across the chow hall as he spotted two of the GD's fiercest knife pushers walk over to Jet, their lieutenant with deadly scowls painted on their faces. They were wearing heavy brown coats, but it was mid-summer, and Toney knew what that meant.

"Neither or . . ." his henchman reported. "It's a young black guy here. He got into a pretty deep debt gambling on a table ran by Bloods, but before the Bloods could move on him and collect the debt the GDs stepped in and paid the tab. He played on their basketball team for a while, but now he refuses to play or pay back the debt they cleaned up. He's a hell of a soldier and they want him down, but he refuses to affiliate with GDs in order to make good. He says the Bloods cheated him and he never asked anyone to step up for him. So basically, it's just their loss."

"So who's he down with?" Toney whispered before sitting his cup back down.

"Nobody. He's a vigilante."

"Nobody?" Toney belched out in disbelief. He knew this was a definite no-no in prison.

He sat in silence as he contemplated and waited for the next move to be played out. Glancing to his left he saw a table full of GDs. They were all young, black and sitting on life sentences or something very close to it. To his right was a table occupied by the Texas Syndicate, fierce looking Latinos wearing khaki shirts heavily starched and pressed, with only the top button fastened to expose their crisp white T-shirts underneath. Their full body tattoos protruded from their necklines and some even spread onto their faces. He looked just a few tables ahead of him at the Aryan Nation and the Dirty White Boys settled at their tables, and then out to the pools of blacks.

Bloods, Crips, Vice Lords, all the way down to Sunni Muslims and the neatly dressed Nation of Islam were present. Both North and South Carolina as well as the Georgia and Florida Boys had pulled together to form sizeable cliques for the non-affiliated.

Lewisburg was one of the oldest and roughest penitentiaries built in the early 1900s in Pennsylvania. A cemetery made of cinder block and barbed wire that very few men actually made it out of. It was for certain that a man had to have an allegiance to something because at the time of inevitable prison war that allegiance would be all he had.

With respect not only being a virtue but also the main ingredient, it wasn't unusual to see this many killers and gangsters in one place without being killed. As long as you minded your business and led with respect, a man could be a man. But today the atmosphere in Lewisburg Penitentiary was thick.

An eerie silence blanketed the room as the men ate. There was no laughter or idle chit-chat. Only the clanking sounds of metal forks hitting the trays as a few men ate, disregarded their trays then vanished.

"He's from North Carolina, just a young, dumb scavenger nigger with a minute to pray and a second to die. He ain't gonna last. Stick with ya own. Reality will soon be his," his man spoke up again.

Toney just nodded his head at the truth of his henchman's words.

'Stick with ya own' was an unwritten rule in all penitentiaries across the land. Toney knew all the rules, all too well. Plus he rarely dealt with blacks. It had to be extreme circumstances or the potential financial stakes were set very high.

Getting mixed up in this wasn't an option. No, at fifty-two years of age Toney was happy to still be surrounded by many of his trustworthy and loyal Dominican friends. Friends who'd die to protect his legacy. Men who still regarded him as the once King of Spanish Harlem. For nearly thirty years Toney had led with an iron fist. And although many of his crimes had been major, so had the contributions he gave back to his community.

He still had smooth olive skin and a head full of shiny black hair that he kept trimmed short and neat. The only signs of aging were the fine gray streaks near his temples. His trademark gold-rimmed Armani glasses gave him a distinguished look. And even wearing starched khakis and steel-toe prison boots, Toney still looked like cash money. His aura seemed to command respect. Although he was now serving a life sentence for his leadership role in the Domacio Crime Family, he knew he'd always be regarded as special.

The federal government had charged him with the RICO Act, which is the racketeering charge used to indict mob figures. They followed it up with another statute called Continuous Criminal Enterprise (CCE). These statues normally followed each other and the government rarely lost its case. Toney never really stood a chance at trial and his final verdict was swayed by his dark reputation and the string of unsolved murders that pointed directly back to him.

With his mind easily settled on the matter at hand, Toney huffed lightly and stood to his feet. He casually retucked his shirt back into his pants to stop his middle aged belly from slightly protruding over his belt.

With a calm wave of his powerful hand he said, "Let's move." In mere seconds Toney was flanked by his crew. He watched the two GDs exit the chow hall as several others came in. He'd decided to get away from the thickening atmosphere. Toney led his crew out of the cafeteria and into the busy hallway with the herds of other inmates scurrying to their destinations. His crew was enroute to the chapel where Toney held a fictitious job assignment that served as a drop point for corrupt officers to deliver him porno books, narcotics and everything he needed to keep him comfortable and relevant while at Lewisburg.

With the GDs now out of earshot, Toney and his closest henchman chatted until they reached the outside walk. It was there that Toney looked up and saw the huge rows of serpentine wire at the top of the twelve-foot fences, and even more rows of razor wire on the grounds that filled the space leading to the next fence. Gazing up, he spotted an armed guard sitting high in the cement gun tower, ready to kill anyone foolish enough to try to escape.

Toney often dreamed about the day he would be released, but he knew there was no way out for him. So all he could do was make the best of it and try to give his family the best advice to stop them from being subjected to imprisonment as well, and that was to always play the game raw. Toney also gave everybody he knew the jewels to beat the Feds. His advice was again, "Play the game raw. Win by any means necessary, and leave no evidence or witnesses for the Feds to manipulate."

Toney's short, unattainable dream was broken as he climbed the stairs to the chapel. His men opened the doors and moved in first. In the midst of hundreds of inmates, Toney hadn't noticed the two GDs as they had quickly slipped in before him. Had he noticed, he would have simply asked them to move their business elsewhere. Every shot caller on the prison yard respected Toney's wishes, except Sunni Muslims and the Nation of Islam community because they cared nothing about the drugs he infested the penitentiary with.

The two young men moved swiftly toward the young black man who had his back turned as he pulled a book from high off the wall shelf. The first GD moved fast, reaching in his coat and pulling from his waistline a belt with a steel combination lock tightly tied to the end. Toney's eyes quickly recognized the head of the sharp knife as the other GD let it slide down the sleeve of his coat. It slid out until his fist firmly gripped the handle, which was made of beige masking tape. He held the knife close to his side as he approached the man, who was totally unaware that his moment of crucifixion was here.

As soon as he was close enough, the first young disciple swung the belt and lock with all his strength. The unexpected lick came across the young man's back and neck area. The painful blow immediately thrust him forward into the bookshelf, causing all the books to collapse on his head.

As his young mind raced to gain composure, the other young disciple moved in even faster. With one swift motion, he swung the sharp shank as if it were a sword. The shank ripped through the man's shirt and embedded in his shoulder before the GD

LIFE 5

dragged the sharp blade across his back all the way to his hip bone. The young man screamed out in sheer pain as he fell to the ground kicking and squirming away in a panic-stricken attack.

The hard blows from the lock continued to pound his legs and back as the young man rushed to get back on his feet. As he rose, Toney saw him struggle to pull out what seemed to be a knife made from hard fiberglass material. With haste he lunged forward at the disciple who held the metal shank.

In a flash, he stabbed the knife into his gut and pushed all of his weight against him. The young GD's eyes widened as he gasped his last breath and dropped his bloody shank to the floor. Blood rushed from the gaping hole in his stomach. The young man pulled the knife out and then stabbed him three more times as the other assailant stared on in shock at the sudden turn of events.

The young man shoved the GD's mangled body to the floor then charged at the other. Toney saw the fire in his eyes, the look of a killer, that all-too familiar look that his own eyes had once possessed. The moment the young man gained his composure, he moved with the intensity and control of a natural born killer.

The Disciple swung the lock desperately in order to protect himself, but the young man ducked the blow and moved away swiftly. When he rose, his feet were firmly planted right in front of his opponent with his shank stuck in his gut the same way. He twisted the knife, yanked it out, and then stabbed him again with his right hand, while his left arm simultaneously wrapped around the GD's back and pulled him even closer, almost in a bear hug. Their eyes met as they were now face to face. The young man fearlessly stared into the eyes of the gangster who had come to kill him.

"If I die, you comin' wit' me! See you in hell, bitch!" He spat a saliva and blood mixture in the man's face just before his own weakened body collapsed to the floor from the sudden loss of blood. The GD collapsed the moment he let him go.

With a stern glare Toney turned and gave orders to his men. "Get the young one up. Take him to the spot. I want Doc to fix him up."

His men looked puzzled, but by the look on Toney's face they quickly did just as told. They all knew that with this decision, Toney was now responsible for his actions and his debts. But most of all he'd have to use his highest influence to cover up this mess and to squash this beef.

Mike Jefferies

8

Chapter Two

Drako

Some of the smartest and realest men I have ever met, I met within the walls of this federal prison. Here, they breathed a new life, hope, and opened my eyes to true 'reality.' From this day forward, I'll never look back, nor come back—alive! I put dat on Diamond!

Drako felt a new surge of energy and strength as he penned his latest entry into his small notepad. Over the eight years he had been incarcerated, Drako kept up with all the highlights of prison, jewels he learned to live by, all the deaths that had occurred, and all the wonderful things he wanted to do for Diamond when he got out because she was the only woman he'd ever truly loved.

Drako was now twenty-nine years old, and the years of incarceration had preserved him; he didn't look a day over twenty-three. His six foot, two-hundred pound frame was chiseled like an ice sculpture. He was not of huge mass, yet lean and buff, a Roy Jones Jr. styled physique, with smooth dark skin that had to be attributed to his good eating habits.

For the last six years, Drako had been a vegetarian and only drank water. He ran four miles a day and worked out vigorously to keep his body in top physical condition and maintain his youthful appearance. Yet his youth slowly but surely slipped by him each day he was still locked away.

After stashing his personal notes under his mattress, Drako got down on the floor in the tiny confines of his cell and began to do push-ups. He would do perfect sets of fifty until his shirtless body dripped with sweat. He'd get up after each set and take the small eight-foot pace from the door back to the wall where a blurry sheet of steel served as a mirror, which sat above the small porcelain sink. To the left was the toilet, and to the right were two bunk beds.

Drako would watch his chest muscles swell up and the veins in his biceps come alive as he flexed and admired his body. He squeezed his stomach and counted the deep outline of all six muscles; this gave him self-gratification. The mean grit he always held became a fleeting smile just before he got back down to do another set.

Toney lay on the bottom bunk and looked on as his cellmate, Drako, exerted this kind of energy every night. Toney knew that Drako was as physically fit as humanly possible, but he also knew this was not just physical for Drako; it was mental. It was Drako's form of meditating as well as venting pent up frustrations.

Toney had observed Drako the day he entered the penal system. Drako was young, wild, and out of control. But most of all he was bitter inside.

Eight years ago, Drako was only expected to have survived one year in prison, but he was smart. Although he was wild, he possessed the heart of a lion and the fists of a gladiator. And was true to whomever he was down with.

A Life for A Life

Toney looked at the long cut Doc had sewn up on Drako's back years ago to keep prison officials unaware. It was on that unforgettable day when Toney recognized Drako had that royal glow in his eyes. He knew Drako was loyal, but had simply been misled.

Since that day, the only wrong Drako had done in Toney's eyes was when he had the word 'Reality' tattooed above that terrible scar. Toney felt like he glorified it by marking his body up. Toney also knew that day had been Drako's wake-up call. Toney had many other inmates patched up, but none had an impact on him like Drako.

Inwardly, Toney chuckled at how proud he was of Drako. They had now been cellmates almost eight years, and though Drako had a dark soul, he also had the skill set to become a criminal mastermind, thanks to Toney's influence. He didn't just teach Drako penitentiary survival, he taught him respect and how to get it, and he expanded his mind to the meaning of real money as he explained the benefits and complexities of white collar schemes. Drako took classes in accounting, marketing, and business management. Toncy made him read books on word empowerment and take classes such as toast masters so that he could learn to speak properly in any setting.

Drako was in awe of Toney as he saw the influence and power he had in the underworld and even in prison. He loved the way Toney spoke and people listened. In any other case, the GDs would have killed him eight years ago for what he'd done to the two GDs. But with just a few words and gifts of narcotics, Toney made it all disappear. The late night stories that Toney shared made Drako want to be just like Toney, but without the misfortune of getting caught.

Drako absorbed all he could and passed the information he learned inside to his only real friend left on the streets, Wiz. Wiz had dabbled in the dope game with Drako as childhood friends,

but had quit. After Drako got busted, Wiz took what money Drako had left and fled North Carolina, going back to his native, New Orleans. He used Drako's money to upstart his long-term dream—an independent record label. He used the rest of the money to make sure Drako and Diamond were okay.

The only love Drako had left in his heart was for Diamond, Toney, and Wiz. No one else mattered. Toney kept Drako's spirits alive in prison, and his only other love was the love letters he received from Diamond, and the money and pictures of how good things were going for Wiz and Red Rum Records.

He grunted as he pushed out the last set of his repetitions. He got to his feet and paced back to the mirror. Grabbing the towel from the sink, he dabbed sweat from his shiny baldhead as he once again admired his body. Drako turned to Toney as he flexed his chest. "Can you tell I'm gettin' bigger?" he asked.

Toney smiled. "You've asked that same dumb ass question almost every night for the last eight years. You know damn well you can't get no bigger. Besides, stop worrying about that. That's not what's gonna keep you on top."

With a cocky smirk on his face, Drako sucked his teeth and said, "I know, but I may have to get in a video and let these cats see just how real this shit is. I 'on know why they don't believe Wiz is gonna embrace me, but they'll see when I get in the business."

Toney sat up, the smile vanishing from his face. "What did I tell you?" he yelled. "Fuck what people think! You *want* them to disassociate you! Stay the fuck away from them cameras! You take your job as head of security for now. Focus on finding your own lane and stay out of the limelight. I've instructed Damien to help Wiz in all affairs. Wiz will be fine."

Toney's response stunned Drako. "But I . . . I—"

"But shit!" Toney wouldn't let up. "Drako, I've shown you the way. Get your own money regardless of what Wiz has. When it comes down to it, Wiz's money is *Wiz's* money. You'll soon be standing next to one of the biggest names in the music industry. Learn what you can. Take what you can from it, but be your own man! I have given you Damien, my most trustworthy consigliere—now use him! Invest wisely and hide the money always. Place your interest in service businesses; you only have to pay Mexicans spit to work for you. Invest in low attention real estate—*lots* of it."

"I know. I gotcha, man. I've been listening. Don't get bent outta shape. I know my days will be hands on with Wiz, but I won't let it make me lose focus. Now, I only got two weeks left in this hellhole, so tonight let's catch up on Vinny Pazo. I'm ready to make that bastard sip Red Rum," Drako said with a sinister grin.

Toney smiled again, loving the sound of 'Red Rum.' Its meaning was 'murder' spelled backwards. He had given the name to Drako for Wiz to name the record label.

Toney lay back down as Drako turned the lights off, and then climbed back onto the top bunk. They began to go over everything in whispered tones as they had rehearsed so many nights. Toney had Damien and his crew closely watching Vinny Pazo for years, and there was only one way to catch him.

Vinny was seventy-one years old now, an Italian mobster who used Toney, and then threw him away after years of doing business. He gave Toney away as a trade to keep himself out of prison. Vinny used his political influences and his dirty ties with the New York Police Department (NYPD) to cover up his involvement in the case. Toney knew it could have only been Vinny's work because the things they knew only Vinny could have told. Vinny never would have given up an Italian without getting killed, but Toney was Dominican and replaceable. Reality became his in the harshest way—a life sentence.

Toney never forgot faces or places, or anything else for that matter. Little did Vinny know that Toney remembered the safe house that Vinny had in Aspen, Colorado. It had been twenty years ago in idle conversation when Vinny revealed to Toney that every anniversary he and his wife visited the hideaway. Every year since Toney's incarceration, Damien made sure that date was met, and the couple was always unguarded.

That thought gave Toney a full-blown erection because he was a good judge of character and knew Drako would handle his business. Drako would kill Vinny and many more bodies would follow. He had taught Drako business and the workings of the underworld. He taught him that after he used people in the underworld to dispose of all traces— "Get a couple mil', then kill; play the game raw!" Drako was ready. Murder was only business in his young mind. Never personal. It was just a necessity to stay on top.

After talking into the late night hours, Toney fell asleep knowing that if he never got freedom again, he'd soon experience the next best thing—revenge!

Drako fell asleep knowing that in just thirteen days he'd be holding Diamond in his arms again. He had plans to eventually be a part of the music industry with Wiz. But he also had plans to keep his word to Toney. He was ready for millions and to give Diamond everything she had ever wished for.

Drako knew he was going to win because he was about to play the game the right way, the only way; RAW.

Chapter Three

Diamond

"Oh yes . . . oh yes . . . mmm . . . mmm . . . mmmmmmm."
Sounds of pleasure escaped Diamond's lips as her hips gyrated.
Diamond's eyes were shut tight as she rubbed her middle finger
back and forth over her clit. She could feel the orgasm building
up as her lover pushed all ten-inches of chocolate man meat into
her tightness. "Oh yes, oh yes! I love you, baby!" she moaned,
feeling his warm hands squeeze all over her soft body. She could
feel his tongue flick over her hardened nipples and then slither
into her mouth as they made love. Her legs spread as her climax
neared. Just as Diamond was ready to tell her lover, "Oh, Drako,
I love you," she felt an unfamiliar hand caressing her breasts and
an unfamiliar tongue slid into her ear. But she realized this lover
wasn't Drako.

Diamond suddenly awoke, sweating in a panic, only to
recognize the heavyset, bull-dyking bitch, Bobbi, trying to ease
her way into her bunk. Diamond hopped out of bed.

"Get away from me, you butchy bitch!" she yelled. Bobbi
jumped to her feet and began to chase Diamond around the bed.

"Come on, Diamond, you know how much I want to taste
you," she begged in a supposedly sexy tone.

The thought disgusted Diamond. "Bitch, stay away from me!
I don't go that way. I'm strictly dickly!" Diamond pounced

across the bed putting more space between them as she continued to back pedal around the bed and fumble her tittie back into her bra.

Those words angered the two-hundred pound Bobbi, who wore a short Caesar haircut like a man. There were no feminine traits about her.

"What the fuck you say? Bitch, I been puttin' up wit' yo' prissy ass for way too long! And now you tryna' play me like you ain't gone gimme a taste 'fore you leave? You best relax 'cause you 'bout to really make me hurt you!"

Diamond looked at Bobbi as they played chase around the bed. Bobbi looked scary and had a terrible resume for raping newcomers and girls without heart. Diamond had made it eight years, and today was no day for a fresh turnout.

Diamond thought fast. "Wait!" she pleaded.

Bobbi seemed to relax as a smile bloomed across her manly face. She could tell that Diamond would rather get her pussy licked than to go home all beat the fuck up.

Diamond dropped her head to the floor as she twiddled her fingers. She timidly made her way around the bed toward Bobbi. Bobbi smiled and then licked her lips with anticipation.

When Diamond reached the head of the bed, she reached under the pillow and snatched out a toothbrush with razor blades melted firmly in place where the bristles once were. Bobbi's eyes widened with terror. Diamond charged at her and Bobbi's fat ass quickly turned to run. Diamond chased behind her. "Bitch, I'm gonna kill your fat, nasty ass before I leave!"

Stricken with fear, Bobbi screamed, "Help! Help!" to alert the guards in hopes of stopping Diamond. But Diamond continued to chase her through the dormitory, yelling and waking the other inmates. Bobbi was out of breath when she finally reached the officer's desk, but Diamond was right on her heels.

A Life for A Life

Diamond had dropped the razor before reaching the desk; she knew being caught with the razor would extend her time. She also realized that Bobbi was 'big for nothin', and her wolf tickets were for sale—only to the heartless.

Diamond was a chameleon, as she had fooled Bobbi into letting her get close to the razor. Drako had long ago taught her to sort through signs of weakness, to fight and to never back down.

She ran straight into the officer's station and clawed Bobbi, digging her long fingernails deep into her face, and ripping away her flesh. The white meat showed first; blood came rushing out right behind it. Bobbi yelled out in pain as she bent over holding her bloody face. Diamond roughly kicked her in the stomach, knocking all the wind from her lungs. Then she tried to finish with a flurry of blows to Bobbi's head, before the guards quickly contained them both. Kicking and flailing wildly, she screamed repeatedly, "That bitch tried to rape me!"

The officers were well aware of Bobbi's reputation. They took Bobbi to the prison infirmary and later placed her in segregation for the eighth time on the same charges.

Diamond was all too tired of prison life; she had been in Alderson, West Virginia Federal Prison Camp (FPC), for five years after she had been shipped from Tallahassee, Florida, for cutting another dyke bitch's face for the same shit.

Often she relived that night through the same recurring dream; it was a horrid nightmare about the time in Tallahassee FPC. She awoke to find herself pinned to her bunk by three women while another dyke bitch licked her pussy. Diamond tried to scream, but her cries were quickly muffled by the heavy hand that smothered her mouth. Tears of pain and rage trickled from her eyes as she felt the huge makeshift strap-on dildo invade her over and over again. The ordeal left Diamond traumatized, but as soon as she gathered the first strands of composure she retaliated with a fury that no one ever anticipated. She ran up and sliced a

line straight down the face of the most feared predator in the whole prison for all to see. The thoughts of what had happened repulsed Diamond and she vowed to never allow anyone to violate her in that way again. Up until that very moment, and mainly because of the way she looked, no one would have ever believed Diamond had the heart or courage to do what she did, but from that day forward her prison legacy was born.

Diamond had to be the most beautiful girl in prison, standing five-foot-five-inches and a curvaceous one-hundred-twenty-five pounds. She had a firm, round ass, tight abs and perky breasts. She had never bore kids, and at age twenty-six it showed. Diamond's mother was as white as snow, but her mysterious father had to be black because his dominant genes gave her skin a golden hue. She had the hair, complexion, and cheery smile of Mariah Carey. These attributes made her loved by men, hated by insecure women, and lusted after by lesbians in prison.

Diamond returned to her section, pulled her soft hair into a ponytail, and fixed herself up, washing away the sweat and dried tears from her face. After climbing back into her bunk, Diamond pulled the blanket over her head and began to weep. Although her days in prison were coming to an end, it felt like the last days were now her worst days. They came slow and hard.

Praying that this would be her last altercation, she began to toss and turn in hopes of another sweet dream about Drako. As far as a lover, he was all she knew. They'd met as orphans in a group home when she was fourteen and became lovers shortly after. In her eyes he'd been her everything and all she prayed for now was better days with him again. Diamond sniffled and muffled her cries as best she could. She wasn't certain what she was going to do upon her release. She knew she could rap a little, but she could sing very well. She knew Drako now had big dreams and somehow he and Wiz would bring them all together. Their lives would surely be in the fast lane of Wiz's accomplishments. Being with Drako was her first priority, but she held small hopes of one day taking a chance with her voice. She knew prison was no place for a woman. Just the thought of ever returning caused her to shiver. *Oh God, just thirteen more days,* she prayed as she pulled the wool blanket tighter and closed her eyes again.

Mike Jefferies

20

Chapter Four

Wiz

On a warm spring day in April, two blocks of Peachtree Street in Downtown Atlanta had been blocked off. At least two hundred hip-hop fans were patiently waiting behind the wooden police barriers and the security team.

Today was the video shoot for one of ATL's hottest new rappers, Trek. He had hella cameo appearances from other artists scheduled, and fans came out in herds to get a look. This video was sure to be hot because it featured Red Rum's most lyrical assassin and CEO. The Street Kings had joined together and were ready to rip up the mics.

The crowd's roar grew louder as they watched Atlanta police officers move the barrier to allow entry of a huge black Hummer with at least twenty-six-inch chromed out wheels.

The huge truck with dark tinted windows pulled up fast and parked. No one got out. All the fans wondered who could be inside. About thirty seconds later, a shiny ocean blue Aston Martin DBS gained entry at the barrier; another black Hummer followed it. The deep blue paint flickered so beautifully under the sun's rays, as the DBS came to an abrupt stop.

Two large men dressed in suits, wearing headsets immediately got out of the first Hummer and stood in front of the foreign whip. The crowd quickly realized they were security. The driver's door opened and one crisp, white, Air Force One touched the pavement. The sports car was fit for a giant, but when Wiz stepped out, he only stood five feet six inches tall. Though short in stature, everything Wiz did, he did in the biggest way. He was the same height and weight of Jermaine Dupri, and within five years of working at Red Rum, their bank accounts almost weighed the same. Red Rum Records was reported to be worth over $100 million strong. Wiz was a street genius, and he did just as his mentors Baby, Puffy, Russell Simmons, and Master P had done. He took Black culture, used his brains, and made what black people have always deserved his *reality*.

"Wiz! Wiz!" the groupies yelled. "I love you, Wiz!" He smiled as he got out and waved to the crowd, all too used to the fame, groupie love, and everything that came with it.

After Drako had left, Wiz did it all legit and never dabbled again. He only used marketing strategies that Drako gave him and he used Damien to reach important figures in the industry where his voice was once inaudible.

Wiz moved with his bodyguards toward the set, stopping so professionally and politely to show his fans love. Flashing his platinum smile as they took pictures, Wiz looked hip-hop immaculate. He had on enough ice to freeze an Eskimo near the North Pole. His quarter million dollar diamond necklace was set in platinum, and so was his custom diamond watch.

Wiz's hair was braided and parted neatly, sixteen cornrows to the back. He always wore his signature ten carat earrings, which bulged like golf balls from his ears. Over his smooth brown skin that gave him a young, handsome and boyish look, he wore his signature platinum Cartier frames.

Wiz had given the fans their moment, which his arrogant ass seemed to enjoy more than they. He knew he was standing at the top of his game. Once on the set, he went straight to the director and got instructions on his cameo appearance.

All the beautiful video girls were in place, all clad in the tiniest bikinis and shorts. He looked over at the green screen and saw Myria posing for the cameras. All the other girls were standing around the set. Myria was the featured girl standing in front of the green screen alone. Wiz smiled because he had gotten her the lead role, and she was surely earning her place in the video industry. Wiz got into place and did all his cameo shots within two takes like a video vet in front of the lens. The next few hours were spent mingling with video girls, groupies, and signing autographs for the kids who waited behind the security lines.

Wiz seemed to glow that day, and everyone knew how much love was in the air when the south united, but that was not the only reason for Wiz to be happy. In one week he'd be sending a limo to bring Drako and Diamond home. Wiz knew he owed Drako for allowing him the opportunity to stay free and conquer his dream. Drako could have easily implicated Wiz into that conspiracy, which had cost Drako and Diamond both ten-year federal sentences.

For a long time after Drako was incarcerated, Wiz often reflected back to that day. He could never forget the perplexed look on Drako's face as he and Diamond exited Douglas International Airport in Charlotte, North Carolina. Wiz was supposed to have picked them up after they had made the successful trip back from Miami, Florida like so many other times.

Wiz had pulled his '87 Maxima up to the baggage claim as usual, but when Drako came out, he continued to walk right past the Maxima. Diamond nonchalantly rubbed her hand across her chest from left to right; it was their signal that something was wrong. Wiz watched their pace quicken as they approached one of the waiting cabs in hopes of a clean getaway.

Silently, Wiz prayed that his premonition had missed. The moment Diamond opened the back door of the cab and threw her Louis Vuitton bag in the back seat, Wiz's intuition became his reality. He realized Federal agents were strategically placed everywhere as they began to rise from their slouched positions in unmarked cars. When the man posing as a baggage handler opened his jacket in order to pull his gun, Wiz spotted the police badge secured to his waist.

His heart raced with panic, because he had never foreseen this part of the game. All he anticipated was the quick cash. Looking back at Diamond and Drako as they got into the cab, Diamond lunged forward and pushed what looked like a gun into the cab driver's neck. Wiz could read her lips as she demanded the cab driver to go. The tires made a loud screeching sound as the cab quickly pulled off, but only made it about one hundred yards before it was sideswiped by an unmarked police car. U.S. Customs agents and D.E.A. agents instantly swarmed the cab with their guns drawn. What had supposedly been the last sweet lick for Wiz had without warning become his nightmare. Wiz didn't know what to do. He just knew that he'd be arrested next. Putting the Maxima in drive, Wiz drove at a normal speed straight past the arrest. He saw agents pull Diamond and Drako from the cab and lay them on the pavement at gunpoint. Neither one of them looked up as Wiz slowly cruised past.

Watching in his rearview mirror as they roughly handled Diamond back to her feet and put her into the police car, Wiz's mind was blank. His heart beat fast, and sweat beaded his forehead as he got closer and closer to the expressway. The moment Wiz got on the expressway he drove directly to his and Drako's house.

A Life for A Life

Wiz knew where all the money was kept and quickly gathered all the stashes. There was almost $150,000 in cash; the jewels were mediocre. Gathering all the guns, he went back out the door and stopped at the first dumpster he saw and discarded them. Once he got back on the expressway he headed for home, back to New Orleans.

The traumatic blow took the life out of Wiz. He'd lost his best friend, and didn't know if he'd be indicted next. All Wiz knew was that what he had just seen was enough to make him know the dope game wasn't for him. He cried real tears and vowed to never hustle again, and prayed that if he made it through this one he'd make what he knew best work for him. He could make hot tracks, spit gangster lyrics, and he understood the business. Wiz was smart; that's how he got his name. He was a cool nerd, a bookworm who knew how to incorporate everything, which is why Drako hipped him to the dope game. They worked well together with Drako being the muscle and Wiz being the silent brain. But from that point on, the only dope game for him would be lived vicariously through his rhymes.

It was almost a year before Drako felt safe enough to contact Wiz through the mail. Once Drako received a money order in the County jail with a Baton Rouge, Louisiana address, he knew exactly where to write Wiz when the time was right. Once they did establish contact, Drako had informed Wiz that the moment they got their bags from the baggage claim, Diamond realized they had been tagged, and it was only a mascara applicator that she pushed into the cab driver's neck. Diamond tried to claim the dope, but the U.S. Customs agents didn't believe her story; they knew she was simply a mule. They interrogated her for hours, hoping to make her the weak link in the chain. The U.S. Customs agents had purposely let them make it all the way through the airport checkpoints in order to see who'd be picking them up, but Drako and Diamond stuck to their story: The 'kiss my ass' story.

They were charged with trafficking five kilos of powder cocaine, and the federal guidelines imposed a mandatory sentence of ten years and because it was a federal crime they were to serve their sentences at the next available prison with bed space. They were moved far away and they never snitched a word to anyone about Wiz. Wiz promised to look out while they were down. If he blew up, he'd have a hell of a gift waiting for them upon their release.

Well, he had blown up, and so today Wiz wasn't just happy to be visiting the black Mecca of the south, he was happy because he was now able to provide Drako a home in Stone Mountain, Georgia. Wiz owned an immaculate ranch-style home equipped with a pool, circular driveway, three-car garage, and air-conditioned doghouse, and you name it. He bought a snow white 760 Li BMW with twenty-two-inch chromed out Ashanti rims and put it in the garage. He had other toys available for Drako to use as well.

Those thoughts seemed to fire up Wiz, and as soon as the director wrapped things up, he and his crew popped champagne. Wiz made sure Red Rum had crates of chilled bubbly to stunt with on every video set. In the private trailers they always smoked big Kush and Wiz had a hard fetish for pretty video vixens and high maintenance groupies. He extended the unlimited supply to them as well and promised all the ones he liked spots in his upcoming videos.

Wiz had watched Myria as she mingled about the set. She was beautiful and gaining rank fast with her five-foot-four-inch frame. She had perfectly augmented c-cups, a thin waist and thirty-eight inches of firm backside. The combination of her golden skin tone and long, dark silky hair is what gave her that exotic look the industry clamored for. She'd been featured in *Black Men's Magazine*; she'd had a back shot in Smooth and was rumored to be in the running for Eye Candy of the year in *XXL*.

Her magazine interviews quoted her, as saying she was mixed with Irish, Trinidadian and African American, but Wiz knew damn well she was just light-skinned with some high-priced ass weave.

Wiz didn't give a shit about her ethnicity. He and Myria rendezvoused often, simply because she was cool. She wasn't with all the silly gossiping or starting industry rumors, and for the moment Wiz couldn't seem to get enough. As long as he continued to throw stacks of cash and lead roles her way, Myria, with her good head and wet pussy knew just what to do to him.

Wiz stood to his feet, his eyes trained on the camel toe in Myria's burgundy bikini as she strolled past him on her way to the trailer. He caught himself swallowing a small lump in his throat as he turned to Damien. "So you think Drako gone be cool with this?" His focus was now aimed over Damien's shoulder watching Myria's backside as she climbed the few steps and entered the trailer.

Damien chuckled, realizing he didn't have Wiz's full attention. "Drako will be more than happy in my opinion." He casually waved the remark away. "He's been gone for nearly a decade. He really needs to feel his way first, and a little time will give you a better opportunity to place him in a suitable position."

Wiz nodded his head, agreeing as he watched Damien slip his expensive designer shades across his dark Latino skin. "For now just give him what he needs. Look around." Damien made a gesture toward the men who'd disassembled the makeshift sets and were now loading up all the featured exotic cars onto flatbeds. "Let him drive any of this shit! Make him feel like it's his as well. Who'd complain about that?"

Wiz smiled lightly. He liked Damien and respected his opinion a lot. Damien was a short, neat man, almost of Wiz's same stature. He was a well-connected, very powerful man when it came to reaching people and getting things done. Business was simply business in Damien's eyes. There were no gray areas. It was always this same straightforward advice that Damien had given Wiz to help Red Rum get where it was today. "You're right. I got him. I'ma make sure he's all good and I'ma make sure he stays free." Wiz nodded, but didn't sound sure of himself.

Damien took a sip from his glass of cognac as he ran an inquisitive glare over Wiz's face. "You don't sound too sure," he said, placing his half-empty glass on the table.

Wiz let out a small sigh as he watched all the models mingle about the set. "I'm just saying, Dame. This shit looks like its all fun and games, but it's work too, and if you don't keep ya eyes open and head above water you can go under at any time."

"You worry too much." Damien took a step closer and kept a careful eye on their surroundings as he discreetly passed Wiz the bag of pills he'd asked for. "Red Rum is winning big! It's the hottest label in the south and nobody is eating without you guys. Just accept what you've worked for and enjoy it."

He patted Wiz on the shoulder and glanced down at his watch. "I have to depart now. My flight is in less than two hours. My business is back on the east coast." Damien gave Wiz a firm shake, and then picked up his briefcase. "I look forward to picking him up next week and finally meeting him," Damien said just before departing.

Wiz watched him disappear through the crowd of set assistants and now partygoers as he strolled back over to the table where Trek, Swirl, and a few Red Rum artists' were still smoking Kush and admiring the thick Georgia women. Discreetly popping a yellow pill just before he sat down, he wished for the magical effect to take hold fast.

Surely, Wiz wanted his childhood buddy back on the streets. He'd heard Drako speak on so many things he wanted to do when he got out. But Wiz also knew his plate was too full to take on any new ventures. With all the controversy Wiz had sparked, Red

Rum was moving at the speed of a locomotive, and Wiz loved being the center of attention. Making sure Red Rum stayed number one was priority, and for the moment tabloid fodder and topping the Billboard chart were his only standing appointments.

When Swirl stepped up, Wiz had downed his head and was running a smooth hand over his fresh cornrows as the tingly sensations overwhelmed his body.

"What up, whoadie? We gonna get some studio time in or what?" Swirl interrupted his thoughts.

Wiz looked up at him through glazed eyes and cockily sucked at his diamond-covered teeth. "Yeah, we gonna get it in." He stood back to his feet feeling recharged. "Just give me a moment and we'll be outta here." Wiz gripped up the bottle of Ace of Spades champagne from the gold plated ice bucket and headed to the trailer he'd signaled Myria to slip into. He knew what he had in mind was going to take a while, but like always he'd find a way to fit it all in.

Mike Jefferies

30

Chapter Five

Drako

At 7:30 A.M. Lewisburg Penitentiary was wide-awake. Everybody was happy because Drako was leaving.

It was in rare cases where men with short sentences even made it out alive, and in all other cases, most men did an average of seventeen years behind the walls of Lewisburg, unless they were undercover snitches for the government.

After Drako had been fully reinvented by Toney, his persona just made people gravitate to him. He had learned how to mask his emotions and not let inmates or prison officials know when he was in a bad mood. Never did he get into heated conversations or argue with anyone, and when people crossed the lines that he or Domacio had drawn, Drako, with no words or remorse, smiled until he got close enough to push his shank into their backs.

Many men had felt the wrath of Drako, but in all cases he had been in the right. Respect and loyalty came first to him and Toney, and today Drako was getting his respect. He had earned his prison stripes, and everybody knew he was far from a rat. He received ten years because it was his first offense and he rendered no cooperation with the U.S. Government. Drako's prison conduct never allowed him to be moved to a lower security

prison. He ended up serving his entire sentence behind the walls of Lewisburg Penitentiary.

Drako and Toney stood dressed neatly in their prison khakis and steel-toe boots. They held their heads high and proud as all the other men stopped by their cell to bid farewell to Drako. Drako shook hands, and for the first time in almost a decade, he couldn't stop smiling.

Shot callers from every set came and paid their respects. Drako had to slightly look up as a huge, light-skinned, tatted-up Blood named Deuce gave him dap. "Man, we love to see one of our own go," Deuce said. He had long cornrows and was from Cali. Drako wasn't a Blood, nor from Cali, but he understood the universal language and that 'one of our own' meant a 'solid nigga'—not a snitch.

"It ain't where you from, its how you carry it," Drako said.

"You got a memory like an elephant," Deuce replied.

"I gotcha, blood. I'm gone send you some flicks of them pretty bitches you like, and I'll make sure you stay chipped up." Normally Deuce would have said, 'Don't promise me shit you know you can't do,' but he knew Drako was keepin' it real as they stared at each other for the last time.

Deuce was the Blood whose table Drako said had cheated him eight years ago, but after Toney had squashed the beef, these two gangstas found a profound mutual respect for one another. Deuce admired the way Drako had stood up for himself. He knew damn well they had cheated Drako. He never thought a young man like Drako would have picked up on the marked cards in the deck as they played lowball, nor did he think Drako would stand up to him.

Deuce was a legendary OG, a gangbanger who without hesitation put work in, in prison as well as on the streets. He was serving three consecutive life sentences for drug conspiracy and the murder of two government witnesses. He despised snitches and preyed on the weak.

Drako had never forgotten the phrase Deuce taught him. Deuce loved the way Drako carried out his swag. He reminded him of himself years ago. He even told Drako he was never going to try him and that the GDs just wanted him in. Deuce hated the GDs, so he used his influence to help Toney squash the beef.

Drako and Deuce used to kick it a lot, and Drako knew he could fuck with Deuce on the streets. Drako was ready to go, but he knew there were some good people he had to leave behind.

As the surreal anticipation grew inside Drako, he could feel that lump of sorrow swelling up in his throat. He knew Deuce, as well as Toney would never see the streets again, but this was no place to get emotional. His mind was made up, and in his heart he knew damn well that he'd look after Deuce a little and he'd surely never forget Toney.

Drako broke the moment when he humorously said, "Man, you better work on them chicken legs." Everybody laughed because Drako always picked on Deuce. Deuce was huge and ripped up top, but had pencil legs. When he worked out, all he worked on was chest and arms. He had what was referred to as the 'California body.'

Everybody moved on. This day was so rare; it was as if some men vicariously lived their release through Drako.

All of the female inmates gathered around Diamond. They hugged her and some even cried real tears. They knew they'd all miss her. Diamond had been like a big sister.

Everyone felt that Diamond should have been a shining star, but up until now she had been a lost star.

When she first entered the system, the other females taunted her. She looked so young, naive and beautiful. Diamond didn't look like she could ever commit a crime. The jealous girls made rude remarks. "Look at that dumb half-breed doin' time for a punk ass nigga;" "Bitch, you stupid! I'da told on his ass!"

Diamond never let words hurt her. She had all the love letters Drako had written over the years. He apologized for involving her in the beginning, but she quickly let Drako know that she loved him and it was her conscious decision to be with him at that time. She made herself believe that she was better off in prison while Drako was doing time. Diamond couldn't fathom the thought of being with another man and knew Drako better than anybody. For another man to attempt to shape this Diamond would cost him his life.

The girls walked Diamond to the door of Receiving & Discharging (R&D). At this women's camp, they could observe the cars pulling up to the front of the prison. They saw the long, white limousine as it pulled up. Emotions ran high. Diamond's sentence had come to an end. The girls hugged again.

"Are you gonna be a singer?" one asked.

"Whatever Drako wants me to be is what I'm gonna be," Diamond said.

"Girl, you better stay writin' us!" another hollered.

Diamond smiled. "Girl, I'ma keep it real. My loyalty is to my man first. I may not have much time to write, but y'all will hear from me or about me. I promise!"

"Hey, do me a favor and hook me up wit' dat nigga Wiz," another girl humorously interjected.

They all laughed as Diamond wiped the tears from her eyes. "Bye ladies. I love you all. Y'all time will come, too."

Diamond turned and went through the door. Inside R&D, she quickly changed. Wiz had sent her designer jeans, Louis Vuitton boots and a matching shirt. Diamond put the jeans on and her body took on an hour glass form that the prison khakis had hidden for so long. Stepping out the door, she saw Wiz. He was all smiles, standing in front of the limo.

Wiz ran up to Diamond and hugged her tightly, then picked her up and spun her around before putting her down. "Damn, lil sis, I missed you so much!" He hugged her again, then pecked her cheek, looking as if he were about to cry.

Diamond took a step back. "Ah, nigga, don't you go gettin' soft on me," she said, laughing.

Wiz quickly caught himself as he returned a smile. "My bad, but you know how it is. It should've been me . . . It—"

She punched Wiz on the shoulder playfully. "Stop it, Wiz! I don't need to hear about that shit now! Now, where's my man?"

Wiz smiled harder. "Damn, girl, you still Drako's diamond. You the hardest lil momma I ever met. You gonna be Red Rum's first lady."

"Don't start with that bullshit. All I want to be is Drako's wife."

Wiz laughed lightly, not at Diamond, but with her. He knew she meant every word. He let go of Diamond and took a good, long look at her. She looked as if she hadn't aged, and he saw her beautiful tone. He couldn't help but sneak a peek at her perky breasts and curvaceous hips and thighs. Wiz smiled inwardly, but he wasn't absorbing the look for himself. He just knew that Drako was going to be a happy ass man.

"Let's go, pronto!" she said, snapping her fingers. "Standin' in this parkin' lot ain't gettin' us no where."

Wiz snapped out of his trance. "Damn, lil sis. My bad. Let's get you away from this place." He placed his arm back around her shoulder and coaxed her toward the limousine door. "When we land in Atlanta, my friend-girl gonna take you shopping. We'll be just in time before Drako arrives."

The chauffeur held the door open as Wiz got in first. As soon as Diamond climbed inside, she unconsciously flared her nostrils at the light skinned, weave-wearing skank sitting on the seat in front of her.

"Hey, I'm Myria," she said, crossing her legs in a shimmering red, short, spaghetti strapped dress that barely touched the top of her thighs.

"Uh-huh," Diamond replied without doing a good job at hiding her distaste.

Myria wasn't even paying attention. She was now holding up a compact mirror and reapplying the lipstick she'd worn off sucking Wiz's dick.

Wiz picked up on Diamond's expression and seized the moment. "Don't trip, lil sis. She know how to put that shit on. She gone get ya back in the game, ya dig?" Diamond just nodded, agreeing. She relaxed and sat back for the rest of the way, but at first glance she knew what chicks like Myria were all about. And wasting time around girls like that wouldn't be a part of her plan.

Back at Lewisburg, 'surreal' couldn't describe the plethora of emotions that overcame Drako when he heard his inmate number blare from the intercom for the entire prison to hear. Drako had said his final good-byes. He told cats they would hear from him on the low. He told them to holla at Toney, and he told the underworld who Toney wouldn't associate with to check on him through Deuce.

"Is we gonna see you on TV?" an inmate yelled out.

"Man, send me some money when you get on," Dub-D said as he stepped up.

"Nigga, is you gone be a model, a stripper, or a bouncer?" the Blood behind Dub-D asked.

Drako smiled, still masking his emotions as he did best.

He had left all the guys in the unit, only allowing Toney to walk him to the door of R&D. When they reached R&D, Toney gave Drako a fatherly hug. He looked deep in his eyes as he patted Drako's shoulder. "I know you ready. I've shared with you things that I will never share with anyone else as long as I'm here. Keep it real out there. Be the last of our dying breed." Toney squeezed Drako's shoulder even firmer. "I love ya, man, as if you were my own son."

Drako had been waiting for those heartfelt words. He looked back at Toney and said, "I appreciate all you've taught me, and for that, I love you too. I'm gone play da game raw! I gotcha. As long as I got air to breathe, you got a dollar and a hand still in them streets. I put dat' on Diamond!"

Drako dropped his head. He couldn't look at Toney and leave him behind. If there was a way to break Toney out, he surely would try, but Drako never pondered the unimaginable.

He stepped through the door, waving his hand backwards over his shoulder, because it was bad luck to look back and speak while leaving out of the prison door. Some said it was what made the doors revolve. Drako went to R&D and slipped into the Timbs and Polo jeans Wiz sent him. He felt good to have some relaxed fit jeans on. He signed his release papers and gave the officers the first smile ever.

Drako walked out the front door of Lewisburg penitentiary and took a deep breath. The air seemed already cleaner, the grass looked greener. He still didn't look back; he didn't want to remember how the front of the pen looked because he wasn't coming back. The chauffeur held the door to the white limousine open for him and he got in. A short Latino man was sitting inside neatly dressed in a cream linen Cannali suit. He wore expensive Italian gator slippers by Mauri, and his demeanor immediately boasted influence.

He reached his hand out to give Drako a friendly shake. Drako noticed the huge diamond ring on his pinky finger and the

expensive Frank Mueller watch. "Hello, Drako. I'm Damien. It's a pleasure to meet you."

Drako shook his hand, but never smiled. He learned never to open up to anyone until he studied him or her first. No hints of emotion would be read from his face. "Where's Diamond and Wiz?"

"Wiz went to pick up Diamond. He gave me orders to pick you up and take you to the airport and get you to ATL safely." Then he smiled. "Unless you'd rather I had picked Diamond up."

Anger quickly clouded Drako's face. "The best advice I can give you, I'll only give you once! Diamond is not to be played with. Let that be the last Diamond joke to come out cha' mouth. You understand? Now if you got instructions from Toney and you playin' da game raw, then we got things to do, but until I say you know me, keep our conversation business. Ain't nothin' personal 'bout us."

Drako sat back and the mean grit transformed into a dead cold stare, which confirmed to Damien that the words Drako had just spoken weren't just a threat, but a promise. Damien looked deep into Drako's eyes. He saw past the neatly trimmed black man. He too saw the same cold death that used to be in Toney's eyes back in Harlem.

Damien now realized how Toney had gravitated to Drako. Every true gangsta liked everything in his own likeness. Damien's next words hit Drako with hesitance. "Very well, Drako, just checking your humor level."

"This ain't *Comic View*! Do my eyes reek humor to you?" Drako held firm.

"Very well. I see. Toney has told me everything. It'll be awhile . . . months before I can introduce you to Vinny. But meanwhile, I will be in touch. I will keep you abreast of my plans or any changes. We will have no more communication difficulties." Damien attempted another smile. Drako still looked unfazed.

When their plane finally landed in ATL, Damien quickly loaded him into a waiting limousine. He gave the chauffeur an address in Stone Mountain, and told him to make sure he was delivered safely. Then he handed Drako a cell phone.

"I'll be in touch—always business, never personal."

Drako nodded and pushed the button to roll up the tinted window as the limo pulled away. He smiled because he knew Damien was the solid truth, but Toney always taught him to instill fear everywhere, and it was best to nip it in the bud about Diamond. He knew he and Damien had a long way to go in life. So it was best to let him know he wasn't playing with a child; he was playing with a solid gangster, armed with a master's degree in crime. A man who was ready to get his at any cost. He lay back and laughed as the limo entered Stone Mountain.

Mike Jefferies

Chapter Six
The Family

Damn, this is nice, Drako thought, sitting up a bit as the limo entered the gated community in Stone Mountain. He was impressed with the pristine landscape and at all of the nice estates that sat a safe distance back from the main road.

When the limo slowed and turned into a circular cobblestone driveway, Drako knew at first glance of the blue DBS that this ranch styled home had to be owned by Wiz.

"How do I look?" Diamond turned to Wiz and asked nervously as she and Wiz spotted the limo pulling into the driveway.

"Stop trippin', lil sis." Wiz smiled. "You look good, girl. Get it together. Drako gonna love you." He watched as Diamond resituated her sheer blouse and then raked a few loose strands of soft hair back behind her ear. She wanted it in a pulled back style how Drako had always liked. He didn't like her hair covering her face. He said he loved to see his whole Diamond.

"Well, open the door," Diamond said timidly.

When the huge oak door opened, Wiz was the first to emerge. He trotted over to the oversized porch and hopped down the steps with ease. In the next flash, he was finally embracing his childhood buddy in the free world once again.

 41

"Man, I can't believe this shit!" Wiz snapped as he pulled back and took a look at Drako. "Man, you still look, look . . . Man, you big as shit!" Wiz seemed lost for words.

"Ain't nothin', man. I was just tryin' to maintain." Drako waved the compliment off with a shrug. "Nigga, we need to talk about yo' shit!" Drako smiled warmly, reaching for the diamond chain dangling from Wiz's neck.

"You talkin' 'bout 'ain't nothin' to it'. . . Hmph!" Wiz let out an arrogant huff.

"This came from pocket change, nigga," he said, taking a hard suck at his diamond grill.

Drako couldn't mask his emotions this time. He was happy that Wiz made it; he felt like because of that very reason he'd made it too. "Pocket change, huh? I like that shit," Drako replied, checking out the rest of the ice Wiz was draped in.

"Don't trip. You know I got you some mean pieces on deck." Before Drako could respond, their moment was instantly shattered when he saw Diamond making her way down the steps.

Oh shit . . . look at how beautiful she is! Drako thought as he bit down on his lip and swallowed his first lump. He held his arms wide open, gesturing Diamond to come to him. He quickly observed everything about her, from her smooth skin to her soft, neat hair, and of course, her banging body. For the first time ever, Drako experienced something so beautiful that it took his breath away.

"Damn baby . . . you're so pretty." He pulled her into his embrace and smiled down into her enchanting hazel eyes.

She first answered with a firm kiss on his lips and said, "I missed you so much, baby." A tear slid down her cheek. Butterflies churned like crazy in her stomach. Drako sensed her jitters.

"Don't cry, baby." He strummed a smooth thumb across her cheek, admiring her skin as he brushed the first tear away. "I love you more, baby, and this time I'm here to take care of you forever, just like I promised." He didn't wait for a response as he slid his tongue into her mouth. This time Diamond lost her breath.

Drako's touch to her was equivalent to Kryptonite's effect on Superman. He was the only thing to make her weak.

"I kn-know, baby," she stammered through heavy breaths as her hands clung to his shoulders even tighter and their kiss became even more passionate. Drako couldn't resist running his hands down her back and squeezing at all that ass she had in those jeans. Just as he was about to lift a hand to her breast, Wiz interrupted their moment.

"Gaddman, partna. You can't do her like that out here." He couldn't hold back his laughter. "Yo, for a minute I believe y'all forgot we were outside." He nudged Drako lightly on the shoulder.

"Damn, my bad." Drako let out a huff, never taking his eyes off Diamond. "I-I did get lost," he admitted and popped Diamond across her juicy hips, followed by a lick of his lips. She hugged him tight all over again and rested her head on his chest.

"Okay, love birds, let's take it inside. I see y'all got lots of catching up to do." Wiz waved his hand, gesturing them to follow him back inside.

As soon as Drako stepped into the foyer, he fell in love with the hardwood flooring and high vaulted ceilings. Wiz had extremely good taste in home décor, Drako realized as they made their way through the living room and headed for the kitchen. Wiz had imported figurines and expensive African masks and swords that sat high on the wall. Plasmas were in every room, and the moment they stepped into the kitchen, Diamond was all over the island stove in the middle of the floor.

Unable to keep his focus off Diamond, Drako turned to Wiz with a knowing look in his eyes. "What's up, man? How long we

gonna hang around here? I'm ready to get to my suite and relax."
Drako cut his eyes at Diamond again.

"Your suite?" Wiz rested his hand on his side. "Man, you
trippin'! You ain't got to go nowhere. You can stay in this house
as long as you like. I want you to enjoy everything in it!"

Damn, that was fast! Drako thought with raised eyebrows.
"Wow, that . . . that, I wasn't expec—"

"Man, I told you I got you, partna, and I meant it," Wiz cut
him off, clearly seeing that his gesture had taken Drako by
surprise.

Diamond stepped up and clung on to Drako. She smiled
brightly at Wiz. "Thank you, Wiz. This is a really nice place."
She had to look around again. "Well, I guess I can go hang my
things in that big walk-in closet," she said, referring to all the
bags of clothes Myria had helped her pick out.

"C'mon, baby." She nudged Drako in the direction of the
master suite.

"Hold up first, lil sis. I'm not done." He motioned them to
follow him down the hallway.

They made their way down a short hallway where Wiz
opened the door that led to the garage. He stepped aside and let
Diamond spot the snow white 760 Li first.

"Haa . . ." she gasped, clasping her hands over her mouth in
awe.

"This is out the gate, baby. I can't see you ridin' no other way
but clean," Wiz said, patting Drako on the shoulder. Drako
nodded his head with a proud grin. He didn't show too much
emotion around Diamond. He was still trying to take it all in.
Things were happening fast and he knew Wiz knew he was
thankful.

"Yeah, that's player shit," Drako shot back and gave Wiz a
firm pound.

Diamond had opened the door and slid into the comfortable leather seat. Noticing the key chain dangling from the ignition, she switched on the power and let the stereo blare at a modest pitch.

Wiz smiled at Diamond fumbling with the gadgets, and then turned to Drako. "Look man, I'ma get out of y'alls way in a short, but I really need to speak with you alone for a few minutes." Wiz's face was full of concern.

"Cool . . . you got that," Drako said, also recognizing the urgency in Wiz's voice.

He followed Wiz down the hall and into a room that served as an entertainment room. There was a wall bar, an expensive billiard table, and an at least eighty-inch projector screen on the wall.

"Sit down for a moment." Wiz pointed to a comfy barstool. "Drako, I want you to know this is just the beginning," he stated, sitting on the stool next to him. "This crib . . . The car is yours. . . Man, any of the shit that's on my plate. It's on your plate as well. I just want you to take your time. You know, feel your way. You got nothing to worry about. I'ma bring you in as Security Coordinator for titling purposes. I'll kick you up a descent salary that's sho 'nuff gone keep you eatin' good for now. After you see things through and I get a few things I'm workin' on out the way, we'll press forward." Wiz's voice was filled with assurance.

"Okay, I can understand that. You know I pick up fast though, and I'm just gone try to get my feet planted while the getting is good. Feel me?" Drako said firmly.

"Yeah, I feel that." Wiz nodded and pulled his Cartiers off and placed them on the marble counter top. "But that's not the issue at hand." He cleared his throat. "Drako, I-I'm just saying, man. Even with all this material shit, I know there is nothing I could ever give to replace the time both you and Diamond lost in that place. I-I just want you to know I thank you for leaving me out here. I—"

"Man, please don't start with that." Drako cut him off with a calm raise of his hand. "It's over and—"

"Just let me finish," Wiz said and hopped to his feet. "Look man, I knew snitchin' was no part of your DNA. That was never an issue. It's something bigger than that, that I appreciate." He took a step closer and leaned against the bar right next to Drako. "I appreciate you giving me the opportunity to do this shit." His glare settled on the far wall. "It's like you never once asked about that money. You never even mentioned it. I still have all the magazine clippings and all the lil things you learned inside and sent me to help get things moving.

"And Dame?" Wiz's voice cracked a bit. "Man, that was a miracle I wish I could thank your man for personally. He's been an amazing asset to me." Wiz paused, letting his sincerity sink in. He then turned back to Drako. "And most of all you never told anybody about the money I started with. Drako, that was real. You know how things—how those kinda rumors do in this business."

Drako nodded easily. He understood how Wiz felt, but the way he'd handled that whole ordeal was simply the nature of his gangster.

Wiz stepped around the bar. He leaned over and picked up a Louis Vuitton duffel bag and tossed it onto the counter. "Just to let you know I never forget. Here's my thanks to you." Wiz smiled and pushed the bag closer to Drako.

Drako stood and quickly unzipped the bag. "What's this?" he asked, looking at stacks and stacks of cash.

"It's all there. A hunned' grand." Wiz smiled cockily.

Drako seemed to be staring at the cash in awe, but for some strange reason something eerie pricked his logic. *I know he didn't just try to pay me back,* Drako thought, standing there feeling temporarily paralyzed.

"You a'ight?" Wiz spoke up, snapping him out of his trance.

"Yeah, yeah, I'm trippin'." Drako tried to brush away the thought with a quick nod.

"Pocket change, nigga." Wiz snapped his fingers again and reached for his ring of keys off the counter.

"Yeah, I feel ya. We'll see, won't we." Drako gave up a weak smile as Wiz seemed in much of a hurry to depart now.

"I want you to get out to Baton Rouge in a few days. I want to show you the new place now that we've moved from New Orleans and plus, I wanna get you acquainted with everybody in the camp."

Drako followed Wiz to the front door as they spoke. "Don't sweat it. I'll be there after I catch up around here, you know that."

Wiz turned and gave Drako dap and a brotherly embrace before he headed out the door.

"Bye Wiz, and thanks again," Diamond shouted, spotting him making his way out.

Wiz winked, "I got y'all, man. Anything, just ask " He turned and headed for the blue DBS.

Drako and Diamond watched Wiz crank up and zip out of sight before they stepped back inside and closed the door behind them.

"Well baby, what now?" Diamond leaned into Drako and raised her arms around his neck. "Why are you so tense?" She nudged him softly. She always had a sixth sense when it came to Drako.

"I-I 'on know. It's just for some strange reason it just don't feel like the Wiz I expected."

"What do you mean by that, baby? I mean, he put us in a nice home and he said he bought the car for you. He said the 760 is all you spoke of while you were locked up." Diamond looked confused.

"I know that. I appreciate everything. He gave me a satchel full of money, too."

"How much?" Diamond asked as she quickly leaned up.

"A hundred G's."

"So what's the problem then?"

"It's, it's just how he said it. He said *'It's all there!'* Like he thought he was repaying me for the money I left behind."

Diamond's expression softened. "Drako, I know how you are. Now baby, I think you're looking too far into it. Of course he'd never feel that way. That money is just a gesture of his gratitude. Put it away for hard times. It don't look like we're gonna need much of anything for a while. Well, except this." She began massaging Drako's dick. "Just get with him soon, but tonight I need some dick." She didn't hold back any of her feelings.

Drako knew she was ready to satisfy him and he was damn sure ready to satisfy her.

"Oh, I'ma get with him in Baton Rouge in a few more days. And don't you ever worry, ma. I'ma always make sure we got all we need."

"Mm-hm," Diamond moaned with heavy lust in her tone. She could feel her magic already working as Drako's dick swelled in her small hands. Anxiously, she reached for his zipper and he literally tore the buttons off her top.

"Damn, I can't wait to get in this pussy." Drako yanked her shirt the rest of the way open, and then flipped her bra over her tittie.

"Mmm!" she moaned, enjoying the feel of Drako's warm mouth as he pushed her titties together and devoured them at the same time. By the time she unbuckled his pants and pulled his dick out, Drako was trying to scoop her up and carry her into the bedroom.

"Wait!" Diamond whined.

"What?" Drako stopped, looking confused.

"Let me suck it first." Diamond licked her lips as even more lust dripped from her eyes at the sight of his swollen, fat dick.

He let her go and let his jeans drop to the floor at the same time. Diamond guided him to the sofa just a few feet away. She pushed him down gently with his jeans still clung over his Timbs. With one look at his huge dick standing straight in the air, Diamond sank to her knees and took hold of it with both hands. "Mmm!" she cooed, licking the pre-cum from the tip at first brush.

"Ooh yeah . . . da-damn, baby," Drako stuttered as Diamond, not wanting to waste another second, slobbered over half his dick and placed it into her warm mouth.

"That's it, baby . . . yeah, make some noise," Drako urged, running his fingers through her stringy hair. He pushed her strands back so he could watch her mouth bob up and down.

"Gllu!" Diamond gagged and plopped the dick from her jaws after trying to swallow too much. "Damn, Drako you taste good," she said, trying to catch her breath. "I'ma swallow up this bone tonight." She went back down onto Drako's long dick with even more intensity and determination to make him cum.

"Gaddamn, ma!" Drako's toes curled as he heard the loud slurping sounds for the first time. Before he realized it he saw drool sliding down his pole. His hips were raised off the cushion and he was feeding Diamond almost nine inches.

"Oh, shit!" Drako yelped, feeling his balls rumble. "Slow down, ma before I—"

"Mm . . . Mm . . . Mmm . . ." It was too late. Diamond sucked at him even firmer, milking every drop from her man. Drako's hips dropped back to the sofa and his head fell back in ecstasy. He was spent and felt light-headed for a moment.

"Damn girl! What the fuck was that?" he asked, still clutching his pulsating dick.

"All you'll ever need," she assured him, standing to her feet.

"Is that right?" Drako smiled.

"Damn right it is!"

"Hmm." Drako laughed. "Well, you know I ain't done with you. Get all that shit off. I want you ass naked. You know how I like it!" he said, wrestling one Timb off with the other.

"You know how I like it, too." Diamond gushed through her even smile and began to strip all the way down.

"Damn! That don't make no fuckin' sense!" Drako sat straight up and couldn't calm himself once Diamond got butt naked.

"Come here," he commanded. "Turn around," he said next. His dick expanded all over again at the sight of Diamond's juicy, red ass. Her skin was flawless, abs tight, breasts perky, but it was her ass that had him stuck. It had to be forty inches of perfection. He picked her up and laid her on the couch. "I'm 'bout to fuck the hell outta' you."

"Good." Diamond draped a leg over the back of the couch and the other to the floor. Drako took one look at her fat shaven mound and leaned face first into it. With both thumbs he spread her lips apart and began to suck her clit. Only the first few slurps came gently. After he got a taste of her sweet cream, he lost control. He licked and sucked deep into her crevice.

"Mmm . . . right mmm. Oh shhiii—right there, Drako!" Her back arched, and her hands clamped around Drako's head like a basketball.

"Oh, shit! Dr-Draako—what are you!" Diamond gushed glaze all over Drako's face, causing him to lick even deeper for a while.

A few moments later, Drako stood to his feet with his dick clutched in his hand. He didn't say another word as he guided himself into Diamond's love hole.

"Oh, Drako. Ta-take your tu-ime," she whimpered as he stretched her to her limits.

"I got you, ma. It's so wet!" Drako held her underneath her shoulders like a harness and continued to sink deeper with every stroke.

"You like that?" he whispered in her ear.

"Uh-huh! Right there, ooh-mmm!" Diamond closed her eyes and bit down on her lip. Her pussy was getting wetter and looser, causing him to plow harder in her juices.

"Take this dick, baby." Drako rose up on his knees and pushed her legs back at the folds.

"Oh, yeah, fuck me, baby. Gimme all that dick! You know how I want it!"

Drako heard her pussy sloshing with her juices at every connection. He knew she was ready. He began to fuck her hard and long like she always liked. "You like that?" He plunged as far as he could.

"Oh Drako!" she squealed. "You hittin' my spot, baby!"

"Gimme this pussy like you missed me!" He jerked her to him, knocking his dick to the back of her pussy. She tried to meet him with every stroke, but it was just too good. He was so deep it felt like he'd discovered new pussy inside of her. Their bodies began to jerk simultaneously.

"Oh, ooh, ooh, Dr-Dra-I'm about to cu—"

"Sss . . . Fuck! I'm . . . me too!" He felt her walls clamp his dick like pliers.

"Oh! Ah! Shit!" they howled at one another as they came together in tremors. Drako collapsed on top of Diamond and they both tried to catch their breath.

"Damn, ma. I can't believe I lived without this for over eight whole years." Drako looked down at her in awe. He couldn't resist kissing her pink lips again.

"Shit, I lived without it, too." Diamond pulled back a bit and gave Drako a sideways look.

"Well, you'll never go without again," Drako said.

"And you won't either. You can have all you want however you want it." Diamond smiled, raising a soft hand to his face.

Hmm, Drako thought, knowing he had the best woman in the world. She'd always been down to please her man. "Well, in that case you oughta' know I'ma want to make love to that pretty ass from behind when we get to our room."

Diamond smiled even brighter. "Drako, you so damn freaky. That's why—"

"I ain't that freaky," he said defensively.

"Boy, I felt you sucking my butt." Diamond giggled. "Now, lay here and hold me for a minute. You know I like that freaky shit." Drako was about to say something in response, but quickly changed his tune. Hell, he liked doing that freaky shit to her and that would never change. He smiled just before he closed his eyes and squeezed Diamond a little tighter.

Although he was ready to cap his first night home off with his woman, he still couldn't shake the strange vibe Wiz left behind when he'd rushed out the door.

Drako was glad to be home, and he knew it was finally time to see firsthand what Wiz had been up to. He made a mental note to pay a little extra attention.

Chapter Seven

Wiz

On the corner lot of a block of some of the most prestigious property in Downtown Baton Rouge, Wiz stood at the top of his three-story, five million dollar, soundproof, state-of-the art recording studio. With his hands clasped behind his back, he paced slow circles on the elegant hardwood floors as he stewed over bringing his most street credible artist into the fold of his latest scam.

Wiz was happy that this structure now served as headquarters to Red Rum, and he was even more proud of everything that had taken place inside so far. Wiz was no doubt, a marketing genius, and for the last year his intuition had paid off in the biggest way. Red Rum dominated all hip-hop publications. Every media music outlet clamored for Red Rum's star power and Red Rum's shows and guest appearances garnered more profits than its competitors by far.

It wasn't easy clawing his way to the top, nor would it be staying there. But the elite feeling it gave Wiz was almost intoxicating. What he needed from Swirl was surely not the first time he'd done it, but if he could get Swirl to go along with his plan it had the potential to be the most profitable scandal to date.

Wiz knew money made the world go 'round and he had lots of it coming his way. He was expecting a call at any minute to close out on a lucrative endorsement deal he'd settle on with Vitamin Water. That was in the bag. That was not his dilemma. The dilemma was that Swirl had been with him for almost a year now. He'd inked him to a hefty three album deal and Swirl had built his brand solely on street credibility, which is what Wiz feared could stand in his way. Swirl was indeed a hood legend. His lyrical wordplay first had him as a local New Orleans celebrity, and today some even regarded him as a hero.

He was now more than hood rich. He'd moved from his home in Magnolia projects and into a nearly two million dollar estate. He now had the means to reach back and help his hood, and that's exactly what he'd done. Swirl was both proud and moral. He donated money to help refurbish parks and recreation centers all over New Orleans. In his videos he only used girls straight from his old projects.

Yep, Swirl is a proud man, Wiz thought, flopping down in his huge cherrywood armchair when he saw Swirl's blood burgundy Chevy Impala whip up to the building on his security screens.

Show time . . . It's all about presentation, Wiz thought as he pulled a fresh box of expensive cigars from the drawer and placed them on the end of the long, cherrywood boardroom table. "All about presentation." He reared back with a grin.

Swirl got buzzed in and stopped by the recording booth on the first level. He then made it up to the third floor where Wiz only held his most private meetings. Wiz was already on the phone, obviously handling the huge endorsement deal that everybody was buzzing about. He held up a finger, signaling Swirl to sit down as he rounded out the deal.

Swirl stepped over to the table and rolled the padded chair back. From his side he pulled out a .40 cal and laid it on the table, carefully making sure the safety was engaged. He then sat down in his chair, reached for the lighter on the table, and relit the blunt of Kush that dangled loosely between his lips.

"I'm sure we'll enjoy doin' business for a long time. As long as the money's right, Red Rum and Vitamin Water gone stay tight!" Swirl heard Wiz say through the phone with a gleam in his eyes.

Pushing his dreads over his shoulders, Swirl exhaled a cloud of smoke thinking how proud and thankful he was for Wiz. Wiz had never given him any bad advice or not made good on a single promise. That's why he felt both privileged and obligated when Wiz summoned him for a special meeting. Swirl was ready to drop his next album. His single had been number one for the last six consecutive weeks. Wiz kept pushing the full album release date back in order to get more exposure and sales before the album finally dropped. It was one of Wiz's ingenious marketing tools that placed him in the chair he sat in today, and Swirl wasn't about to question his grand scheme. He was assured Wiz had his best interest at heart.

"I'm glad we understand." Wiz stood up, adjusting his Cartier frames on the bridge of his nose. "Great . . . Yeah, I know. We'll be in touch soon." He ended the call and turned to Swirl.

"Damn, It's raining money 'round here, whoadie," Wiz said, glancing at some of Swirl's new tattoos that now ran down to his fist.

"Fuckin' right! I can't wait to ink me a shoe deal or somethin'. I'ma make that third ward stand up, ya heard?"

"Whoadie, you comin', and I'ma make sure you get there! Swirl, you gotta push units! All the big people see is numbers, just numbers, baby!"

"Man, the streets fiending for these gangsta lyrics. Can't nobody spit it like me," Swirl shot back defensively as he sat up and placed his blunt down in a big crystal ashtray.

"That's what I'm talkin' 'bout, whoadie!" Wiz explained. "I know you the hottest nigga in the south and one of the hardest in the country. I ain't never doubtin' that, but you missin' the bigger picture—dollars is what makes sense! You wanna be able to drop a 100 G's in your grill? You want money like mine? Exclusive contracts, endorsement deals, and enough groupie love to make you not want any more? Then move units!"

"Yeah, I know my shit gone be gold in no time."

Wiz smirked at Swirl like a kid who was lost. "Gold? Gold is old 'round here, whoadie. You need to be platinum! Look, whoadie. I'm 'bout to put you down on some shit me and my people talked 'bout that could really help boost your first week's sales."

Swirl picked up the blunt and relit it as he tried to pretend like he knew the deal and was in control of the situation.

"Look, Swirl, I spoke to Bless at Take Money Records. His hottest artist is Fatt Katt. Me and Bless both feel the same . . . you are 'bout to be at the height of your peak as far as entering the game on a maintstream level, and so is Fatt Katt out on the East Coast," Wiz said. "You and Fatt Katt movin' more units with your singles than anybody, and that's according to a check through SoundScan. But at this point, if we had some controversy, we could almost double, maybe even triple our unit sales!"

"Controversy?" Swirl replied, slightly puzzled.

"Yeah, controversy! Somethin' for niggaz to talk about. Beef, hate, all that good shit that sells albums," Wiz replied, followed by his self-proclaimed genius smile. Swirl just sat in silence.

"*Source* been waitin' to interview you, as well as a few other publications that I formerly wouldn't allow—until now."

Swirl smiled at the thought of another interview and photo shoot.

"Slow down, Swirl. I see you glowin'. You gone get in the mag, but I need you grittin' hard on all the shoots. Let 'em know ain't nothing funny 'bout making money. I also need you to say 'Fuck Fatt Katt' to my man Joshua. He's the columnist of *Source* who'll be interviewing you." Wiz watched Swirl's smile slowly dissipate.

"Wiz, I ain't got no beef wit' dat' nigga. I fuck wit' his music. What his fat ass say 'bout me?"

"Nothin'! As a matter of fact, he said the same things 'bout you. See, Fatt Katt understands. This shit is just marketing. It's giving the people the entertainment they're not supposed to ask for. WWF Wrestling is worth a billion dollars because they know how to give a show, not 'cause it's real! You gotta give them what they askin' for."

Swirl caught on fast. He pondered for a moment and then said, "What Fatt Katt say? I 'on wanna start no shit that could ever get too big to say on wax. Wiz, you know I'm from the streets! No matter how much paper I get, my heart ain't changin' for no man!"

"Swirl, I got you. We gonna keep it small. Just say that you know *personally* that the nigga fakin' and without them ghostwriters he couldn't be a backup R&B singer. His album's gonna drop two weeks after yours, but with a diss song directed at you. You'll both reap the benefits, and as long as you and him know it's harmless, then it's harmless. Just don't kill him too bad with that slick wordplay you got."

"Wiz, you know lyrically I'll assassinate that fat fucker, and it's hard for me to hold back my flow."

"I know that, and he does too, but he's still hot! It's a helluva business move. I consulted with Damien and he loved it too, so let's not drag our feet any longer. We missin' bread right now! So you wit' dis' money scheme or what?"

"Whoadie, I'm 'bout dat' paper! You know I'm wit' it!"

"Good, good. First off, I'ma call Bless and let him know the deal. Next week he's gonna have Fatt Katt call *Vibe* and *XXL* in response to your interview. A few weeks after that, he'll also tell his side to *Source* mag. We'll fuel this shit a few weeks, then we'll find a way to truce this shit after we move these units."

Swirl smirked. "So that's what's really up? Wiz, you a bad mothafucka!"

"Nah, I'ma genius, and you will be, too. I'ma teach you this shit. Now, let's go over everything. Then I'ma call Joshua right here and grant him that exclusive interview. I'm expectin' my financial adviser, Dame and my man, Drako shortly."

Wiz picked up the phone. He lit a big ass Cuban cigar as he always did when he thought he had accomplished something. Then he dialed Bless, the CEO of Take Money Records in New York.

"Everybody is happy . . . Sure, sure. Go ahead and tell him it's underway . . . Ha, ha, ha! Let's make millions!" Wiz laughed into the phone, blowing a cloud of cigar smoke large enough to hide his little ass sitting in that big ass chair. "Good, good. Gettin' money ain't just a New York state of mind! Whoadie, just get at me when you see how SoundScan blow da fuck up!" Wiz shouted into the receiver before he hung it up.

"Well, Swirl, I did my part. You ready to do yours?"

"Hell yeah! Let's get these millions, whoadie! I'm handlin' mines, ya dig!"

Wiz was all smiles inside and out. He carefully walked through the beef-sparking statements with Swirl and was confident that Swirl would be convincing. "You made for dis' shit. You a business man," Wiz coaxed on as he picked up the telephone receiver. He pressed one button, and as soon as the phone rang, he put it on speakerphone.

"Hello?"

"Josh, what up? This Wiz."

"I was expecting . . . I—I mean, hoping you'd call."

"Well, Josh, I feel it's only right to give the fans the real shit. I mean, give 'em our side of what's really goin' on."

"What about Swirl? What can you tell me?"

"I can't tell you shit 'bout Swirl. Well, at least not better than Swirl can. That's why I'ma let Swirl do an exclusive interview with your magazine first. But whoadie, if you edit this shit into somethin' my man ain't say or leave shit out, we *won't* be back, understand?"

"Oh sure, sure. Is he there now?"

Wiz nodded his head to Swirl as an indication to speak up.

"What's happenin'?" Swirl spoke straight into the speakerphone.

Reclining back in his chair, Wiz began listening to Swirl answer questions and lay down the harmless beef. He was happy Swirl was now on board. Wiz felt that this was just bringing entertainment into the hip-hop game. He smiled as Swirl got hyper and played things all the way through. Choosing Joshua's gossiping ass had been his best choice because he knew that Joshua lived solely for the growth of industry scandal.

Once the interview was completed, Wiz mashed the button to disconnect. "Whoadie, you did good. You playin' da game now. Niggaz already know you gangsta, and now you 'bout to see millions in no time."

Mike Jefferies

60

Chapter Eight
Drako

After Drako's flight had landed him at Louis Armstrong International airport in New Orleans he felt relieved. It had been over a week since he'd seen Wiz and several ideas had crossed his mind. Drako was hungry—no, he was thirsty and hungry and ready to stand on his own two feet. He'd now been telling himself this for days.

As soon as he made it through the busy terminal and reached the taxi stand he spotted Damien standing next to an awaiting limousine. Damien extended his hand for a firm shake the moment Drako stepped into his space.

"Hello, Drako." His smile was warm. "I hope your flight was pleasant."

"How long is the ride to Baton Rouge?" Drako gave him a weak shake and kept his focus on the business at hand. He was ready to check out Red Rum headquarters firsthand.

"Just about an hour. That will be enough time to fill you in on a few things. Just business—still not personal."

Drako showed no emotion as he savored the way Damien respected his gangster. They both got in the limousine and cruised away.

Drako felt like sightseeing, as he always wanted to enjoy the Big Easy. But that thought was quickly dismissed as Damien popped open the briefcase, handing a stack of pictures to Drako. "These are pictures of Vinny Pazo. Some are of the cabin he has in Colorado, and the others are to show you the difference in his security when he's home in New York rather than far away where he thinks nobody would recognize him."

Drako studied the photos. It looked as though Vinny was rolling deep. "It would be almost impossible to touch him in New York with that many bodyguards around him."

"I know, and that is why it's most definitely important that we touch him in Colorado. It's a one-shot opportunity. We get him then or never, Drako."

"What else you got on this piece of shit?"

"Here's a map of the area, some aerial photos, and my written strategy to gain entry and control of the retreat."

Drako read over the notes and pondered their potential. "What kinda tools we using?"

"I suggest Mac 10s with silencers. I prefer .45 shells, but whatever else suits you best will be available."

Toney had always told Drako that Damien had access to every connect that he once held. Damien's professionally laid-back demeanor was magnetic to crooked business tycoons. Most of them owed Damien a favor or felt that they were doing Toney a 'solid' when they rendered their hands to Damien.

"Hmmm . . . Well, I'ma need a vest for sure. And I want some hunting knives and a couple of .40 Glocks." Drako even asked for night vision goggles and some more things he felt were unnecessary and most likely unattainable to Damien.

Damien grinned. "You'll see that most of what you've asked for I've already thought of." He handed Drako another list of weapons and items he felt they would need. At the top of the list read 'night vision goggles.' He read down the list and saw that

Damien was well prepared, and his plan had been thoroughly researched. Drako liked his style a little more, now that he had spent a moment with him.

"I'm wit' this vibe. Wit' this much potential, we gone make it work. I'ma make sure Toney gets to smile a lot of nights off this one." Damien smiled at the comment.

Drako observed Damien closely. It was easy to see that Damien surely had a powerful aura about himself. He was very clean cut and kept a short neat hair cut just like Toney. Both times Drako had met him he wore nice tailor made linen suits and expensive alligator slippers. None of his jewels were big and gaudy. They were small and impeccable V.S. Diamonds. He spoke so eloquently about any topic. Drako knew that Damien understood dark power well and hoped that he'd one day be an integral part of his plan on his way to the top.

"Yo Dame." Drako sat up straighter and decided to spark a subtle conversation. "Of course, you know I've been enlightened on most of the things you can do." Damien looked at him with raised brows. "I'm saying it all with the best of intentions." Drako smoothly raised a hand, emphasizing to Damien that he came in peace.

"All I'm saying is when I get some real paper on the table I want to dump a lump on you. I want you to formulate me some legitimate companies." Drako crossed his leg and reared back on the seat again. Damien didn't respond. "I'd like to do something to cut in at Red Rum, but I don't want to just stop at that. All my eggs won't be in one basket. Plus man—I feel it. I'm telling you. It's millions of dollars circulating out here and I know I can get in."

"Hmm . . ." Damien let out a small sigh. "I understand clearly, but it's gonna take some real start-up capital to get you stabilized in the fashion you're speaking." Damien's face was flushed with doubt. Drako quickly picked up on his expression and was about to address it, but Damien spoke up first.

"Drako, I'm not going to waste time or lead you on here. I'm sure Toney would advise me to help you and help you as soon as possible. But in all honesty, I cannot understand why we're discussing this if you don't have the start-up funds yet." He looked down in his briefcase and shuffled some papers as he tried to hide the annoyed look on his face. "Furthermore, I don't understand why you don't have the money already. It was my understanding that you somehow had a major input in acquiring the tools needed to upstart Red Rum from the start." Damien exhaled a sort of aggravated sigh, hoping Drako didn't feel as though he'd overstepped any boundaries with his personal opinion.

"Nah, Dame. It's all good. I'm just taking a careful approach, but trust me. I know Wiz more than most. Once we figure it out, he gone put it down for me."

Damien half smirked at Drako's straight forwardness. "Oh, well, maybe you just need to find patience for the first year or so." Damien shrugged his remark off easily.

The first year or so? This nigga must be crazy, Drako thought. "Yeah, well maybe so," he said, still keeping his thoughts to himself.

"Baton Rouge, we made it," Damien announced as the limo cruised through downtown.

Once the limo stopped, Drako stared up at the nice three-story establishment. "Is this Red Rum?" He didn't seem very impressed.

"Yes, this is it. The brain of the South," Damien retorted proudly.

A few moments later, he had disarmed the alarm and they stepped inside.

A Life for A Life

When Drako stepped into Red Rum headquarters he was met with surprise. Music blared from the piped-in speakers and everyone inside seemed to be in a festive mood. "What's good, Damien?" a nice-looking caramel-complected woman who looked to be in her early thirties asked as she stepped up to him.

"Same as always I'd say." He spoke politely to Dianne, the hairdresser who also served as stylist for several of the rosters up and coming artists.

"What's the occasion?" Damien asked casually, seeing a few more people than usual.

Dianne gave him a baffled frown. "You know Jay-poon got released this morning." She shook her head and waved Damien off as she pivoted and headed down the hallway. "You know how it goes down here," she shouted, switching her thick backside with every step.

"Damn, how'd I forget—again?" Damien emphasized. "That kid gets locked up at least once a month and each time they celebrate as if he'd . . . Just forget it." He dismissed his remark. "It's just image crap." Damien gestured his head for Drako to follow him.

They walked down the first floor hallway aligned with plaques and framed pictures of some of Red Rum's greatest moments. Drako trailed him up to the window of the glass recording booth where Jay-poon, Choc-money, and a few other artists were engaged in a freestyle cipher. Scantily dressed women paraded all about the building and the scent of exotic weed wafted in the air.

Damien seemed unfazed by everything except the beautiful black women. He smiled, clearly in awe as most of them passed him by. Reaching the elevator, Damien pressed the button and turned to Drako. "You'll get used to it. It's just a day in the life." They stepped into the elevator.

Wiz was upstairs in his big armchair. He'd observed Drako and Damien on his security screens as soon as their limo stopped at Red Rum's doors. He had cameras all around the perimeter as well as inside his facility. He used his remote and switched his screens to internal vision and was now buzzing them into his office as he watched them step off the elevator on his private floor.

Spinning his chair to face them, he greeted Drako with a platinum smile. "What up, Drako? Welcome to Red Rum headquarters." Wiz held that proud smile.

"No doubt." Drako nodded coolly. "Guess ya can't judge a building by its shingles. This is a nice place." Drako was picturing the sleeping quarters and gym Damien told him about on the second floor.

"Well, let's not be strangers." Wiz stood up and looked in Swirl's direction. "Drako, I'd like you to meet—"

Drako let out a light chuckle. He was already gripping the hand Swirl extended his way.

"What up?" Drako said.

"We eatin', baby. Every thang good, ya heard," Swirl said, reclining back comfortably in his chair with tons of swag.

"Well, I guess ya right. Swirl don't need no introduction. He 'bout ta be a household name when he lock down this mainstream." Wiz gave a confident wink.

Drako nodded, maintaining his cool. He knew Wiz was exactly right though, because with one glance of the brown-skinned, tatted up cat in the wife beater, Drako recognized him immediately. Drako spotted the red rag hanging from his pocket, but even before that, he knew Swirl was a Blood to his heart.

A Life for A Life

"Well, I guess I should be introducing you to Swirl, huh?" Wiz switched tunes. "Swirl, meet Drako, our head security coordinator." He tossed out Drako's informal title.

"He's going to man everything and see to it that we have a proper game plan to get out as well as we have to get in." All the humor had left Wiz's face. Today, Drako's reputation was to go without saying. Wiz had informed everybody close to him several weeks ago that Drako would be assuming this position.

"Welcome aboard," Swirl said in a very welcoming tone.

"Well, I just want to brush over a few things." Wiz extended a hand toward the seats on the other side of the table, offering Drako and Damien a seat.

In the next moment, he was catching Swirl and Damien up on all of Red Rum's upcoming projects and concerns. After that ended, he promptly went on to enlighten Drako about his first job coming up in just a few more days. They pored over the details, and it was certain that Drako was overqualified.

"Alright." Wiz began to sum up the short meeting with the swagger of an army general. "So, any more concerns while Red Rum's table is open?" He held his arms a little wide. No one spoke up. "Well cool, 'cause I'm starved. And I need some bubbly!" He stood up. "Let's go celebrate a little with Jay-poon and the team." Wiz smiled and laid a hand on Swirl's shoulder.

"Everything is lookin' up." He winked at Damien, but was referring to Swirl's allegiance. "Innovation and persistence always pays off." Every Diamond in Wiz's mouth was visible due to him smiling so hard. "Looks like Swirl gone be dumpin' the next hunned' on his grill soon." Wiz patted his shoulder proudly and stepped toward the door. Damien gave a sly wink, indicating he knew Wiz had swayed Swirl into his scam. He decided not to tell Drako. Maybe one day he'd let it out, but today he felt best by taking all the credit and star power his ingenious plans had brung his way.

LIFE 67

A few hours later, Drako had seen every inch of Red Rum headquarters. And from the little time he'd spent mingling so far, he could only imagine how draining it would be to live out this lifestyle night after night.

Drako not only understood the streets, he also understood the game of life. He recognized that most of the females were hangers-on—groupies that drifted from one Red Rum event to the next. There were several young artists signed, but not yet released, and it was already clear that their priorities were sex, parties and industry scandal. Everyone he spoke with had a story to tell or a rumor to spread.

Sitting down on a padded stool near the booth, Drako watched on as the festive night unfolded. The weed continued to spark and the bubbly poured while the MCs auditioned song after song. Drako's eyes were now stuck on a tall, curvy chick who stood just a few paces in front of him swaying her hips to the beat. She made sure Drako took in a good look before she turned and sauntered up to him.

"Hmm, haven't seen you around. What's your name?"

"Drako," he said casually. "And you are?"

"Single," she answered with a sexy nibble to her bottom lip.

Drako smiled lightly. "Yeah, that was cute and so are you." He nodded, glancing at her from head to toe. "But I just got here, I ain't into nothin'."

"You down with Red Rum? What are you? Some kind of A&R or something?" Drako saw the sparkle in her eyes just as he'd seen it in the last two vixens that hoped he was someone who could help jumpstart their careers.

"Somethin' like that. But single, not tonight, ma."

She smacked her tongue against the roof of her mouth. "Well, you're a cutie. I'ma have to keep my eyes on you." She smiled.

"I'll see you around." Drako winked and headed over to the bar. He wasn't concerned with any of the pretty and mostly willing women that were on hand tonight. He was trying to keep up with Wiz, who was hands down the center of attention. Other than slipping away with Damien a few times, all Wiz did was frolic and flirt with all the pretty women.

Ready to toss a few thoughts at Wiz and wrap things up so that he could get back home to Diamond, he stepped over to Wiz. "What up, playboy?" He gave him dap. "If everybody works as hard as they play around here you'll be rich for a long time." Drako cracked with a smile.

Wiz chuckled and took his lips off the bottle he'd just turned up. "We on top of this shit! We on top of everything!" He sat the bottle on the counter and picked up a perfectly rolled blunt from the ashtray. "We put out hard music and we stunt this shit for real!" He flicked a lighter to the leaf.

"Ain't no doubt. You got shit movin', and everything is first class. But all I'm tryna say is you got to have order too, partna." Drako's tone was sincere. "I see you got artists who'd just as well hang out here, smoke and party for the next two years before they finish up a complete album. Man, you gotta make them boys stay in the booth and make it count! They should be making you money, not costing you money until they come up. You gotta pay attention to these little things. The cost of riffraff can trim—"

"Whoa, daddy. Pump ya breaks. You act like you ready to be CEO," Wiz said jokingly.

"I might be." Drako winked. "You know I ain't slow. I see shit. Especially potential. I got some people in mind I think you should eventually meet. And I want to talk to you about helping me start this—"

"I got you. I got you!" Wiz said, exhaling weed smoke. "Feel your way around the studio first, then spend a lil time in the yard. I know you know the street and that you're smart, but you just jumpin' off the porch wit' this here." He looked at Drako for a moment. Drako noticed that same glazed over glint in his eyes again. "You have to do like I did. It won't come to you overnight, but believe me it's gonna happen. Believe me, I want ta see you wit' it like nobody else."

Wiz's focus shifted across the room. He saw Myria prancing his way. "Loosen up, man. Live a little first. I'ma get you on track soon."

Drako could clearly tell Wiz's whole tune had changed. He wasn't lending any thought to what he had to say at this moment.

"Dig what I'm sayin'?" Wiz said, pulling Myria into his arms and promptly running his hands down her back and over her ass. "It's everywhere you look." He snickered and kissed Myria on her lips.

"I'm good, partna. I'm all good." Drako gave him a wink and stepped away as Wiz began to grope her lustfully.

A short while later, Drako had said his good-byes and was headed back to the airport. He was ready to get home and give Diamond his assessment of Red Rum. He was proud of Wiz for sure. He recognized and respected the influence he had over his camp. Clearly, Wiz lived the hard life of a rock star. Also, he recognized within five minutes of meeting Jay-poon that he was simply a studio gangster—an ongoing publicity stunt for Red Rum. Drako didn't plan to mix a lot of pleasure with his business. He didn't use drugs at all. His fix was getting rich and his mind could only process getting it quick!

By the time his flight landed in Atlanta he'd made up his mind. He now had Wiz's best interest at heart. He had a few ideas that could easily be beneficial to both him and the label. And he'd also formed a connection with Drip, someone who could definitely be an asset to Red Rum.

All of this would come fast and as a surprise, but the next time he saw Wiz it would be time to get down to business.

Chapter Nine

Wiz

At two in the afternoon, Wiz was awakened by the constant vibration of his cell phone. He finally reached over after a long night of exhaustion from alcohol and kinky sex, and answered the call.

"What up, son?" Bless yelled excitedly. "Man, Swirl's shit did 1.8 mil' already!"

Wiz quickly sat up and turned away from Myria. "When did you check? Last week! You late, baby. Swirl done hit double, ya heard. This shit is goin' through the roof!" Wiz lied.

Wiz laughed a little as he listened to Bless on the other end. "Look, whoadie, I'ma go ahead and release my album early. I'm feelin' the timing, but we need to talk. I'm gonna hit you back later. I'm in a meeting, plus I gotta be in Memphis by 7 P.M. Swirl's got a concert and BET is gettin' at me hard about doing their commercial on the campaign to stop downloading music and buying bootleg CDs. Shit's been hectic, whoadie. You know the life we live." A few "uh-huhs" and "I gotchas" later, Wiz hung up.

His next call was to Damien.

"You still in Atlanta?" Wiz asked as soon as Damien answered. ". . . good. How long before you can meet me at Justin's? We need to talk. My plane is leaving at 5 P.M. I got an appearance at Swirl's concert in Memphis. Plus I gotta be there tomorrow for BET . . . Good, good. I'll see you in an hour." He disconnected the call and lay right back down.

Myria sprawled her sexy leg over his as she snuggled closer, rubbing her soft, freshly-manicured nails over his chest. "You at a meeting, huh? I don't know why you would hide anything from fakin' ass Bless."

"Girl, that wasn't no goddamn Bless for yo' nosey ass information!" Wiz huffed, only to get a light laugh and a sexual gyration from Myria's warm naked body as she cuddled closer.

"Wiz, I ain't silly. I know what's up. He calls too much on your private line—puleeze! I ain't even got that number. He always spittin' that 'son' shit! I see him and fat ass Fatt Katt fakin' it on TV all the time. You know I couldn't care less. All I care about is this." She began massaging his morning erection to make sure her point was clear.

"Myria, all you do is lay there and play sleep wit' yo' nosey ass! Stop screening my goddamn calls! You 'on know shit!"

Myria giggled. "Whatever. All you gotta know is you don't have to worry about me."

"Shut the hell up! I'm milkin' this industry! Your position is to stay milkin' me!"

"Well, don't I just love my job," Myria said with a smile as she slid down Wiz's stomach to send him off with a smile and something to think about on the plane.

Wiz enjoyed her kick-starting his day. Afterwards, he and Myria quickly showered. He jumped into one of his outfits he had stashed in the hideaway home he had Myria staying in, and then gathered the rest of his things to leave.

A Life for A Life

"Wiz, I'm kinda hungry. Can I go to Justin's with you?" Myria asked.

Wiz inwardly sighed because Myria had begun to nag him. She already knew the answer, but he still responded, "Myria, don't start! Here yo' ass go again wit' dat' *we an item* shit!"

"No, I'm not! I'm just hungry! Plus I'ma be here—bored all day!" she whined.

"Look at you! You standing there naked and I'm dressed ready to bounce! If yo' nosey ass was listening, you'd know I'm supposed to be there in an hour, which leaves me twenty minutes!" Wiz looked at the sad, dumbfounded look on Myria's face and decided to end this meaningless conversation. He went in his overnight bag and handed her a stack of hundreds that had to be close to six G's.

"Here, take this money, go shopping . . . buy a dog if you're lonely, but let me do me, dammit! You need to stop acting like your pussy is gold! You ain't impressing me. I want a ménage a trois. How 'bout makin' that happen wit' yo' precious ass?"

"Wiz, please don't talk to me that way. You know I don't do girls, and your attitude is not impressing anyone. I'm the only one here. You're hurting my feelings." A tear welled up in Myria's eyes. Wiz quickly seized the moment and hugged her.

"Be cool. You just need to stop naggin' me. I dig you, but I dig this paper, too. I need my space, so stop tryna crowd me."

"I'm sorry." She looked at Wiz's handsome face. "Do you, baby. I'll call you in a day or so."

"I gotcha, lil mama." Wiz popped Myria's ass before pecking her soft lips. He saw the smile return to her pretty, golden face as he turned to leave.

Myria smiled inwardly, happy because she had gotten good dick, a stack of money, and a new-found hope that if she slowed down, one day Wiz would love her back.

Twenty minutes later, Wiz pulled up in front of Justin's in downtown Atlanta in a rented Suburban. He was met by Damien and two bodyguards. Wiz got out of the truck and greeted them. "What up, Red Rum?"

"All is well," Damien replied with a smile. "You're really enjoying the city of Atlanta, huh?"

"Ain't nothin' like fresh Georgia peaches," Wiz said with a smile as they entered the upscale restaurant and received VIP treatment.

"So you staying with Drako?"

"Yeah, yeah," Wiz quickly lied and changed the subject. "Look, Dame, we need to talk, but we got to make it fast. I'm on a tight."

"I understand," Damien responded as he pointed security to the table across from him and Wiz.

As soon as they sat down, Wiz got to the point. "We gotta spend money to make money. Swirl is at 1.8 mil' and slowing down at SoundScan. It's been seven weeks, and I want to certify him as double platinum by his eighth week. This will boost his future sales and put him in a class with cats like Ludacris. And it'll open doors for endorsement deals and a bunch of other money-making shit."

Damien thought for a brief second. "How do you think we can boost those sales in a week?"

Wiz grinned before responding. "That's just it, I don't! Damien, I want you to buy the other 200,000 units. We'll get it all back a couple times over in the end, feel me?"

"I'll have it done in no time," Damien replied, understanding the plan.

"Cool."

Just then, their waiter strolled up. They ordered quick appetizers and a bottle of chilled champagne.

"You know I don't mean to be rude, but I gotta make this snappy," Wiz said.

"No problem. I'll meet you in Memphis later tonight, and I'll keep you posted on my progress with the units ASAP."

"Good." Wiz threw back a gulp of bubbly.

They picked over the appetizers. A few minutes later, they shook hands and went their separate ways.

"Look, Bless, I'm tellin' you, man, nothin' could be better. Can't you see? Swirl done moved two million units already! He's certified. A guaranteed sell-out money-makin' hit!" Wiz spoke through his cell phone while traveling in a charter jet.

"You sure about this one, son? I mean, it could go either way. They may not even buy it," Bless shot back, uncertain of Wiz's proposition.

"Look, Bless, I ain't never gave nobody bad advice. What you gotta realize is timing can be just as important as the lyrics and tracks. We in this shit to get money, and I'm tellin' you there's still more cake to be baked!" Wiz took complete control of the conversation as he continued to press his scheme.

"Bless, I'm tellin' you, it's always the artists beefing, but we're two CEOs who can spit it! Ain't nothin' like two giants gettin' involved with this beef. Man, they gon' eat it up. Plus, once the two heads call a truce, everybody gonna follow! I got BET's ear right now. We can truce this shit out on *106 and Park*, *Testimony*, and some mo' shit! Anyway you spell beef, it spells paper! Plus, we can turn it off wheneva'. Man, is you feelin' this money train or what?"

Bless paused before responding. " . . . I'm feelin' you, son. Let's get dis' money and finish dis' shit!"

"Good, good. I'ma set the tone tonight on stage in Memphis once I get the crowd crunk. I'ma announce my album release will be early, and you know it's a lil sump'n sump'n comin' at you on this one."

Bless laughed. "Oh yeah, well guess what, son? I'ma murder yo' ass on wax for this, so get ready. Here it come!"

They both laughed at his fake threat. "Yo, Wiz, check it. I need a lil somethin'. You know that shorty, White Chocolate featured in Swirl's "Kill 'Em Slow" video?"

"Yeah, what up?"

"Nah, son, I'm just saying shorty phat. I'm tryna see her or that other shorty, Myria, I think her name is. Who she fuckin' wit'? What's it hittin' for?"

"Oh, White Chocolate," Wiz responded at the thought of Bless shoving his dick down Myria's throat. "She cool. She ain't cuttin' like that. She way phatter than that stuck-up ass Myria. Just be cool; I'll slide her the number and make her feel important. I owe ya a lil sump'n anyway.

"But that's small to a giant. Let's look at this money. That's what's big. When this shit is over, we gon' have a party in Morocco bigger than Puffy—I'm talkin' 'bout bein' the first niggaz to stunt on another planet, ya dig?"

"Son, you burnt out. You say anything! We'll see, won't we?" Bless replied with a chuckle.

"Bless, I ain't stuntin'. I mean exactly what I say. Just follow suit . . . my plane is about to land. I'll be atcha'—one!" Wiz hung up the phone as his plane prepared to touch down in Memphis, Tennessee.

Shortly thereafter, he and two bodyguards Drako sent to meet him were enroute back to the set where the taping for Swirl's video was underway.

A Life for A Life

Wiz beamed with pride as he stepped onto the busy set. He saw Swirl's tour bus and the bevy of fine women he'd chosen to complement his video. Of course they were all straight from New Orleans and they all showered Wiz with mad love. He waltzed straight over and sat in the open seat next to the director as they wrapped up the last take.

He saw that Drako had roped off a designated area to provide Swirl and his assistants' a little more personal space than normal. Drako posted security near each entry point and he gave orders through his headset.

"Man, you got it lookin' real professional," Wiz admitted as Drako stepped up to him.

"It's nothing hard about it. Scope out the spot, then cover your investments." Drako offered up a light smile and some dap.

"Indeed." Wiz smiled back. Drako could see his eyes traipsing over the set for which girl he was gonna choose for the day. "Well, you know me. It doesn't change often. I need to unwind a little before we make this concert tonight." He sucked his diamond grill as his eyes settled on a fine light- skinned Creole chick with hair hanging to nearly her butt.

"Well." Drako looked at his watch as Swirl stepped beside him. "You got about four hours to get it in before we hit the FedexForum." He was referring to Swirl's concert.

"Oh, we'll get it in." Wiz chuckled and glanced Swirl's way. "Man, who is that broad?" He pointed to the girl he'd been scoping.

With one glance Swirl said, "Man, don't waste your time. That's April, she just a pretty hoody. She ain't nothin'. Plus, that's Jay-poon's jump off."

"Hmph . . ." Wiz huffed. "We'll see."

Swirl nodded at Wiz with a grin. "Forget all that. I'm telling you it's nothin'. Now let's go spark up. I wanna be right for this show."

Wiz adjusted his frames and stood to his feet. He was eager to start the party in Memphis.

"Hey, look man." Drako stopped Wiz in his tracks. "I need to holler at you before you get caught up."

"What's goin' on?" Wiz's forehead wrinkled up a bit. He sensed a hint of urgency in Drako's tone.

"Look man, I got some great ideas. I see a few things that could really help out around here, and I need you to take a moment to sit down with me on them."

Wiz nodded his head in the direction of the trailer. "Well, come on. We can sit down for a quick moment while—"

"Nah, man. That's part of what I'm saying." Drako spoke firm but sincerely. "I ain't tryna run the business or your life; you do what you like. But as for me I ain't wit' all the blazin' and wild parties. I'm just trying to get my shit in order. I was thinking maybe you should let me handle the management arm. This way I could work with the artists a lot closer, but not be solely responsible for their day to day functions. You, I mean, this label—these artists need structure. Why don't you take that responsibility off of yourself and place it on me?" The smile melted from Wiz's face as Drako's thoughts registered in his mind.

"Wait. Hold up, man. I really think you moving way too fast. What you think you can run Red Rum better than me?" His unexpected response surprised Drako.

"Nah, player. It ain't nothing like that. I'm just saying from a business aspect I see—"

"Business? Come on, man. Red Rum didn't make it this far with a man who don't know business." Wiz now had a sour look to his face. "Drako, all I asked you was to be cool. I got you, man. My plate is a little full, but believe me, I know what ta do."

Drako didn't even respond. His mind was still trying to understand how the hell Wiz could take offense to someone like himself giving him sincere advice.

"Gone and do what you gotta do," Drako said, masking his thoughts. He didn't want to say or do anything stupid until he figured out where this sensitive side of Wiz was coming from.

"I'ma wrap things up out here." He turned and walked away, seething internally with disappointment.

Drako went about his security duties as discussed, but he watched Wiz, Swirl, and the camp with a new outlook for the next few hours.

It seemed as though whatever kind of cannabis Wiz had smoked in that trailer made him forget all he'd said. He acted as though he'd never heard any of Drako's requests.

The Red Rum camp partied hard until it was nearly time for the concert.

Drako and the security team led the camps' entourage through the backstage entrance, and as always, Swirl brought the crowd to his feet with his gangster lyric performances. When everybody was sure the show had reached its peak, Wiz busted out and tossed his shirt into the crowd. The crowd roared into a frenzy. Wiz was now blazing his 150 carat diamond Red Rum charm. He immediately blasted on Bless and Fatt Katt, and then announced his album to drop soon.

The concert and the stunt with Bless turned out to be a complete success. Drako snapped a rack of pictures of the finest women Memphis had to offer and of Swirl's scantily dressed dancers backstage for Toney, Deuce, and his friends back in prison.

Drako stayed close as the party moved to Beal Street for a while, but then ended in the private suites the camp had reserved at the ritzy Peabody Hotel. Drako was ready to get to his suite where Diamond awaited him.

Wiz was already enjoying his suite with the two ladies he'd spent most of the night partying with back on Beal Street. He knew his night would be long, and so would Damien's, whose suite was just across the hall. But first thing tomorrow he had full intentions to meet with Damien about Drako again.

It was late, past noon when Wiz walked the two ladies he'd partied with to the door. He had to get one more feel of her soft ass just before he sent her on her way.

Damien came waltzing up with his briefcase in hand just as Wiz dismissed her. "Hey. Isn't that Jay-poon's girl?" Damien turned and squinted, trying to get another look as the ladies disappeared down the hallway.

"I-I 'on know. If it is, she didn't mention it ta me." Wiz couldn't even look Damien in the eyes.

"Hmm . . ." Damien huffed suspiciously, watching the ladies step onto the elevator. He turned and walked through the door.

"So what's the business?" he asked, politely standing his briefcase next to the recliner he sat in.

Wiz secured the door and turned to him with a sigh. "Dame, I think I'm soon going to be faced with a real dilemma here." He walked over and sat on the couch in from of Damien. "It's Drako. Man, I know he ain't happy. I know him too well. I know he's a smart man. Smarter than you or anybody would think until he opens up to you. I feel something brewing inside him. He wants to get it out and prove to himself and Diamond that he can do things . . . the right things in a big way." Wiz nodded his head in certainty.

Damien reclined back casually and calmly crossed one leg over the other. "And you say that to say?" He held his hands apart as if awaiting a response.

80

"He wants an executive position, a stake in the company so to speak. He ain't used to being an underboss, not even to me. He's a leader, and I know I owe him—"

Damien laughed.

"Do you find something funny here?" Wiz asked angrily.

"No, no." Damien chuckled again. "I apologize for my outburst" He grabbed hold of his briefcase and stood up. "This is too personal. I cannot advise you from a personal point of view. I never will." Damien fished a ring of keys from his pocket and headed for the door.

"And I'm not asking you to give me personal advice now, dammit!" Wiz shouted. Damien stopped in his tracks and turned around. "I've got a major issue here. One with a true friend, and I'm simply asking you what's the best way to go about it, that's all!" Wiz hopped to his feet. "You've been my go-to-man for everything else. Even the shaky shit I can't share with anybody. So why the fuck can't you advise me now?" He snarled.

"Very well then!" Damien sat his briefcase down with a thud. "You *don't* go about it, damn it!"

"You what?" Wiz looked stupefied.

"I said you *don't*, damn it!" This time Damien stepped right up to Wiz's face.

"Now, I can give you bullshit or I can give you the truth. And the truth is that signing Drako's name to anything connected to Red Rum at this point is the most pathetic thing I've ever heard. Don't you realize he just got released from federal prison? Don't you of all people know why he was convicted? You know firsthand the things he's kept to himself, and you're a smart enough man to know that if the Feds had one shred of evidence to prove you used drug money to start up Red Rum they would use everything in their power to destroy it!" Damien stood as stone-faced as Wiz had ever seen him.

"I'm certainly not saying don't help him, but a stake, a signature. A tie-in that strong I would not want to be a part of." Damien cleared his throat after hearing the crack in his voice.

Wiz thought for a lingering moment. He'd recalled when Death-Row had affiliation problems, and then Murder Inc. Without much thought he knew Damien was all the way right.

"Well tell me, Damien. What can I do?"

Damien reached for a glass off the bar, filled it with water, and took a seat and a moment to think himself.

"Wiz, there's a lot at stake here. A hundred plus million dollar entity. This is not peanuts. I've been with you a long while. I've only given you my best." He swallowed a lump in his throat. "I like Drako a lot, too, but in all honesty, I've given you the best advice. Throw him some money to help him through. But as far as a percentage, any businessman knows that's gonna take some time."

"What do I tell him meanwhile?" Wiz asked, full of disappointment.

"Wiz, for one—in this business—hell, any business of this magnitude, you have to be a shrewd businessman." His expression softened a bit. "Put it on paper. Hide behind contracts. You can have things drawn up and it'll take months for various accounts, etcetera, to be cleared. You can buy yourself at least a year by doing so. I think you should give all that you've accomplished here a window of at least that long."

All Wiz could do was down his head as he took it all in. He wanted to help Drako for sure, but it would have to be done the right way. He wasn't about to let his personal feelings sway him off of his fortune. Feelings of guilt had made him want to confide in someone. He knew the ecstasy pills and codeine syrup he'd tried for the first time over his three day binge had him anxious and geeking for more when Drako approached him. But he wasn't sure if his reaction had been an appropriate one.

A Life for A Life

Wiz was now reassured that he'd handled the situation just right. Drako, for the first time in his life would have to learn to be the underboss. He'd hate to deceive him behind paperwork and lies, but in the end he knew it would be for the best. For now Wiz planned to stay focused on his own schemes. Keeping Drako blind to that was enough all by itself. Once he finished his plans against Take Money Records he told himself he'd figure out a safe way to eventually cut Drako in.

Mike Jefferies

84

Chapter Ten

Drako

Drako had accessed his keycard and quietly slipped back into his suite. He was first met with the sweet smell of Diamond's body spray before he found her fast asleep in the middle of the king-size bed with two low burning candles flickering softly.

Slipping out of his Timbs, and pulling his shirt over his head, he ran a loving gaze over Diamond's creamy smooth skin that peeked from beneath the satin sheet. He loved everything about her from the bottom of her pretty feet to the fine roots of soft, stringy hair in the center of her crown. He watched as she began to stir a moment and then turned over on her side, feeling him near.

She didn't even open her eyes when she scooted over a little to make room for her man. Drako was down to his boxers when his weight settled on the mattress beside her. The moment his head hit the pillow, her hand slid across his chest and clung to his shoulder. She moved in close, now resting her head on his chest.

He'd first hoped to come back and tell Diamond all the good things he'd seen at Red Rum and how hard Wiz worked, but the more the day unfolded, the faster those hopes seemed to fade. He kissed her forehead and ran his hand down her back until it rested on her butt. A million thoughts raced through his mind and none of them were good. The only thing good to him right now was what had always been good to him and that was Diamond.

She raised her head to look at him. "You okay, baby?" She placed a hand on his cheek, turning his face to hers.

"Yeah baby. Just tired. It was a long day," he lied, turning his gaze back to the ceiling.

She watched him close his eyes, and she closed hers.

"Get some rest, baby." Drako coaxed her back to sleep with a slow caress up and down her spine.

He thought about confiding in Diamond, but then thought better of it. His job was to take care of her and please her. Not cry to her about Wiz or the fucking label. No, instead of complaining he decided to first figure things out.

A lot of things he'd seen at Red Rum didn't sit well with him. But even more than that he thought he saw some things in Wiz he'd never hoped to see. He was almost certain Wiz was using harder drugs than weed. And he saw that his celebrity status had him powerstruck.

Drako heard the uncertainty in Wiz's tone; he sensed the fear filtering through his eyes. Wiz knew all too well the desires Drako had in mind, and being a good judge of character he felt that Wiz was not going to help him in that capacity anytime soon.

Letting out a small sigh, he peered down at Diamond once again, still trying to figure out if Wiz's motive was fueled by jealousy, greed, or just plain ignorance. At that moment he didn't give a damn. All he knew was he felt much more than just slighted. He felt betrayed, and now giving up or giving in wasn't an option. His plan was to always win. He thought better than to show his hand just yet.

Swallowing another lump and his pride simultaneously, he decided to stick around Red Rum and play his role until he could get what he was due. Because of their long term friendship and the bond Wiz shared with Diamond as well, Drako would give

Wiz the benefit of the doubt. A sensible window to make things good. But if his premonition was right about Wiz, friend or foe, Drako was going to make him pay dearly.

Toney had always told Drako that plan number one wasn't any good until plan number two was complete. Drako already had plans number two and three unfolding in his head.

With or without Wiz, Drako was determined to have all he envisioned. He was going to take care of Diamond, showering her with the world. Just then another thought struck Drako, and he nodded his head one last time. He knew there was one thing that would sting Wiz in the worst way. Tomorrow, Drako would start realigning his priorities and Wiz wouldn't have a clue. Drako had just been pricked the wrong way and there was no turning back. His mind was already playing the game—raw!

By checkout time, Drako was eager to get back home. Once his plans started unfolding in his head they wouldn't seem to stop. They were still materializing in a big way as he sat on the bed and watched Diamond pull a form fitting pair of designer jeans up over her thong. She turned to Drako snapping her jeans at the waist. "What are you up to?" She couldn't hold it in any longer. "And why are you looking at me like that?" she asked, wearing a baffled expression.

Drako stood up, reached for her and then pulled her into his arms. "'Cause I love you so much," he said. *And because you'd be perfect for this scheme,* he thought to himself as he planted a kiss on her cheek.

"Un-huh . . ." She tilted her head, still giving him a sort of suspicious eye. She didn't like the sound of his voice when she'd heard him call Damien and arrange to meet with him so soon.

"Why you got to run off to meet Damien so fast?" she whined. "I've been cooped up in this hotel for nearly three days. I was looking forward to us getting out a little tonight."

"It's going to be okay. It won't take long. I just really need to check on some things that are better not spoken over the phone."

Diamond smacked her lips dismissively. "Whatever Drako." She shouldered past him and grabbed her purse from the bed. "Let's just get outta here." She headed for the door.

Drako was sitting in a comfortable leather recliner in his entertainment room trying to press another two hours off the clock before he was to meet Damien at a small sushi-bar near Downtown Atlanta. He was channel surfing with his remote in hand when his cell phone rang. Reading the caller-ID he was happy to know it was either Toney or Deuce calling to check on him and the outside world once again.

Hearing Toney's voice spill through the recording, he pressed 5 to accept charges.

"What's good, man?" Drako tried to sound upbeat. Toney laughed.

"Fuck kinda trick question is that. You know my position and I can't think of but two things that could make it good. Freedom or the next best thing to it." Toney chuckled, trying to convey his words as a joke over the monitored prison phones. But all the while Drako knew the next thing to it meant revenge. Revenge against Vinny Pazo.

"You know I only hope the best for you." Drako was telling Toney in code that he was still committed to the cause. "I'm gonna be sending you some pictures soon. I'm gonna send you some paper, too. I just haven't gotten around to it yet, 'cause things really haven't worked out the way I planned just yet."

Toney held the phone in silence for a moment. It went without saying that Drako obviously wasn't met with the lump sum he'd hoped for.

"Oh . . ." Toney's voice cracked with a hint of despair. "Drako, we spoke about times like this. Money, as well as ego can ultimately be the root of every man's evil." Toney sighed. "Learn what you can and take the lesson in stride. And stop allowing your right hand to know what your left hand is doing at all times. I know you're a smart kid. You got all you need." He paused a moment.

"Can you remember the last thing I told you about life?"

"Yeah." Drako cleared his throat and sat up straight. "I'll always be my own man, regardless of—"

"Then I know you'll be just fine." Toney didn't even allow him to finish his sentence, indicating that Drako was thinking just right. "And don't worry yourself with sending me no fucking pictures. I'll just be happy knowing that you're free and living the life you finally deserve."

"Just don't think I forgot you. I won't be like the other cats you see come and go. I'ma be steady on my grind." Those words caused Toney to smile.

As expected, he figured Drako's life would quickly be overwhelmed and consumed by Wiz's star power, but all in all he knew Drako was still on board.

"I'm sure I'll hear good things from you soon." Toney rounded up their conversation at the beep of the one minute warning.

"No doubt, man. Just hold ya head and stay up."

"Of course."

"One." The phone went silent. Drako pressed the end button now feeling a wave of even more determination. Toney had dealt with Tycoons worth millions for all of his life. He'd explained to Drako how money and power often changed people. Drako just never thought it would affect him and Wiz. He was now doubly assured of what he needed to do.

He reached down and picked up the untouched Louis Vuitton bag of cash Wiz had given him. So far he'd lived off an additional ten thousand dollar stack of cash Wiz tossed him the first day he visited Red Rum.

Drako unzipped the bag looking over the money again, hoping it would be all the decoy he needed since he was about to rob the bank without using a gun. He zipped the bag back up and headed for the door.

Spotting the SUV, Drako pulled his BMW along side it and hopped in the truck with Damien. "I 'on fuck wit' no sushi," Drako said, giving Damien dap as soon as he was settled in. "And I didn't call you here to waste either one of our time." Drako held a firm glare.

"Well, what's so important that you feel the need to tell me?" Damien leaned over and turned off the stereo.

"Look man, I need some help and I need you to move fast."

"What kind of help?" Damien knew Drako knew his MO.

"I need to get Diamond some proper ID. I need a clean profile of a Caucasian woman about her age to begin with."

Damien smirked easily and reared back in his seat. "Well, I'm sure you know I deal with some of the best identity thieves in this country." He clasped his fingers together proudly. "That shouldn't pose a problem. I'd just have to find a woman of similarity in another state."

"Good. I'm gonna also need help doctoring up a resume and finding her a job."

"Hmm . . . I see." Damien nodded and stroked at his chin a moment. He turned to Drako. "What you're asking, Drako. Are you sure you're ready for that?"

Drako sucked his teeth and exhaled. "Look man, I got this. I can handle anything I decide to make myself a part of. I'm not about to sit around and wait for no fuckin' handouts. I ain't no roach ass nigga or a leech!" Drako pounded a fist onto his thigh. "Wiz is gone get that money right in due time. I'ma just give him the opportunity before I decide to smash on his ass." Drako didn't smile a centimeter.

"But right now I ain't got no fuckin' year to wait on mine. I ain't got months to wait. I got a hell of a plan and I need about ten million to be comfortable. With all this goddamn money floating around I can see it in my sights! I see it, I'm claiming it, and it's gone be mine within a year!" Every word he spoke sounded matter of factly. "Just keep our business here and it'll be all good."

"You don't have to tell me that," Damien replied firmly. "I'll have your best interest at heart."

"Good, but like I said, I really need you to move fast on this. I got to get this thing moving."

"Be cool." Damien smiled. "When I tell you I got you, I mean I got you! Nothing makes me prouder than a man who holds his own."

Drako was all smiles underneath the hard face he wore. He knew Damien wasn't Toney, but his heart was just as black. Damien would keep Drako's secrets and was down with everything Drako had in mind, which made him feel that he was the closest thing to Toney he had on the streets.

"I'll be shootin' you that startup capital in a few weeks." Drako gave him another pound and a wink and reached for the door handle. "I'll be in touch." He got out the SUV and closed the door behind him.

Damien put his SUV in gear and pulled away. *One year! Ten million? Fuck!* he thought to himself, remembering the hunger in Drako's eyes, just as he remembered the loyalty as well. From that moment on, there was no doubt in his mind if Drako would stay committed. Damien couldn't wait to catch a break in his schedule so he could go visit with Toney and catch him up on things.

With Damien officially helping Drako with his plan, he was wondering how in the hell Diamond was gonna take it all in because the first step on his way to the top would definitely require her assistance. "Shit!" He pounded the steering wheel as he approached his gated community.

Diamond sat straight up in bed, letting the sheet drop from her breasts. "I don't give a fuck, Drako!" She snarled at him causing her cute little nose to flare. "You know you done that bad and you coulda' handled that better! How the fuck are you gone wait till we get through fucking then spring that weak shit on me?" Her chest still heaved up and down.

"Look, ma, I know I shoulda' told you sooner, but I had to think this shit through." He kept trying to clean up his mess just like he'd been doing for nearly the last ten minutes.

"Diamond, I'm telling you, I feel like Wiz playing me. He shoulda' done more. This gaddamn house ain't in neither of our names. The car is registered to Red Rum Records and even if he called himself paying me back, that funky ass hunned' grand ain't even as much as we left him." Diamond knew Drako had a point. She wasn't tripping over the other small politics about the fake beefs Drako believed Wiz was orchestrating to keep his brand in the media's eye. But she was concerned if Wiz may have started dabbling in hard drugs.

"Well, maybe all that is right, but it don't give you a reason to hold back on me. You've been planning this shit for days! You don't think I felt how tense you were the other night when you made it back to the suite?" She flopped her head back on the pillow and looked at the ceiling. "And now you're asking for my help?" She nodded her head in disbelief.

"Baby, I'm telling you what I need from you is really simple. I just need you to take the job for thirty to maybe forty-five days. There's no risk involved. I'm telling you, identity theft is not detectable until *after* the crime is done." Drako reached out and began to rub her side soothingly.

"That still ain't the point." She pushed his hand away. "I stand by your side because I love you and I want to, not because you persuade me. Don't play me like I'm slow. I'm not a fuckin' chicken head!" She snatched the covers back and hopped out of bed with her hands on her hips. "You try to play me like one again you'll be sorrier than you ever imagined!" Drako's eyes slid over her breasts and down to her mound before she turned and stormed off to the bathroom and slammed the door behind her.

All he could envision were the two sexy dimples at the top of her butt before she vanished. Drako lay back down kicking himself in the ass for not telling Diamond first. He knew she was a cold trooper. Diamond was his everything, the best part of him by far. At first he'd hoped not to need her, but to get started promptly on the goal he'd set, it was inevitable. He knew Diamond trusted him and believed in him, and she knew him well enough to know that there was no turning back for him. She was mad and he just hoped he still had her support. He decided to work on plan three in his head.

✧ ✧ ✧ ✧ ✧

A while later Diamond had soaked in a warm bath of bubbles and stewed over everything Drako had said. She knew Drako was smart and would surely not risk putting her in harm's way. Even though she was pissed earlier she felt she should have at least heard him through. After drying herself off and moisturizing her skin she slid back in bed right in front of him. She reached back and pulled his strong hands around her waist. He snuggled up close to her butt again. She pulled a few strands of her damp hair back behind her ear. "Lace me, baby," she whispered in the dark. "Teach me what playing the game raw means."

Drako kissed her softly on her neck. "It's easy, ma. We gone rob these banks without a gun." He palmed her tittie. "All you got to do is listen."

"Just lead, baby. You know I'll follow."

Drako smiled. He knew in his heart Diamond would ride till the end. He began to give her the game from top to bottom into the wee hours of the night. Then he made love to her to seal the deal once again.

Drako fell asleep a happy man because he knew soon and very soon it would be game on.

Chapter Eleven

Wiz

"Y'all stop arguing." Wiz raised his voice and tried to regain his focus on the situation at hand. After she comes up, you go down." He stared at the light-skinned chick to his right.

She smacked her lips, sat up a bit, and continued to massage Wiz's balls while her friend took full control, bobbing up and down on his big dick.

"Mm . . . yeah, that's better," he said, running his fingers through her short styled cut. "Oh yeah . . . Damn . . . mm!" He was getting back into it. "How you say her name again?" he asked the light-skinned girl while holding her friend's head with both hands now.

"April. Her name is April, I'm Tyrienna," she corrected.

"Oh, yeah . . . that's—oh, good . . ." He felt himself about to explode. "Take it all!" he grunted. "Don't waste a drop!" He closed his eyes and jizzed down her throat.

"Mm hmm! You got that bomb head." He smiled down at her as she milked him dry. "And you the bomb, too, April." He winked at the light-skinned chick again.

"My name's not April!" She tossed her long hair back over her shoulder with attitude.

"Whatever. My bad. Y'all do each other." Wiz slid from between the two women and hopped out of bed. He was already

running late, but he knew he had to make it to the set. He'd received a phone call yesterday that didn't sit well with him at all. His intentions were to come to St. Louis and party hard for two nights leading up to the video shoot, but he ended up cutting things short and finding two chicks to help mellow his mood.

"Hey," he yelled over his shoulder when he reached the bathroom. "Y'all better kiss and make up by the time I'm done in here." He watched the dark-skinned chick smile and lay on top of the other girl.

"That's what I'm talkin' 'bout." He thought out loud and stepped in the bathroom. He quickly cleaned himself and tried to ready his mind for a long day. He needed to speak with Damien first about his ongoing troubles with the IRS. Also, he still had some unfinished business with Bless and Take Money Records that was eating him alive.

After leaving his suite in a dash and making it to the set, Wiz felt as though the sun couldn't have shone more beautifully in any other place than it did on him. He was in front of the green screen that had been placed on Memorial Drive in front of the historical Gateway Arch in Downtown St. Louis. Today was the making of the second video of Wiz's latest album, and it featured one of the Lou's hottest rappers, Lil Breezy.

Drako stood to the side, hardly even noticed as he called shots through his headset to the rest of his security team. Drako snickered as Wiz pulled off his T-shirt and tossed it toward the camera, which was his signature move. Wiz worked the camera, and the directors usually captured his two-step performance in one or two takes. The moment Wiz became shirtless the green screen was bombarded with all the sexy dancers that Wiz had chosen. Each girl wore a blood burgundy colored bikini, a trademark of Red Rum.

One by one, each dancer performed their sexy moves in front of Wiz. The last girl to do her thing in front of him was surely the featured vixen. Standing in place, she wound her hips in the direction of the camera, and then turned away from Wiz, facing the camera. She began to jerk her arms and hips simultaneously until they met in unison at a sexy rhythm. The look on Wiz's face and every other spectators face confirmed that she had seized the show.

As soon as the director yelled "cut," White Chocolate stopped dancing. The set assistants quickly ran over and handed Wiz a towel to dab the sweat from his face.

Wiz turned to White Chocolate with a smile. "Damn, lil momma, I think you just made *XXL's* eye candy of the month." White Chocolate slapped Wiz's shoulder playfully.

"Wiz, you so crazy, but I hope you're right. I could use the exposure."

"You ain't gone have no problems. You hot right now. You got that look." His eyes scanned down her body. "And I hear niggaz been tryin' to get at ya."

"For real, Wiz?" She crossed her arms and raised a brow with excitement.

"Hell yeah, you know I 'on play them type of games." He gave her a firm glare. "Look, we 'bout to head over to Pink Slip after Breezy's girls shoot this last take. If you want me to fill you in just come on by."

She smiled even wider. "Say no more," she chimed back. She turned away adjusting her bikini from crawling back up her ass as she sauntered away in a hurry.

Wiz was trying to catch a good look at her body. She wasn't petite like Myria. She was rather tall, five-ten with a trim waist and as thick as a woman could be without being considered fat.

Her 40-inch plus hip measurements made her an ass connoisseurs dream. With her cinnamon brown skin and hair that dropped to the center of her back, Wiz could see exactly how she'd once captured Swirl's attention, but also why they kept her in front of the lens and why Bless had inquired about her.

"Stop fiending off Swirl's girl!" Drako stepped up close and caught him off guard with a sharp whisper.

Wiz was surprised, turning to Drako with a devious grin. "Nah, man. It ain't like that. I–I just didn't realize how fine that bitch was really built." He nodded his head in wonderment. "Fuck it. You can't have 'em all," he said as he and Drako stepped off the set to let Lil Breezy wrap up the final take.

"So when did you realize they been tailing you?" Drako asked Wiz about the two men he'd pointed out. He'd spotted them tailing the entourage shortly after they'd touched down in St. Louis.

"Man, trust me. They ain't shit!" Wiz shrugged at the thought. "It's just them fake ass hip-hop cops. They done put together a task force to follow rappers around. They been doing that stupid shit for years. They never build any cases that amount to shit. A gun charge here or there. Find a lil pills or weed and drag a niggaz name through the mud is about all it ever amounts to." Drako leered at Wiz, taking it all in carefully. He'd heard speculations about the hip-hop cops, but he didn't really know if it was all together true.

"Well, if it ain't no big deal why do you seem so uptight?" Drako could normally detect when there was something more to what Wiz was saying. Wiz wasn't good at masking his emotions at all.

"Nah, man. It's nothing really. And it definitely ain't 'cause of them." He turned a small foldout chair to face the green screen and took a seat.

"So what the hell is it then?" Drako turned a chair himself and sat down to face him.

"Look, I got a call from my accountant. The fucking IRS wants to subpoena my tax returns for the last six years."

"What the fuck?" Drako thought with wide eyes. "You mean to tell me you being audited by the Feds?" He bolted back to his feet before he knew it.

"No . . . no, sit back down." Wiz looked around a bit, urging Drako to keep it cool. "It's not like that. I think it's like procedure and them nosey bastards have the right in this country to open your books at any time. Hell, they opened Bill Gates, Zuckerburg and—"

"And?" Drako's tone was loud and over powering. "You ain't nan one of them! You're a fucking black man, which means anytime the Feds, the IRS, to be specific, steps in and wants to see your books—you just got audited, dammit!"

Wiz thought for a short moment with his head hung low; then he looked back at Drako. "And it still don't make a fuck!" He sucked his diamond grill arrogantly. "Red Rum is squeaky clean. All the dirty money washed away years ago, lil daddy. I ain't did shit but grind since you left. This shit come from the hustle. My head hustle, not the muscle. I ain't took shit from nobody! They just hate to see a black man with this much power. With so much influence over an entire genre." His chest seemed to swell with pride. "And now they believe taking it is like disarming me." He nodded his head, feeling sure of his assessment.

Drako never interrupted him. He wanted Wiz to spill his guts. He was now assured that Wiz was blinded by his overwhelming success and was addicted to making the headlines.

 99

Drako nodded his head at Wiz's ignorance. "You love this shit," he said flatly. "Not just the money, but the fake shit that comes with it." His response jolted Wiz, causing him to look at Drako with wide eyes, but Drako pressed on. "Man, I'ma tell you once. You better open your eyes to this shit. To what's going on around you. I can't find no humor in taking these Feds lightly. These are the same people who print the money and the same people that will take every goddamn penny you got!" Drako huffed, letting his words settle in. "What you need first and foremost is a real person who knows their shit and can be trusted to handle your books.

"Then you need to sit Jay-poon and them clowns down and continue building a respectable brand. You don't need these cop, hip-hop police, or whatever the fuck you call 'em sleeping on your front porch."

"Stt . . ." Wiz sucked diamonds and came up with a nasty smirk. "Like I said, fuck 'em! It is what it is at the Rum. Shit come our way, then its shit we handle! I—"

"Hold the fuck up, nigga! Who the fuck you think you talkin' to?" Drako barked, causing the rest of Wiz's words to freeze in his throat. "Yo, straight up, man. I'm just here trying to tell you something good, and this will be the last time you look clean through me." Drako sat straight up with his jaws tight.

"Hold up, man. I'm–I'm just sayin' be cool. I–I know what my plan is for this company. Shit, I–I know my plan for us." Wiz changed his whole tune. No matter how high or blind he was, he knew firsthand what would happen if and when Drako was pushed over that line.

"I know you got a plan." Drako had an attitude and was doing his best to curb it. "But don't come at me wit' that gangsta shit. You and I both know you ain't 'bout that. You a businessman, you make great beats, and you can portray whatever you like. Just don't come at me sideways. Now if you ain't clean I suggest you get that way."

"Drako man, I ain't doing shit. I ain't the cause of all this—"

"Look." Drako cut him off with the raise of his hand. "Ain't no need in tryin' to sell me on shit. I see right through your charade. You don't think I know all this shit between Swirl and Fatt Katt is behind your hand? All the shit he talk and you ain't once spoke to me about us trying to see 'bout him?" Drako nodded his head knowingly. "Man, cut that fake shit out before someone really gets hurt. Jay-poon a bitch and everybody he talking about is not playing the same games as him." Drako stood to his feet.

"And another thang . . . I hear well. Don't come out ya mouth with no more slick remarks about you built this shit. I caught what you said about you got it with your head hustle and not your muscle. I remember you used to always say you're the brain and I'm the muscle. Nigga, don't forget the muscle is what helped you keep it."

"I ain't mean nothin' by that. Real talk, man, I was just tryin' to cap slick, ya dig?"

"Whatever, man. I heard you and I'ma be waiting patiently to see what that plan is you got for us." Drako booted his chair aside. "Well, since it's a wrap around here I'ma skip Club Pink Slip. I'ma head back and get some rest. Me and Diamond got things to do tomorrow."

"Cool, I'll call ya in a couple days," Wiz said lightly. He thought about giving Drako dap, but then thought better of it. He knew Drako was a little pissed and as a businessman he didn't want to give in or make Drako feel like he was spooked by him.

Wiz let out a breath as he watched Drako walk off the set still giving orders to his security team he was leaving behind. Wiz told himself soon he was gonna end the beef wars. Maybe Drako was right, but for now he had to finish what he started.

Looking at Drako climb into the Range Rover and zip away, Wiz knew sooner or later he had to do something big. Even if Drako wasn't used to it, Wiz believed that he could handle it just right. He'd also seen Drako holding back his anger and he damn sure wasn't up for fighting that fool if it ever came to that. But at the end of the day, Wiz was a man just like him and he'd damn sure find a way to handle his business. "Fuck it!" Wiz said aloud, standing to his feet as he saw White Chocolate come out the trailer. *A hunned million dollars strong.* He thought about his bank account with a smile. *Pocket change, nigga!* He smiled further as White Chocolate neared him.

"You riding wit' me?" He'd already reached for her wrist.

"Sure." She whipped up a bright, even smile.

"Cool. The gold Maybach right there." He pointed in the direction and they were out.

Chapter Twelve

Wiz

By the time the Maybach crossed the bridge and entered Brooklyn, Illinois right outside of St. Louis, Wiz had cut into White Chocolate. She was yapping away, telling Wiz all of her business about how she and Myria, *his girlfriend*, as Myria and obviously those close to her seemed to believe, were best friends.

"Yeah . . . yeah, that's good, lil sis," Wiz responded, hardly paying attention to what she'd said. "I know you're gonna go far."

She blushed a little. "Do you really think I have a—"

"Look," Wiz cut in firmly. "Just being straight up, I normally wouldn't be doing this. But I see you really doin' your thing and I just think with what you're workin' wit' you oughta' get all the work you can." He gave her a sly wink as he sucked at his diamonds and fished a card out of his pocket. "Now, my stay gone be real short at Pink Slip. I'ma get you in, show my face, and then I have ta keep on pushin', so we won't have a lot of time to talk." He passed her the card. "But when you get back to your hotel I want you to call this number."

She looked down at the card then back to Wiz as her whole smile disappeared into thin air. "Wiz, I appreciate the work and all, but it's not that way with me. Please don't take this the wrong way. You're a handsome man and I've heard all the big things about you, but me and Myria—"

Wiz cut her off with his laughter. White Chocolate looked even more puzzled.

"Wait a minute." He seized the moment trying to hold in his laughter. "I ain't tryin' to go there either. This ain't my number. This is that nigga Bless' number." Her eyes bulged for a brief moment. "You know I 'on really fuck wit' them clowns, but a reliable birdie told me he checkin' for you hard!" He looked at her with a serious expression when the chauffeur brought his Maybach to a halt in front of the club.

"Look, I know it's a lot of paper laying over that way and I just hate for you to miss out on account of our beef."

A rainbow-sized smile zipped back across her face. "For real, Wiz?"

"Get that money, lil sis. All of it. He a sucka!" Wiz smirked deviously.

"You too real, Wiz." She leaned over excitedly and gave Wiz a hug.

Wiz copped a sly feel of her ass. "And you fine as a muthafucka for real," he said with a dead serious stare to her cleavage. She sat up, quickly adjusting her shirt.

"Yep, I 'on know how I let you slip by." He nodded his head and licked his lips. She cleared her throat, breaking his trance.

"Wiz, don't go there." She tried to change topics. "You know Myria really wanted in on this video."

"Look, stop talkin' 'bout Myria. She cool, but she's not my girlfriend. We're just friends. Myria has to realize she can't be in every video. She's gonna burn herself out. She already being spread too thin. What Myria needs to do is stop nagging me and open up to new things. Why don't you teach her how ta do that?"

"Hey, no argument outta me. I understand." White Chocolate gave in.

"Good, now worry about feeding yourself . . . let's get inside."

When Wiz and White Chocolate made it through the door of Club Pink Slip, Damien was already seated at the table reserved for Red Rum. He and Lil Breezy sat surrounded by a flock of beautiful women.

"What up, durrty?" Breezy slurred as he stood and extended his hand.

"Easy money, ya heard," Wiz shot back, seeing all eyes on him. "You and Red Rum . . . we got a lot of big thangz ta do, ya heard. I want you on somethin' real gangsta wit' tha boy Swirl real soon."

"Oh, fa sho' dat'," Lil Breezy snapped back, looking at all the ice Wiz sported like only a hundred million dollar nigga could.

"Say, check this out." Wiz adjusted his frames with one hand while pulling White Chocolate a little closer with his other. "This here is first class," he said, referring to White Chocolate. "I want you to take care of her while she's in the Lou, ya dig?"

"Shiit . . . no problem, durrty." Breezy shot him a wink and stepped aside. "Have a seat." He extended an arm, watching White Chocolate take a seat in VIP.

Wiz's eyes traipsed over the room in search of something pretty enough to catch his eye. He knew his stay at the club wouldn't be long. He'd gotten what he needed from White Chocolate and pushed her through the door into good hands. Now all he had to do was let Damien enjoy himself for a while and they'd be out.

Wiz took a seat while Damien made his way to the stage to tip a few dancers. He ended up at a small table where he received lap dance after lap dance until he'd given away the entire stack Wiz had provided.

The club's atmosphere was nice. Dancers in every direction. Ballers out having a good time and the security was tight.

"Gimme another stack." Damien came up to Wiz with a desperate look in his eyes. Wiz laughed at him. Everybody at the camp was circulating the rumor of how turned out Damien was over black pussy. Once he'd gotten a taste, he couldn't get enough and there was nothing anyone could say to slow him down.

"Come on, Wiz, just one more stack. You know I hardly carry any cash." He looked pitiful, peering back at the girl who'd just been dancing for him.

"Man, it ain't that." Wiz fanned his huge pinky ring in her direction. "That ain't shit. Hit tha delete button on that bitch. I got something special lined up for you tonight." Wiz stood tall. "Let's blow this place. We need to talk."

"Shit!" Damien huffed. "This better be good!" He stomped over to the table, took another look at the girl, and then grabbed his coat.

A few moments later, Wiz's Maybach was trailed by Damien, security, and a Hummer filled with some of St. Louis's prettiest women. Wiz had already had Bless on the line. "Damn, son. Yo' lil ass rolling in money!"

Wiz smiled. "What did I tell you, player? I'm out here in St. Louis now. We just wrapped up a shoot earlier and I'm gettin' so much love it's ridiculous!"

"And you should be! You opened with over eight hundred thousand in the first week. Where are your numbers now?"

"Man, I been so busy countin' paper I ain't had time to check," Wiz bragged.

"Yeah, yeah. I feel you. I'ma be droppin' in about two weeks. I spoke with the heads at Def Jam yesterday."

"Hold up, Bless." Wiz sat straight up. "You cuttin' ya own money short! You need ta push that shit back at least another two to three weeks. You gotta let them streets anticipate. I didn't wanna drop so fast, but I spit it first. It was all in timing, baby!"

"Ya think so?" Bless sounded unsure.

"What did I tell you about SoundScan?"

"Yeah, man, you been official."

"Always . . ." Wiz sounded cocksure. "Now, I suggest you call back up to that head office and talk to whoever you need to. Just tell 'em you don't feel that your single has reached its full potential in sales."

"Yeah, man, you right. I'ma let 'em sweat for this."

"Now you thinkin' paper," Wiz capped, knowing he had Bless right where he wanted him. "But look though, I just passed the Dome, so I'm almost at the spot and you know I got a couple shorties ready to play."

"Shit is crazy out there." Bless sounded excited.

"Damn right it is. And you know I couldn't forget you. White Chocolate gone be hitting ya up real soon."

"And shorty gettin' round trip tickets to New York City," Bless shot back with a cackle.

"I can't blame ya, she thicka than a mothafucka!"

They both shared a laugh.

"Look, B, I'm out."

"I'll holla at ya, soon. And I'll see ya at the Source Awards."

"One." Wiz ended the call.

"Whew!" He reclined back, letting out another sigh of relief. *That went over well,* he thought. Now all he needed was a few minutes with Damien to wrap his long day of woes up. Wiz felt a little bad for bartering one of Swirl's jump-offs away, so to speak. But he told himself fuck it! Swirl had plenty of women

just like her and she probably didn't mean shit to him anyway. And besides, he'd rather envision her with those round trip tickets much more than Myria. He smiled to himself.

A few turns later, the Maybach had once again cruised past the Arch and was parked in front of valet at the exclusive Ritz Carlton Hotel in downtown St. Louis. Wiz directed security to escort the women upstairs and he asked Damien to sit in the Maybach for a quick chat.

"Whatever this is better be good!" Damien said again.

Wiz got right to the point. "Most of this shit is going good. I'm glad you were able to buy up Swirl's units, but there's been something else on my mind. The shit just been troubling me."

Damien sat up, seeing the look on Wiz's face. "What is it? Get to it."

"First off, the IRS is tryin' to audit me. They're checking my returns for the last six years."

Damien smiled. "Is that what you're worried about? All you gotta do is keep a clean paper trail on your money."

"My accountant says they're using frivolous excuses to justify their actions. They're acting like I have hidden accounts."

"That's nothing." Damien gave his shoulders a weak shrug. "Look how they fuck with Don King. What you gotta do is just learn their procedures and stay abreast of tax laws. These fruitless IRS probes are normal."

Wiz pondered a second. "Good, I was makin' sure we on the same page. Now what's really fuckin' with me is I still feel like I'm missing money!"

Confusion clouded Damien's face.

"Look, Dame. I mean, Swirl made his cake off this beef shit and so did Fatt Katt. Matter of fact, they got rich! I done made even more than them by coming behind them with this, and the nigga who gone get the most gone probably be Bless, 'cause he following up my shit!"

"And?" Damien asked.

"And? And I ain't gettin' a fuckin' dime from Fatt Katt's units!" Wiz fumed. "If I did eight hundred plus my first week, Bless gone do the same or better! How da' fuck can I not feel left out? I'm the nigga who put this shit together, and all that nigga screamin' is 'good lookin, son!' Good lookin' my ass! I know the nigga ain't gone kick back shit! And if I'm the brain, why should I have to miss out on all that paper?"

"Well, what do you suggest?" Damien crossed his leg and sat up.

"You remember what we was talkin' 'bout a long time ago? I believe some shit I kicked to you ain't impossible." Wiz reached for his gold cigar case. "I been doing my homework. Dame, you just gotta outthink a cat. He ain't giving up shit no matter what we say, so I wanna try and bootleg that nigga Bless' shit. Can you imagine that shit on the streets two weeks before it's released?" Wiz's voice dripped with desperation.

"Wiz, you are certainly thinking crazy. How are you gonna come up with a fully audible copy of his CD?"

"Dame, it's mostly covered. I got Bless tryin' to push his shit back two—three more weeks, which at the least gives us the window of one month from today. Secondly, we both know the masters go straight to the distributor. The distributor is the only place to steal one copy. All we need is one copy. I got a list of names of some employees, and for the right amount of money, somebody will leak one disc.

"My only problem is I can't try nobody. You know people in New York. Set the tone; 30 G's for one single copy. If you get a bite within a week to ten days, that'll leave us about two weeks to get our cut off the top!" Wiz took out his Cuban as Damien pondered his plan in silence. He lit the cigar and blew out a cloud of smoke. "So what do you think?"

Damien's response came slowly. "It could work, Wiz. I mean, you got young people, and for that kinda money for a task so easy, someone could easily fall weak to greed. Moving them won't be a problem. It'll be similar to crack on the streets of Harlem."

"Dame, I need ya to do your best and move fast! That nigga gotta pay one way or the other. I'd rather it be off da' top! Trust me, in the end, he ain't even gone miss them lil ends."

Wiz let out another cynical laugh before inhaling his Cuban once more. He exhaled, blowing the smoke directly at Damien.

Damien waved the thick, gray smoke away from his face. "You win. You did it again. You're a brilliant man."

"Nah, Dame, I'm a genius!" Wiz clarified.

"You may very well be, but so am I. I want you to pay me off the top. You can start by telling the tallest chick you got to hook up with me as soon as we get upstairs!"

Wiz laughed. "You got that. Matter of fact, I'ma make sure you get yo' first chocolate ménage a trois right here in the Lou!"

Damien was going to work for Wiz as best he could, but tonight, all he could think about was satisfying his libido. "Okay, okay, I got you. Tomorrow."

Damien got out of the Maybach resuming his lustful thoughts until they reached their suite, while the last thought resonating in Wiz's head was Bless' voice asking, "Or either that shorty, Myria, I think her name is. What she hittin' for?" Wiz laughed as he thought to himself, *For you, my friend—a couple mil'!*

Chapter Thirteen

Drako

"Windows can't get no cleaner, shawty," said the grinning worker at the auto detail shop. He had just detailed Drako's 760 Li and watched as Drako carefully inspected the job.

"I want extra air freshener. Make it vanilla aroma today."

"You got it, shawty," the man said, quickly spraying the carpet with the scent.

"Call me Drako, pahtna," Drako said as he tipped the lil man a $50 bill.

"You got dat' too, balla—I—I mean, Drako."

Drako just shook his head as he closed the door and pulled away with a proud smirk on his face.

He felt good as he whipped in and out of the heavy traffic of Peachtree Street in Downtown Atlanta. Drako wasn't just happy because it was another beautiful sunny day in the ATL. He was happy because three weeks had passed, and all his plans were coming together.

Damien had been helpful in successfully finding Drako a clean profile. Drako had opened up a business account and the account holder's name he utilized had been dead for almost a

year, so there would be no infractions. Drako had deposited all of the $100,000 into the account. He would live off his salary for now.

Diamond had a clean profile as well, and was now employed as a trustworthy employee at Hertz rental car at Hartsville Airport in Atlanta.

A few miles later, just past Lennox Mall, and having bumped three more hot TI tracks, Drako steered his BMW into the parking lot of Kinko's. He sat patiently until he saw a well-toned, petite-framed white woman exit the door.

She had medium length blonde hair, neat wire-framed glasses over her blue eyes, and was dressed casually in a denim skirt that fit her hips rather nicely as she walked up to Drako's BMW. She handed him a manila envelope as she leaned over in his window and kissed him on the lips. Drako tongued her back for a few seconds, and then broke the kiss. "Damn, girl, you gone make a nigga catch jungle fever!"

"Boy, you know I ain't no fuckin' white girl!" Diamond said sharply.

"I can't tell! You got blonde hair and blue eyes."

"Yeah, that may be right, but the only thing giving me away is this bubble. You ever seen a white girl with an ass this fine?" Diamond teased as she turned around and displayed her derriere.

"A'ight, ma, I got it. Stop teasing me or you gone end up being back real late from lunch."

"Boy, you too much! Listen, I gotta get back. There's a lil over fifty receipts in there. I get off at 3 P.M., but I want to stop by Lennox Mall on the way home, so I'll see you no later than 6 P.M. Oh yeah, stop by Cheesecake Factory and get me some cheesecake with extra strawberries on top." Diamond smiled as she leaned back in and kissed Drako again before he could even respond.

"You got that. Anything else?"

"No, baby, just be done with that other stuff 'cause you need to spend some time on your Diamond tonight."

"A'ight, but one other thing."

"What's that, baby?"

"While you're at the mall, I need you to buy some looser skirts and maybe some looser pants; that pretty ass of yours gettin' too much attention!"

"Drako, ain't nobody thinkin' 'bout me except you, baby. But okay. No problem."

"A'ight, I'll see you in a minute," Drako said, finally dismissing Diamond and watching her jump into her small rented Toyota Camry.

They both pulled back onto Peachtree. Diamond made a right turn on her way back to work. Drako, with TI blasting, hit the Cheesecake Factory and then headed straight home.

As soon as Drako pulled into his garage, he felt the relief of accomplishment. He quickly went into the kitchen and began to look over the day's receipts. He was proud of Diamond; she was playing her role nicely. At first, Diamond wanted a job at Visa headquarters, but he had told her that would limit their access to only Visa credit card numbers and information. Drako then quickly explained that he'd learned in prison that the best and most overlooked place was right under their nose—a large rental car establishment. The information on a rental car receipt could be deadly if it ended up in the wrong hands.

Drako had instructed Diamond to steal all the receipts from a day or so before. Those receipts were all placed in boxes and put on a shelf and not even thought of again until weeks later when they would all be shredded.

Each day, Diamond would steal as many as she could conceal, and during lunch break she'd photocopy the receipts at Kinko's for Drako, and then return the originals. No one would ever realize anything had been tampered with.

Drako thoroughly studied each receipt; they contained pertinent information such as full name, driver's license number, date of birth, home address, race, height and weight, and best of all: The full credit card number.

He was especially searching for black males with large bank accounts. He'd be very observant of birth dates; twenty-eight to forty years old. He'd often use addresses of upscale property to clue him in on their income and he always looked for common last names such as Jones, Brown, Williams, and Taylor, so that he could open up other accounts in their names and utilize their accounts without drawing attention.

He had already found three names for himself and one for Diamond. He passed them to Damien to get a full profile such as bank account balance, job titles, and traces on their spending patterns and account deposits and withdrawals.

Drako had been studying the receipts for almost three hours when Diamond arrived home. She came into the kitchen where he had the table covered with receipts, all spread out in separate piles for what he thought each receipt could be used for. Diamond smiled, pleased to see Drako, who only raised his head for a second to offer a light smile and a "Hey, baby," before dropping his head right back to the receipts.

"Baby, don't you see me standing here with these heavy bags?"

Drako looked up. Diamond had two large Neiman Marcus bags, one in each hand.

"Put 'em down; I'll bring 'em up in a minute."

Diamond sucked her teeth and dropped the bags. "Drako, never mind these. I got four more in the car. You need to get them, and you ain't finna' do that mess all night. I get those every day."

"A'ight, ma, I got you. Just a few more minutes. Plus, you need to get out of that wig and take that pancake makeup off ya face, unless you want me thinkin' 'bout a white girl," Drako joked.

"So you got jokes, huh? Well maybe in a *few* I just might not feel like telling you about this rich ass black man who seemed to love this white girl when he tried to holler at me today."

Drako whipped his neck around faster than a watch dog, giving Diamond his full attention. "What the fuck he talking to you about?" Drako barked with beady eyes.

"Oh, don't even trip. Just keep taking those *few* more minutes you was needing," she remarked with an attitude. She picked up one of the bags and sashayed to the bathroom, and promptly closed and locked the door behind her knowing Drako was right on her heels.

"Open this door, girl!" Drako banged twice.

"Go get the bags, Drako. I'ma need a *few* minutes now." She tried to hold in her giggles. Drako banged on the door again, but then his footsteps quickly shuffled away.

I bet he'll pay attention next time, she thought with a laugh and turned on the shower.

Pulling the blonde wig off her head, she shook her tresses out and then took off the glasses and removed her blue contacts. She stepped into the shower and began to wash away the pale compound that easily made her pass as an all-American white girl.

Drako got the bags from the car and went to the bedroom where he lay on his back in their oversized bed. He was doing his best to keep his thoughts on the situation at hand. However, he continued to find himself lightweight mad. It wasn't that he didn't trust Diamond. He just knew how pretty she was and how

aggressive men could be. Then the fact that fat ass Fatt Katt was now sitting on *106 and Park*, blatantly throwing shots at Swirl, Wiz, and the entire Red Rum camp wasn't helping either.

Unable to steer his thoughts away from Wiz, he switched off the plasma and closed his eyes. He hated that he nearly showed his hand to Wiz a few days ago. He'd thought viciously about slapping Wiz right out of the chair he sat in. But he knew it would have been a wasteful move at that time. Drako had never realized what all he'd stepped into when he stepped through the doors of Red Rum until that day. He had no idea the Feds already had Red Rum in their sights, nor the reality of what Wiz's antics could attract.

From the moment Drako pulled away that day, he was contemplating ahead to plan number three. Plan one was already set to get his money now. Drako had never hoped to revert to the things he had in mind, but with what he needed to accomplish his goal, he felt there was no other way.

Toney had explained the complexities, the benefits, and the punishment if one were to get caught. In comparison to drugs and hard crimes it was merely a slap on the wrist, and in Drako's mind the huge payday he was looking at far outweighted the slim chances of him getting caught. His schemes seemed like free money and Drako was damn sure gonna take it! Yep, plan one would hold him for now. Plan two was to get his from Wiz, and if it came down to plan three he'd exact revenge on Wiz where he knew it would sting. If his premonition was right, he knew exactly what Wiz didn't want to share. Those plans would come in due time. He sat up as Diamond stepped out of the bathroom. She stood there with her natural hair hanging past her shoulders. Her hazel eyes were back and she had on sexy yellow lace bikini underwear.

"Brang yo' ass over here, girl," Drako barked again. The smell of her fragrance hit his nose, and a wave of emotions swept over him. On the one hand he was jealous, but on the other hand that rested in his lap he felt his erection swelling more and more.

"So what the fuck you tell that nigga?" His eyes trailed her ass as she settled on the edge of the bed beside him. Diamond smacked her lips lightly and folded her arms. She was turned on by Drako's twinge of jealousy, but knew better than to play with it too long.

"Drako, stop it. I was just messing with you."

"Fuck is you playing like that for? You meant ain't—"

"No, no. He did try to holler, but I coulda' told you better."

"So what's the point then? Why you telling me now?"

"'Cause I think I may have stumbled up on something." She got up and went to retrieve her purse from the dresser as she said, "When he came in to pick up his car he asked them to check it first, which left him at the service counter with me for nearly twenty minutes. He got to yapping away about how he was this big time general contractor and that he was building a federal prison in North Carolina. He was bragging about how the government pays him nearly four million dollars a month to have the prison ready within the next year. "She rummaged a piece of paper from her purse and came back to the bed.

"So what did you say to that trick?"

She smiled. "You mean, what did I *do* to that trick? I tricked him like I was supposed to, baby. I smiled enough to make him bump his gums just enough to where I believed him, and as soon as he left I got a chance to copy that single receipt right there in the office." She passed Drako the piece of paper.

Drako quickly scanned the copied receipt with a careful eye. The man's name was Scott Smith. He was black and his address was located on Sardis Road, in Charlotte, North Carolina.

Drako smiled and thumped the paper. "This just might be my man." He hopped out of bed and went straight to call Damien.

"I got a good feel for this one," he said, dialing Damien's number. Drako knew this address was on a prestigious side of town, which was always a good sign. He fed all the information to Damien, telling him he was eager to start traffic on some heavy accounts soon.

He hung up the phone with high hopes and turned to Diamond who'd been listening attentively.

"So what now?" She sat on the bed in Indian style waiting for the next step.

"Trust me, baby, this shit simple." He sat down next to her. "All you gotta do is have the heart along with the smarts and it's like taking free money. I gotta couple of sweet schemes and in a few months they'll all pay off big!" Drako nodded with confidence and rubbed a hand up her thigh. "This shit is happening every day, just played out in different ways.

"My first lick is the simplest. I already opened a frivolous account and tossed that funky hunned' grand inside. And right now I'm putting the finishing touches on the web page for a company that sells expensive antique artifacts and things. I've also plugged in with Paypal so we can accept credit card payments. And now that you have access to all of those credit card numbers all I have to do is charge them to the account."

Diamond seemed surprised. "I get it. You're gonna be the manufacturer and the purchaser."

"Exactly. Then after about the twenty-fifth day I simply clean the account out and vanish. It's normally about thirty days before a customer is notified."

"And you can burn up those Internet cafes."

"Of course I will, and when I get through with my personal laptop I'll just burn it up and be done with it."

Diamond nodded her head, still following Drako's lead.

"Now the next jobs are a lil more complex, but at the end of the day you use the same tools to get it. It's just as easy, except they'll pay off even bigger. This is where I'm talkin' 'bout robbing banks without a gun." He noticed Diamond perk up a bit ready to hear all the details. "Damien has both of us accounts to use. All we're gonna do is steal those people identities for the next few months. I'm going to open up an account in their name, except in another state. We won't be withdrawing any money; we're just gonna ease our own money into those accounts. We won't get any attention doing that. All I need you to do is look pretty and use heavy traffic on the account. Always use the same manager so you can build up a rapport. The people we're profiling are similar to our looks. We can easily do things to conceal our identity and fit the bill as them. You can be that pretty white girl for a while and maybe I'll grow some hair." Drako winked, still rubbing that comforting hand on her thigh.

Diamond nodded in finality after taking it all in. "Sounds sweet to me," she chimed, lying down on her side. She knew Drako had researched his plan thoroughly.

"Anything else?" She glanced at him with a sexy nibble to her lip.

"Yeah . . ."

"What?"

"Get them panties off." Drako reached for his buckle.

Diamond smiled and raised her hips from the mattress.

Mike Jefferies

Chapter Fourteen

Toney Domacio

The tall, burly corrections officer rarely rendered a smile as he observed the long line of visitors while they signed themselves in religiously for visitation each Saturday. He often wondered why these beautiful women would dress up in their best to even come waste their time to see criminals, which he often considered to be scum.

His jealous heart often made him turn away women as he exercised the only power he ever held. He'd say their dresses were too short, their shirts revealed too much cleavage, or the entire ensemble was too revealing. This temporarily brought self-gratification to his jealous, lust-filled eyes. Deep down inside, he fought with himself to figure out why any sensible woman wouldn't want an honest, hard-working man like himself.

He ran the metal detector over them all and made certain women removed their shoes, emptied purses, pockets and anything he felt could be used to smuggle drugs inside. He only rendered a slight smile to very few visitors just as he always did to Charles Nobles.

"Hello, Mr. Nobles," the officer said as he disregarded the metal detector and let him sign the book as usual.

"Good Morning, Officer James," the fuzzy-haired middle aged man with thick glasses replied with a smile. He quickly moved on to follow the next officer who would lead him into the actual visitation room now that he'd gained clearance.

Charles Nobles smiled at the CO, but not because it was a good morning. He smiled because under the funny-looking toupee and non-prescription glasses, Damien had passed successfully as the modest-dressed, middle-aged man for years, coming to visit Toney Domacio. Damien knew today was gonna be another pleasant day for Toney.

Under the guise of Charles Nobles, Damien made his way through Lewisburg's visit room. His feet traced the same path back to one of the tables near the far wall in order to sit as far as he could from the officer's desk. In about five minutes, the infamous Toney Domacio was escorted into the visit room. He was once again dressed neatly in fresh pressed khaki's and shiny steel-toe boots. He shook Damien's hand and pulled him in close for a brotherly embrace.

Toney broke their hug, smiling down at Damien's toupee. "How's everything goin'?" He held back his chuckle as he slightly adjusted his Armani frames.

"Pretty good." Damien shot Toney a knowing glare as they both quickly sat down. "I'd say even better than I expected."

Toney wasted no time about his interest. "So how's Drako doin'?"

"That's what I wanted to tell you about most, of course." Damien smiled behind the punch bowl thick glasses and reached into the bag of popcorn on their table.

"Well, let's see," Damien began. "Wiz put him in a nice home in Stone Mountain. He also purchased the 760 Li Drako had spoken of." He popped a few kernels and glanced at the officer who was paying the pair no attention.

"Is that it?" Toney didn't seem too moved.

"No, no, that's not all." He swallowed the kernels and continued. "He's gotten himself a pretty stable position within the label. Drako is the head of his security team, and I'm telling you he is tight-knit." Damien's eyes lit up a little.

"What else?" Toney asked, eating up Drako's success.

"Wiz hit him with some petty cash. Most guys in his predicament would've probably laid back, blew it and held his hand out, waiting for more to be placed there. Well, obviously that didn't wet this kid's whistle." He glanced at Toney briefly. "He's smart though, and pretty humble I'd say. He claims he's got skill to flip it and when he does he wants me to invest a chunk into some legitimate companies."

"Okay, and?" Toney tossed out sarcastically.

"There is no 'and' to that. I'm already on top of it. At this point I know of a construction company he could buy into and perhaps a cement company he could gain control of. I'm looking at a couple other things as well, but I'm going to incorporate everything under one umbrella for tax purposes as well as discretion when that time comes. He'll make a pretty good income and in a few years he could be financially stable from that alone. His hang-up is he has his mind set on roping off damn near ten million dollars in one year!"

"Well, you just make sure you give him all the help he needs. Give him the assistance you'd give me, dammit!"

"Be easy, Toney. I've got this. I understand. You couldn't have chosen a better friend," Damien said to ease the tension in Toney's voice.

Toney cleared his throat and thought for a moment. "What about Diamond?"

"As far as I can see she's fine. I don't speak on her. He has a way about that girl. I mean, she is pretty, but damn . . . I think she may be his weakness."

"She's not his weakness; she's his motivation, damn it!" Toney snapped just that quickly. "All he wants is money and power and to be able to provide her with whatever he thinks she deserves."

"That's fine, but I—"

"Damien, don't look at her with those kind of eyes!" Toney cut in with a stern glare. "I know your ways. Just remain his friend as you are mine. He'll be fine. Trust me, the kid is smart and he has the natural instinct to see things coming."

"I understand. I see things in him, too. Most people seem to think that he's just another street savvy thug. He has that quiet, easygoing temperament until he's provoked. Well, I see past that. I can't ignore the loyalty in his eyes, nor can I ignore the death! He's special. He wears some type of wings. I can't say what they are just yet, but in time I hope to see."

"I'm sure." Toney dropped the popcorn and raised a soda can to his mouth. "He's everything I thought he'd be. He just wants money and ain't taking no for an answer. Tell 'im I said thanks for all. You're right . . . I could have never chosen a better friend. Yesterday, I received the money he sent. Tell 'im I owe him forever." Toney sounded slightly choked up for words.

"No problem. I'll help him get it forever. And I'll make certain he knows of your gratitude." Damien smiled and shook Toney's hand in reassurance.

"Visitation is now over," the CO announced. "All inmates, please say your good-byes and move to the right wall. Visitors, please form a line along the officer's desk."

As the two made their final embrace Toney whispered the address to a new post office box where Damien could deposit funds for the crooked officers to keep bringing in his steady supply of contraband. As soon as they broke the fleeting hug Toney stepped back and said jokingly, "Charles, you oughta really look into getting your hair cut."

"Fuckin' wise guy, eh?" Damien smirked. He smiled just before reassuring Toney as always he'd stay in touch.

A few seconds later, Damien was back in line with the devoted women and many children who became fatherless to the system. Toney was escorted out of the visitation room.

Once again he endured another strip search and full cavity check. He stepped back into the corridor of loud noise and a life of imprisonment. Toney spoke to all of his associates on his way to his cell where he closed the door behind him. He lay on his bunk and folded his hands behind his head as he stared off at the ceiling. All he could focus on was how happy he was for Drako. He wanted him to stay in just the direction he was going. Toney knew this was it for him. And even though there was a lot going on at Red Rum Records, he just hoped in his heart Drako would keep his word and not become like the many guys that left and he never heard from again.

It had been well over a decade so far for Toney, but with Drako home, just maybe he was another step closer to feeling final redemption. Toney knew that Damien was also a great judge of character. His assessment of Drako had been just right. And Drako surely did have wings. Which kind? Only time would tell. Toney dozed off with a peaceful smile upon his face.

Mike Jefferies

\

Chapter Fifteen

Red Rum

One month since Wiz had dropped his album, and three months since Swirl had dropped his album, both now had multi-platinum units sold just two days away from the infamous Source Awards. Red Rum headquarters was in a frenzy. Swirl, Damien, Drako, Diamond and Myria were there. Everybody was there except Wiz. The topic was about the nominations. Swirl was in the category for Breakthrough Artist of the Year. His single "Resurrection," featuring Wiz, was up for Collaboration of the Year. "Kill 'Em Slow," directed by Lloyd, was up for Video of the Year. Wiz was up for Artist of the Year and Producer of the Year, and "Born Ta Stunt" was up for Single of the Year. Everybody was happy to know that Myria was up for Video Vixen of the Year.

It felt like family today at Red Rum. They had long tables of catered food offering chicken wings, crawfish, finger sandwiches and colorful fruit displays, and not to mention the nonstop bubbly and free supply of exotic weed. They all joined in the festivities as Swirl and other artists took turns stepping up to the mic and freestyling over sample tracks. They made up hooks as they went along, and they even persuaded Diamond into singing all the hooks.

Everyone was enjoying the scene. Damien fiended for the
New Orleans dancers who Swirl had invited. He snuck a peak at
Diamond whenever possible, and was happy to see Drako being
festive for a change.

Drako loved to see Diamond perform and never dissuaded her
from showing off her talent. She even rapped short bars and was
spitting them at the smaller artists. Drako looked at Diamond,
who was so beautiful to him. She wore cream colored Roberto
Cavalli pants and a low cut shirt. The form-fitting pants made her
curves impossible to ignore. She killed the ensemble with a pair
of matching Vero Cujo ankle boots with platinum ornaments. To
Drako and to a lot of others, Diamond was by far the prettiest
woman in the house.

Myria sat across the room, feeling like she was the shit. She
had shown up in an all red form-fitting plunge cleavage one-piece
body suit by Versace. Her fire-red lipstick matched her red
stiletto thong boots with gold Versace tassels. Myria sported a
fresh pair of Chanel shades that added a sassy look to her
persona, but underneath, she just wanted to make sure that her
puffy eyes went unnoticed. Nobody would have ever noticed,
because Myria's head-turning ensemble revealed every single
curve that her body held. She gracefully sauntered her well-
sculpted hips around the office trying to gather any information
on Wiz's whereabouts, and which one of these skanks had been
trying to suck on his dick like a leech.

She answered the telephone every time it rang. "Red Rum
Incorporated, Myria speaking. How may I direct your call?"
Nobody paid much attention because that was her normal
disposition when Wiz would leave her for days at a time.

The only person who really paid her any mind was Diamond.
She'd hated the salty looks Myria had thrown her way.

"Not right now," Drako simmered Diamond down earlier
when he saw she had every intention of slapping Myria silly. "Sit

down; don't pay her silly ass no attention. Wiz done bruised that girl anyway. You way too classy to go out like that. I'd much rather see you have a good time. Now gone and let her see you shine." His words landed firmly on Diamond before she stepped back into the booth.

Damien watched the whole scene play out with lust in his eyes. His dick had bulged so many times at the combination of Myria's whining voice and the way her hips bounced with each step. Damien couldn't understand why she was so hung up on Wiz. She was beautiful and could easily get a man to take care of her every need. Hell, he had even told himself he'd be that man if only she asked. Damien kept Myria in his sights as she strolled about the studio.

"When is Wiz comin'?" Swirl yelled to Damien as everybody applauded Diamond's live rendition of Ashanti.

"Dame, Wiz gotta see Diamond! She ain't even in the industry and can sing hooks better than any female out there! She can rap better than a lot of these broads that's signed, too." Swirl turned to Drako with a smile. "Why you 'on get Wiz to sign her? She could be a star!"

"'Cause she don't work for Wiz; she don't work for nobody," Drako replied flatly. "That diamond is just for me. Let me worry about her."

"Swirl," Damien interrupted. "It's going to be a minute. Wiz may not even come. He called me from Miami this morning and told me it would be late if he makes it." Damien shot Swirl a look that told him to leave Drako alone.

Swirl felt the vibe and went with it. "That's cool by me, ya heard."

Damien was still watching Myria as she vanished from the studio. He then announced, "Is everybody pleased?" Then he let them know he'd be at their disposal until Wiz arrived. A few minutes later, Damien vanished from the first floor studio as well.

Damien went up to the second level and searched until he found Myria standing in one of the sleeping quarters in front of the vanity mirror with her head down. Damien thought he had heard her softly weeping. He crept up behind her, slipping his arms around her waist and snuggling up to her soft hips. "Let me take care of you, Myria," he whispered as he tried to kiss her on the nape of the neck.

She quickly turned around, pushing him away. "Get off, Damien!" she yelled, only to get another advance as he tried to roughly grab her by the waist and pull her into his arms.

"Come on, Myria. You know I can take care of you. I'm the real muscle making shit happen around here. I'm the one who put Red Rum together!"

Shoving him again, she was shocked by his actions. Myria never knew Damien harbored these sexual desires toward her. His dick was stiff and throbbing as he pressed up against her.

"Are you crazy, Damien? Stop playin'! You know damn well me and Wiz is an item!" she argued.

"An item? You and Wiz ain't no fuckin' item! You're just like every piece of ass Wiz gets every night!"

"You don't know shit! You don't know what Wiz tells me or all the nice things he does for me!" Her voice perked as she wedged free from the vanity.

"I know he's got other bitches, and they ain't in a room cryin' because they can't find him. Why don't you wake the fuck up and let me help you out and you help me out."

"I wasn't crying, and I know them other bitches don't mean shit to Wiz." She took a nervous step backwards.

Damien's tone turned harsh. "You silly bitch! Come here! Wiz ain't gonna know, and if he does, he won't care!" This time he forced his weight on her and tried kissing Myria roughly on her mouth. Myria twisted her head from side to side in an effort to break free, but quickly determined that she couldn't free herself, so she bit down on his lip.

Damien yelped out in sudden pain, instinctively shoving Myria's petite body. "I'm telling Wiz, you perverted muthafucka!" she yelled as soon as her butt hit the hardwood floor.

Damien knew it would be almost impossible for anyone downstairs to hear her, but someone may have wandered up the stairs. He ran and slammed the door and locked it. He saw tears running down Myria's face. Damien knew she wasn't game, and raping her was far from his mind. But it was clearly on hers as she scooted her back against the wall and cringed with fear. "Listen, Myria, I wouldn't hurt you. I'm truly sorry." Damien began to lie in an effort to dissuade her from telling Wiz or worse yet, Drako.

"I just know Wiz is catching feelings for you and I wanted to see if he could really trust you, or if you were like all these other groupies that mean him no good." Myria continued to cry, but Damien still approached her slowly and comforted her. "Myria, you must believe me. I was just testing you. I mean, of course we can't tell him about this, but now I can always speak highly of you." Damien's voice had returned to its normally eloquent tone. "Myria, answer me. You can trust me.

"I bet you didn't know Wiz was having an exclusive party at Black Gold before the awards, huh? I bet you didn't know about the party he's going to have afterward at his mansion in Florida."

"Mansion?" Myria's voice cracked as she stopped crying and wiped the tears from her face between sniffles.

"Yeah, mansion. See, it's going to be exclusively for his closest friends. I mean, you have to do what you have to do to get there, but you know I'm going to tell him you should be there. Shit, you should be his main lady, his *only* lady, and I'm making

out the list with him." Damien had her undivided attention, just as anyone who held information on Wiz did.

"Myria, get up. Get yourself together. Wiz will be here shortly and you need to make an impression. Don't you wanna be there, beautiful?"

Myria nodded in response to Damien's smile.

"Good, then put your shades on and act like the video vixen of the year. I apologize again. I want you to take my card and anything you need from me or I can tell Wiz in regard to you, you got it. But if you don't keep this between us, you know I'd have to deny this encounter. I'm just trying to do what's beneficial for both of us. Do you understand?" Damien placed the card in her hand and folded her fingers over it.

Myria didn't say a word as she took the free information card. She put it in her pocket, turned to the mirror, and adjusted her clothes back neatly. Raking her hair back into place, she placed her designer shades back over her puffy eyes. She turned and walked to the door. When she touched the handle, she looked back at Damien. "You just had your free pass. Don't try it again." She slammed the door knowing Damien could very well be useful one day.

One hour later, at 8 P.M. sharp, the CEO of Red Rum entered the building. Everybody was happy to see Wiz, and the party started up again. Diamond sang and Wiz was shocked to hear how beautiful her voice could be in a studio. Wiz saw how sharp everybody was dressed, and he loved the atmosphere of family that his studio always held at times like these.

Wiz eyed Myria, and with one look, it was easy to see that she exuded more sexual power than any female in the room. After calling her over, he couldn't help admitting to himself that he'd missed her, but he just couldn't make time for her in his busy scheming schedule.

"What up, lil mama?" he greeted, wrapping his arm around her. "Damn, you smell good, and you look nice!" Myria only responded by nodding. "I know you miss me," he went on, "but we gone get to it after I catch up on things 'round here, so be cool." Myria, feeling so happy and safe in his embrace, smiled and nodded again. He sweet-talked her a little while longer, rubbing her ass while calling for a meeting of the Red Rum roster.

Everybody proceeded up to the third level meeting room. Myria peered over his shoulder and directly into Damien's eyes with an 'I told you so' look as he passed by. Damien took that look as a 'you better not try nothing or I'ma tell' stare, but he just kept it moving and hoped for the best. Myria walked Wiz to the second level where he stopped to momentarily grope her badly missed body. Myria flushed with heat to Wiz's touch as she said, "Wiz, I really need to speak with you. As soon as the meeting's over, baby."

"Do ya?" Wiz smiled. "Let me call the shots around Red Rum. Don't sweat it I need to holla at you, too!" He palmed her ass a few more moments with that devious grin just before he stepped into the elevator that took him straight to his office.

The meeting was short; he just went over a few things they should expect at the Source Awards and how he thought they should represent the brand at the red carpet event. They touched on some security issues with Drako and Wiz enlightened them to a few exclusive parties taking place around South Beach after the main event.

After everyone was excused, Wiz was sort of surprised to find Drako still seated in the conference room.

"Good job, Drako," Wiz complimented, breaking the ice. "You really got this outfit looking good and running smooth around here."

"You know me." Drako stood up and walked down to the head of the table where Wiz was seated in his big armchair. He sat his hips right on the ledge of the desk in front of Wiz.

"What's on your mind?" Wiz asked quickly.

"I need some more money," Drako said, stone-faced.

Wiz's brows furled a bit. "Already? What about your—"

"Already?" Drako smirked, raising his tone a bit. "What happened to just ask? What happened to pocket change, nigga? Is you got problems all of a sudden?" Drako held his arms open, waiting for a response.

"Nah, man I was just thinking you was a'ight for now."

"Well, I ain't a'ight just yet." Drako smirked. "I want Diamond to pick out her own furniture and maybe I'd like to buy my woman a car or just have the option to do something impulsive."

"Yeah, I feel you. How much you talkin'?"

"Another hundred grand, big time." Drako stared straight in his eyes.

"Hmph." Wiz smirked with a cocky suck of his diamond grill. *I know this nigga don't feel like he pressing me?* Wiz thought.

He could see Drako searching his face for the pain his request would have on his pockets. Wiz made sure there were no signs to read.

"No problem, I'll get that to you ASAP." He brushed some imaginary lint from his shoulder and reached for the Cuban cigar on his desk.

Drako stood back up and smiled. He patted Wiz lightly on the shoulder. "I see it; don't trip it. I won't hundred grand you to death. This oughta hold me till you come up wit' that plan you was talking about." Drako chuckled and turned away. "I'll see you in Houston," he yelled back over his shoulder on his way out.

"Tell Damien I need him, would ya?"

Drako ignored him and went on through the door. He'd had fun watching Wiz cower, which he didn't try to do, but he saw clean through Wiz's facade. Drako didn't feel the least bit bad. He needed a little more play money to further out his scheme.

Wiz watched as Drako went downstairs and grabbed Diamond and headed for the door. *You wanna play head games? A'ight then. I know just how ta string you along. I'm a hundred million dollar mogul and 'that,' my friend, you gone learn to respect.*

Wiz had a sinister grin when he spun his chair around as Damien waltzed through the door. *What's up with that shit eating grin?* he thought of Damien's face.

"Well?" Wiz asked with an anxious glare.

"You did it . . . *we* did it. I got the copy and the units are being pressed up as we speak!" Damien amplified his excitement. His guilty conscious was just ready to give Wiz news to make him happy enough not to pay Myria any attention tonight. "You are a brilliant man," he complimented further.

Wiz was already sparking his cigar. "I told ya so. Now watch how that kinda money stack up!" He exhaled with a smile.

"Hey, do me a favor on the way out would ya?"

"Sure."

"Tell Myria to come up here and make a note to have that black Bentley Coupe that I never drive detailed. I want it delivered to Drako's place real soon."

"How soon?"

"Before he can think to ask for money. Let's give 'im something to occupy his time." Wiz snickered.

"Will do." Damien dismissed himself.

As soon as Myria stepped into his office, Wiz was all over her. The X-pills Damien left him were already taking effect. He'd just kissed her lips and pulled the Chanel shades off her face when he noticed her puffy, red eyes. "What the hell is wrong with you, girl?"

"Why didn't you invite me to your party or to your new mansion?" she blurted out and started crying again.

"Party?" Wiz had a busted look on his face. "Mansion? There you go listening to them rumors again."

"Rumors, huh?" She looked at him with pitiful eyes. "You don't think I know when Swirl and nem' trying to speak around me in code? I know what they're hiding," Myria lied.

Wiz let out a weak sigh. "Myria, you gotta stop trying to be on every fuckin' set!" He didn't argue anymore. He knew she knew the deal. Myria was extremely nosey. Very observant. And Swirl had just slipped his lip in front of what Wiz called a human tape recorder.

"Be cool. I'll get you there." He lifted her up on the desk, zipped her suit down the back and started peeling it away.

"You promise?" she cooed, making his dick swell faster.

"Yeah," he said without giving it a mere thought. "Now, come on and gimme some pussy."

"Oh yeah, fuck me good! I want it right on your throne!"

Wiz nailed his dick in her on his desk for a good while. Then just as she'd wished for, they fell asleep butt naked, intertwined in his big armchair.

Myria fell asleep a happy woman, while Wiz was deciding if he should sever ties before things got any worse.

Myria was becoming a pest, rather than an asset.

Chapter Sixteen

Drako

"Thank you, Mr. Smith. Again, it was my pleasure to be at your service," said the bank manager.

"The pleasure is always mine," Drako replied with a smile just before he insisted on leaving. He was ready to attend the Giants game at Meadowland's Stadium, the same Giants that he and the bank manager loved so much. The bank manager happily shook Drako's hand before retreating back into his office.

Drako, who now donned a neatly trimmed full beard, horn-rimmed glasses, and a blue Hugo Boss suit, walked as inconspicuously as all the other customers. He had chosen UBS Warburg Investment Bank in Stamford, Connecticut. He had heard good reports on their upscale services. Scott Smith had turned out to be Drako's man. He was the owner of a very lucrative construction company, and a well-known general contractor for industrial sites, having capitalized on minority contract bidding rules.

His real bank account was held at Bank of America, based in Charlotte, North Carolina. A report of his account transactions revealed that for the last four months, between the first and the fifth the Federal Bureau of Prisons deposited a check anywhere from $3 to $4.1 million into his account.

As Drako exited UBS Warburg, he was happy to be passing so easily for the third time as the humble rich brother.

Back in New York, Diamond was in heavy makeup, posing as Mary Williams. She was working with her white male bank manager at Citibank on the corner of 1st Avenue and 68th Street in Manhattan. Mary Williams was a thirty-three-year-old white woman who had inherited two large apartment buildings in Boston from her late husband, who was thirty years her senior when he passed. Her original account was held in Wachovia Bank and Trust in Boston, Massachusetts. She didn't receive a big monthly payment like Scott Smith, but she had a hefty $10 million account and all her apartment buildings were paid for. Diamond easily passed as the thirty-three-year-old white lady to the fifty-something bank manager. She smiled as she politely thanked him for being such a gentleman. She turned to walk away wearing a long, gray dress that did nothing to accent her physique. Diamond was also proud as she'd deposited the cashier checks totaling over $50,000 for the third time now.

Drako and Diamond arrived at their Plaza Hotel suite at the same time. Diamond laughed as she saw their reflections in the large wall mirrors in the lobby. "Drako, you know you look like a knock off Muslim sneaking a white chick into a hotel."

Drako smiled, looking in the mirror and noticing their true resemblance to her comment. "Shut up, Diamond. I think you do wanna role-play or something," he snapped back.

"Well, perhaps I just might." She added a little sass to her walk as they approached the elevator.

"I 'on know how you'd imagine a nigga stronger than me."

"Well, maybe not stronger, just a lil more powerful and since I'm supposed to be a white girl I was thinking you could be Barack Obama."

Drako smiled. "Well, that is the most powerful man on the planet. I guess you could be Sarah Palin and I'd be the first nigger to knock dick to the back of her pussy." They both laughed as Drako pulled Diamond to him and tongued her down. They'd forgotten all about their costumes until the elevator opened and out stepped a sorta plus-size African American woman with pretty flowing natural dreads. She immediately turned her nose in the air at the frolicking interracial couple and hissed a curse on her way by.

"Oh well. Too late," Diamond said as they stepped on the elevator.

Just as the elevator doors were closing and the lady peered back, Drako leaned over and kissed her again. They laughed all the way to their suite.

Diamond had quickly showered and got out of her costume. She came into the room and Drako was busy on his laptop. "Drako, do you *have* to tonight?" Diamond whined.

"Look, ma, it ain't much. You know I got this thing started up and I got a lot of chargin' to do. I only got twenty days to break these cards."

"Drako, it ain't that hard! If you do fifty cards a day and only charge $1,000 cash to each card, that's 50 G's a day, 500 G's every ten days—$1 million in twenty days, and Drako, you gone charge some people more than a thousand."

"You got that right!" Drako smiled and kept on pushing the keys of his laptop.

"Well, I suggest you keep the charges low. I mean, it's supposed to be thirty days, but some credit card companies notify early on certain sporadic purchases that don't match spending patterns."

"I know that. You seem to know a lil somethin' too. What the hell was you doing in prison again?"

"Hell, I was in federal prison. I was listening! But forget all that. Drako, you said when we come to New York to handle our business that we were gonna shop and you were gonna take me to Club 40/40!"

"Diamond, you did go shopping, and you bought the same shit you could've bought back home in Atlanta!"

"So what about 40/40 then?" Diamond argued.

Drako took his eyes away from the laptop, giving his full attention to Diamond. "Come here, baby."

Diamond slowly walked over. Drako took her hand and directed her to sit on his lap. He made sure that he held eye contact.

"Look, you know that I'd never lie to you," he said calmly. "I wanna give you the whole world. I took you shoppin', and I wanna go to 40/40. I mean, clubs really ain't my thing, but I know you like to get out. I like to see you happy, and I like to show my diamond off." He paused to interlock his fingers with hers and pulled her closer.

"Diamond, going through receipts is tiresome and tedious, but you know this is important to me. Tonight I just wanna go try to play these Internet cafes. I gotta be back up early. You know my people's on lockdown are important to me, too. I gotta send Toney some pictures and a few books he requested. I gotta send Deuce some loot and pictures, too, and I wanna be rested up, baby. You know I gotta do the security for the shoot in Houston in two days, then put something right back together for the Source Awards."

Diamond still didn't respond with words, but her eyes told Drako she understood him clearly.

"I just need you to work with me a lil more. We'll be back to handle these accounts and I'll take you to the 40/40 club, I promise. I love you, ma."

The 'I promise' was enough; the 'I love you' completely melted Diamond. Tears began to well up in her eyes.

"I'm sorry, Drako," she replied softly. "Your things are important. Sometimes you just spoil me—you givin' me *everything.*"

"Don't cry, baby; you too pretty for tears." Drako gently wiped her tears away. "You ain't spoiled neither, ma. You just gettin' what you deserve. Get used to it, baby. I ain't even got started yet. Soon, I'ma be able to take you wherever, and not have to report nowhere. Then we can club everywhere. Feel me?"

Diamond nodded and laid her head on his chest. He stroked her soft hair and rubbed her back.

"I'ma buy you a car real soon—any kind you want." He kissed her softly on the forehead; then he picked her up in his arms and carried her to the bed, where he lay her down.

Diamond didn't say a word. She watched Drako change into Rocawear jeans, a hoodie, and a fresh pair of Forces. He grabbed his list of credit card numbers, clipped his cell to his waist, leaned over and kissed her on the forehead.

"I'll be back in a lil while, ma." She just nodded again as she stared into Drako's eyes

When Drako got to the door, he heard her say, "I love you. I'll still be up whenever you get back."

"Soon, baby, soon."

Twenty minutes later, Drako sat in the Internet cafe two blocks up from Times Square. He logged onto a computer and for almost two hours charged credit card number after credit card number to the account held by his fictitious business.

As soon as the black side of his heart felt content, he got up and drove straight back to the hotel, where he held Diamond all night—no sex, just true love, which made the other side of his heart feel content.

Mike Jefferies

Chapter Seventeen

Wiz

Zipping down Biscayne Boulevard in his blacked out Lamborghini Gallardo, Wiz's confidence had reached as high as the clouds. He'd been partying it up on South Beach for the last two nights leading up to the annual and controversial Source Awards.

His entire roster was now in Miami and ready to enjoy the exclusive party he'd put together for tonight at Club Black Gold. There would be over one hundred exotic dancers and an unlimited supply of everything else, all on Red Rum's bill.

Putting on his turn signal, he whipped into the right lane as he spotted the neutral location he'd chosen to hold a brief meeting that Bless had requested. Wiz wanted to make sure he looked his damn best as he turned into the exotic sports car dealership and headed to the back of the building where there was a long bay of car ports. Taking another quick glance through the rearview mirror, he smiled at the thought of the supersized diamond earrings and the enormous bracelet he wore. "Presentation is everything!" He snickered and ran his tongue across his iced-out grill.

Spotting Bless' silver Rolls Royce Phantom, Wiz steered right into the bay almost making their bumpers kiss. As soon as he stepped out his door, the suicide doors of the Phantom kicked open and out came Bless with a mile wide smile.

"Ay yo, son, you killin' 'em." He gave Wiz dap and a man hug. He then looked the icon up and down from head to toe.

"Say baby, this here ain't nothin'. I 'on even call it stuntin' no more. It's an everyday way of life with me, ya heard." Wiz sucked diamonds and held his signature smirk. He had a gift of making others believe everything he did seem to happen effortlessly.

"I can respect that. Ain't no hate in my blood," Bless responded, trying to hold back the starstruck spell Wiz left him in.

"I finally meet the man with all the plans." Wiz looked over Bless' shoulder as Fatt Katt lifted his three hundred and fifty pound frame out of the Phantom and approached him.

"Yo man, I'm glad you took a minute to come see me." Fatt Katt extended one of his heavy hands as he got close.

"Ain't nothin' to it, baby. I love bumping into money." Wiz winked, seeing his presence had somewhat mesmerized Fatt Katt on first glance as well.

"Man, I just had to meet you and thank you," he said humbly.

"I know tomorrow we gotta play it through at the award ceremony, but I just needed to let you know that if you hadn't put this down I wouldn't have gotten all these nominations."

Probably wouldn't have gotten any, you fat bastard, Wiz thought.

"Like I told Bless—" Wiz smoothly brushed a thumb across his nose to place emphasis on his pinky ring. "Everythang I touch turns to gold."

Wiz smiled down as he heard two little tennis shoes hit the pavement and a little boy ran straight over and clamped on to Fatt Katt's leg. With one look Wiz gave in. He loved kids and the thing that got him most was he looked just like Fatt Katt's 'mini-me.'

"That's your lil man, huh?" Wiz watched Fatt Katt hoist the kid up into his arms.

"Yeah, this my lil champ right here." He smiled down at his son and tickled at his stomach. "This the only one eatin' wit' me till I get to the top," Fatt Katt said seriously.

"We had a lot of rough times before my career took off. Just me and him a lot of nights, so that's why I'ma make sure I stay true to those who helped me." His chubby little boy clung an arm around his neck.

"You thinkin', big, baby. I see you got long-term dreams and a long way to go. Now, tomorrow I can't say what you'll win this time 'cause the boy Swirl got big numbers, ya dig?"

Fatt Katt smirked. "It's cool, I got patience."

"Good." Wiz smiled and gave him dap again. He sorta liked Fatt Katt's style. He could tell Fatt Katt came from nothing and probably was once even grimier than he rapped about on his songs. But the thing Wiz saw in his eyes was that he was both focused and hungry. With the right guidance and marketing, Fatt Katt would have the East Coast on dead bolt for years to come.

"Well, I got a standing appointment." Wiz looked down at a watch that had so much ice on it he couldn't tell the time. "I'm heading over to Black Gold. I wish y'all could be a part of it, but don't worry. As soon as we wrap up we gone do somethin' way big, ya heard?"

"Word . . ." Bless cut back in. "We'll see ya, son. Glad you could make it."

Wiz threw up the deuces and swaggered back to his Gallardo with even more swag than he came with. He pushed the start

button, popped the two pills he had in his pocket, and washed it down with the rest of his bottle of vitamin water.

As soon as he turned back on to Biscayne he tossed the empty bottle out the window.

Fuck them lames! They ain't beatin' Red Rum in any category! He mashed the accelerator causing the Gallardo to fishtail a bit. When it straightened up, he was on his way to Club Black Gold.

When Wiz finally made it through Club Black Gold he was pleased to see everybody happy at his expense. He knew this party would be the talk of South Beach and tabloid fodder. He'd invited all the right people. Damien was again losing his mind over such a huge assortment of dark-skinned women. Drako was soaking up the scene and Swirl was right by his side. He'd told Swirl about him going to finally meet Fatt Katt and Bless in person. Swirl had shrugged it off and said "Fuck them clowns." He'd expressed to Wiz that he was done with the fake beef after this. He felt he was too real and had rather stay true to his fans than participate any further, regardless of the money. He had no plans of ever meeting Fatt Katt. Wiz would have to find some other artist to carry out any more wax wars. It made Wiz no mind because with the 150,000 bootlegs he had pressed up with nearly a 100% mark up, he'd already had his money in the bank. He laughed to himself at what the thirty thousand dollar offer had gotten him.

He was torn from his thoughts when Drako stepped up to him. "What's up?" Wiz spoke first. "Enjoying yourself, I hope."

"It's all good." Drako nodded lightly. "But man, it's 2 A.M. It's about a wrap for me. I told Diamond to get in at a decent hour. I wanted to be rested up for tomorrow. It should be a big day for you and the camp."

"You right, man." Wiz agreed and gave Drako dap. "I'ma cut loose in a minute myself. I just wanted to make sure everything went over well here."

"See ya on the carpet then." Drako turned and headed for the door.

Wiz exhaled a sigh, contemplating his next move. He'd been trying to get a read on how Drako was feeling now, but Drako just seemed cool and unfazed. *I better still keep my eyes on him. And try ta do something to keep him that way.*

Wiz nodded, settling on his next move. He decided not to pop any more tabs. Instead he chose to head over to Myria's suite, cool her jets, and catch a little rest for the big day ahead.

On the morning of the Source Awards, Drako was awakened by the sound of Diamond's sultry voice as she moved about the room. Apparently, she was indecisive about which ensemble to wear so she laid about four dresses out. She had also picked two suits out for Drako to choose from.

Drako broke her happy spell. "Damn, ma, you up early and sho' nuff vibrant. You forgot to tell me where you went last night."

Diamond first met Drako's question with a fresh smile, and a playful giggle as she leaned over and pecked his cheek. "I'm glad you're up, sleepy head. Now you can help me out, 'cause I don't know what to wear, baby."

"That ain't answering my question, Diamond." Drako rose up on an elbow.

"Drako," she tried to whine in her sexy tone, but Drako's expression still meant business.

"Baby, me and Dianne hung out here, and then we went to Club Z-No and Cobars for a little while. And to answer what you wanna know. Yes, I got lots of compliments and plenty of looks. No, I didn't dance, and yes, the only man I'm attracted to is lying in front of me."

Drako's frown melted away as he lay back down.

"Just checkin', ma. And to help you out, I think you'll steal the show in any of them dresses. You can't go wrong." Diamond grinned and went to the closet to choose her night's attire.

Last night Myria rested so peacefully knowing that after Wiz partied he came straight to her suite. He didn't want sex or anything; he said he just wanted to hold her.

When Wiz woke the next morning, he saw Myria sleeping like a peaceful child. He liked the way she behaved behind closed doors, but his conscious knew that she was becoming jealous when she saw him with other girls. He softly nudged her awake. "Get up, girl."

Myria felt so good to Wiz as she snuggled her warm, naked body closer like she always did, not wanting to let him go. "Girl, we got things to do. I got a few appearances today, and you need to look your best when you take that Vixen award."

"Baby, they ain't ready for your girl. I'ma make them bitches look like they don't belong in the category," Myria chimed as she began to kiss down Wiz's chest.

Wiz stopped her. "Not now, Myria. Maybe later. I 'on wanna be drained today. I need to tell you that I got a few seats left. The whole Red Rum roster is gone be on front row. You and two vixens Swirl chose have seating arrangements with us. You won't be next to me, so don't start that 'item' shit. You know cameras make news. I just want you to be on your best behavior and represent well for the hard-workin' video sisters. And don't forget to big-up the label."

"I won't, baby, and I'ma be on my best behavior, a fuckin' diva tonight!"

"'Pose to be a diva *every*_night!" Wiz snapped.

"Anything for you, Wiz. Anything."

Slightly puzzled, Wiz gazed into Myria's eyes and asked the question he often wondered. "Why da' fuck you like me so much?"

She shrugged. "I don't know. I can't really pick just one thing . . . I mean, when I first met you, you weren't corny. Plus you be looking out. I know I should be doing more, but I tried singing and it's hard in this industry. It's been three years, and everybody wants some coochie based on promises. At least you do keep a sista working."

Wiz smiled. "Shut yo' Irish ass up, girl."

They both laughed. "Wiz, we always have a good time together. You know how to make me and my body smile. I guess that's why I like you so much."

Wiz pecked her on the forehead. "Let me see that diva then, startin' today."

He reached out and strummed his thumb across her soft cheek as she laid her head back on the pillow and closed her eyes again. Wiz swallowed another hard lump. He didn't know if it was because he was just sobered up, but staring at Myria all he felt was guilt.

Wiz had plenty of women every night, but for some strange reason none of them made him feel like Myria. In bed and out of bed everything she did for him felt genuine. He knew her screen persona didn't define her at all. Myria was beautiful both inside and out. And it was those feelings that he didn't like. He now realized that he had some type of feelings for Myria. He wasn't in love, but she was something his pride could never share. He

exhaled again, dismissing the thought that he could treat her any better. That thought would be a waste of time. He was already in love, in love with being on top and everything that came with it.

He peeled the covers back and slid out of bed.

By 7 P.M. the Red Rum roster was exiting out of limousines and walking the red carpet to enter the Miami Arena. Everybody was dressed in the best clothes. Drako had on an eggshell-white tailor-made linen suit and a matching derby with a burgundy feather on the side. He wore it slightly tilted, exposing his burgundy skully underneath, which matched his burgundy Mauri gators and belt.

Diamond was the epitome of elegance, clad in her shimmering sequined $10,000 burgundy strapless gown by Versace with a pair of silver four-inch heels. Her burgundy toenail polish and lipstick accented her ensemble with class. She wore her hair in a pulled-back style, showing off her elegant earrings and her platinum cloak chain at her neckline.

Wiz sported a cream colored Cannali suit, and he flossed his best jewels. He sported his golf-ball-sized earrings, and tonight was the first night he donned his new $2 million diamond bracelet that he'd recently added to his collection.

Myria got out of the limo and was temporarily blinded by the bright camera flashes. She wore a sky blue dress which criss-crossed in the front, leaving her flat stomach exposed and her back out. She had baby blue sandals to match as well as oversized platinum earrings and accessories. Myria's whole outfit was exclusively designed by Kimora, and given to her as a personal gift after she did a sexy layout for the Baby Phat line.

Wiz made sure Dianne and the rest of the roster were dressed in the same fashion. Swirl was already inside, and Damien was not a part of the roster. Red Rum was escorted in and seated in their respective reserved seats, and the show took off with a blast.

As soon as Trina and Trick Daddy opened the show then announced the first performance, all the lights in the arena went dim. Seconds later, track lights around the stage came on, heavy fog engulfed the stage, then a blood burgundy Magnum wagon with candy paint rolled out on stage and stopped. As soon as the suicide doors flipped up, the beat to "Kill 'Em Slow" dropped and Swirl hopped out and onto the stage with a fury.

Lights zipped at the stage from high in the sky and the crowd responded with an uproar to Swirl's electrifying performance. Swirl waved his hands in the air and extended his mic to the crowd as they sang his hook.

Nodding his head to the track as if it intoxicated him, Swirl began to bounce on his toes as he dripped the hardest lyrics off his album. The crowd was on the edge of their seats as Swirl's magnolia dancers swarmed the stage in their bikinis.

Wiz sat proudly seeing the way Swirl unfolded the night with so much energy and confidence. He watched the crowd stand to their feet, screaming for more as Swirl tossed his shirt and exited the stage.

The curtain fell and the camera flashes ceased momentarily as Trina hit the podium again in a new dress and began the award ceremonies between acts. In no time Red Rum's nominations were announced and Swirl was the first one to win. The entire arena applauded as clips of "Kill 'Em Slow" flashed across the huge projector screens.

Swirl turned to Wiz and gave him dap; then he turned to Lloyd. "You directed it, baby, let's go."

"Get up there and represent," Wiz urged them quickly. "Let 'em have it."

Swirl had changed after his performance. He now sported a $3,500 gray Armani suit and his neat braids hung just over the

back of his collar. He wore platinum Cartier frames, and when he spoke into the microphone the world got a closer look at his new diamond and platinum smile.

"Thank y'all." Swirl clenched the award and pumped it in the sky. "Y'all know I don't write nothin'," he spoke humbly. "I just want to say thanks to y'all. Y'all know who I do it for—the streets, not just to eat! We gone keep puttin' out good music. So stay with me. This one goes to Red Rum, all my fans, and of course dat third ward, ya heard. Y'all know what it is . . . soo!" He kissed two fingers, raised them high, and exited the stage feeling like he'd just accomplished the proudest thing he'd ever achieved in life.

Wiz nodded his head again, feeling prouder and prouder of his camp. Gucci Mane and Young Jeezy put down a hell of a performance before Swirl along with Wiz claimed the second victory for collabo of the year with "Resurrection." This time the floor cams panned down on the whole Red Rum crew. Another barrage of camera flashes erupted, causing Drako to turn his face in the opposite direction.

"Everybody up," Wiz ordered. "This is our moment. Let the world see who's eatin' big, ya heard!"

Diamond tugged at Drako's arm. "Let's go, baby."

"Nah, ma. You go ahead. I'd rather see how my baby looks on stage from here." Diamond smiled as she got up and followed the camp on stage.

Swirl and Wiz hugged on stage as did the rest of the camp. Swirl and Wiz both held the award high in the sky.

Wiz stepped back, feeling a feeling like he had never felt before. He felt elite, he felt grand like the icon he was. He did not feel nervous about the millions of viewers watching him. Nope, in his mind he welcomed it. He fiended for more!

Wiz stepped up to the mic dripping with poise, confidence, and Red Rum swag. He thanked God, the fans, his camp and all the way down to his distributors. Promising Red Rum had lots more on the way he ended his speech like a seasoned vet. He peered over at the Take Money camp who'd been nominated, but hadn't won anything. Then he looked to his proud brand he'd built and held even more pride.

As they exited the stage he told himself he was done with the faking after he summed things up with Take Money. He knew he'd signed raw talent and he'd built Red Rum so big that it couldn't be denied. He chalked up the little scamming he'd done to grab a couple mil' here and a couple mil' there to be no worse than what the other big fish had done to get to the top.

Wiz couldn't shake the high this night gave him. He felt like Swirl was his own blood. He loved how Diamond and Myria had stood by his side like two angels. Then he looked at Drako and realized how much work and industry politics caused him to miss his old pal. Tonight wasn't the night, but he made a mental note to reach out to him soon.

It wasn't long after the crew was seated when Swirl beat Fatt Katt out for Breakthrough Artist of the Year. Everybody except Wiz and Drako accompanied him to accept his award. Myria made sure she stood close by and made sure the camera got a good thirty seconds of her splendid ensemble. Swirl's 'thanks' were brief this time, and he exited the stage like a seasoned vet.

Wiz lost Producer of the Year to T-Pain and Artist of the Year to Jay-Z. The last award of the night was Video Vixen of the Year. Myria sat nervously as her name was announced, along with White Chocolate, Ebony, Lyric and Azzereya. Then, Trina took the envelope from Trick and announced: "The Winner for Video Vixen of the Year is . . . Myria Coles!"

Myria jumped straight out of her chair and grabbed Swirl's hand. "Come on, Swirl, it was *your* video!"

Swirl smiled. "But it's your time to shine. Go ahead and represent, baby girl."

Myria gracefully sauntered up to the podium to accept her award. Tears brimmed her eyes as she tried to remain composed throughout her speech. She thanked God, all the magazines from *Smooth* to *XXL* to *King*. She thanked Baby Phat, and most of all, Red Rum—for discovering her onscreen talent. Myria was nervous and happy as she spoke for the first time in front of such an overwhelming audience, but she pulled through *and* nailed that runway strutt all the way backstage.

TI closed the show with another hellafied performance and light show. Then Benzino came out and ended the ceremonies. He thanked all the participants and promised an even better show—same time next year.

"We did good and we looked *great!*" Wiz told his camp. "I want y'all to stay that way, 'cause tonight I didn't clean up, but in four months, we gone hit that red carpet in Cali at the BET Awards. I'ma sweep up every category with a mothafuckin' broom. Believe dat! Now, let's hit the real after-party!"

Chapter Eighteen
The After Party

The entire Red Rum entourage had walked back across the red carpet and were shuttled away by the line of awaiting limousines. Drako had casually slipped into the door of the last limo where Damien was awaiting.

"Great night for the camp." Damien beamed with excitement. "And now it's time to really kick back and celebrate!" He gave Drako a firm shake as soon as he was settled in.

"Well, I just wanted to find a private moment to bring you up on my latest thoughts as to old Vinny." His smiled turned wicked.

"Cool." Drako nodded without much enthusiasm.

He crossed a leg and listened in as Damien fixed himself a drink from the limo's wet bar and went back over the same basic plan, except now he had a better idea as to how to gain entry even faster. Drako liked the idea, but hated that Damien still hadn't settled on a solid date to finally pull the caper off.

"Sounds good." Drako nodded. "Just let me know when to go."

"Very well." Damien smiled wider, recognizing the cold in Drako's eyes at the thought of clamping hold of Vinny's throat.

"So how about the start-up capital?" His eyebrows rose a bit. "I've been looking into some very stable things. Service business, just like you asked. I see a lane for us to buy right in and see steady profits in no time."

Drako cleared his throat and smoothly cracked his neck from left to right. "Yeah, well, I just need a few more seconds and I'll be getting that right to ya. Things are in motion," Drako assured.

"You said time is of the essence. I'm waiting on you now . . . Well, enough about that. I think it's about time for the real party to begin." Drako watched him pull out a plastic bag of what looked like nearly 100 yellow pills. He quickly fished out two pills, popped them and chased them down with the glass of brown liquor he'd poured.

"What the hell you takin'?" Drako squinted.

"Relax." He waved Drako off a bit. "This is nothing hard. Just a little X."

Drako smiled. "So that's what's up with your horny ass."

Damien took the joke lightly. "Oh yeah, this is the feel-good drug. You know, tabs, thizzin', rollin', skittles, whatever you wanna call it. The ladies and the whole industry love it."

"Well, you won't have to worry about me. Drako don't use nothing. I'm my own drug. I barely take a social drink."

"Oh, I wouldn't dare offer you any for personal consumption, but if you're interested in monopolizing on some more fast money, I have a friend that can get you the best wholesale prices between here and Canada."

"Naw, Dame, drugs ain't for me. No kind. I mean, I used to push coke, but that shit is done! It's too slow. Too many other avoidable risks, plus the Feds got that guilty by association shit. It's called conspiracy and the time they're handing out outweighs the crime by far."

"No Drako, I'm not suggesting anything street level. I'm talking about serving those on another level, people in the

A Life for A Life

industry with big money who don't have easy access, but need to stay under the radar. Do you have any idea how much money and pills are secretly passed through these industry gatherings?"

Drako peeped the glossy look in Damien's eyes as he paused to let his offer sink in. "This music industry revolves around sex, drugs, and parties," he babbled on. "I want you to give it some thought. My friend will be at Wiz's party tonight. If you decide to do some networking, I can have this thing set up in just a matter of days."

Drako sat straight up looking deeper into Damien's eyes. "How long have you known this guy?"

"Oh, for years. Our story goes a long way back." He seemed to poke his chest out with pride.

"Good." Drako wanted to be sure he had his full attention. "Now listen to me well. Drugs always come back to haunt you, and I can't have that. Man, when I tell you I'm playin' da game raw, I mean just that! Please don't misconstrue me for anything less. Now, I will *take* every pill he's got, but he'll never see one dime. Nor will he be sitting on the opposite side of an oak table testifying against me in two or three years. Now, if you wanna help me set that up . . . or leave it alone, that's my only offer."

A dumbfounded look made its way to Damien's face. "I-I was just offering you a hand."

"Yeah well, hands like that need to be chopped off after you shake 'em. If you wanna keep 'em, keep 'em away from me."

Damien decided to fish another pill out of his bag to go with the fresh glass of brown he'd just replenished. Drako reclined back and kept his cool.

"Well—" Damien took a sip and changed topics. "Like I was saying earlier, we could try one of three things with Vinny." He dropped two cubes of ice and began to shake them around in his glass. "Now, which do you—"

"Look man." Drako sat back up with a cold glare. "I ain't with all that talkin' 'bout what I'm gone do. That shit ain't a part of my demonstration. Just put the shit together. Get me there and I'ma put it down!" He cracked his knuckles and sucked his teeth, fully irritated. "That shit making you talk loosely. Don't talk to me 'bout that 'til you got everything on the table, understand?"

Damien thought a moment and then said, "Yeah, understood." He cleared his throat. "Let's just enjoy the night." He popped the next pill and said nothing else until the limo slowed to a stop.

When Drako glared out the tinted window he spotted the two large wrought iron gates leading to Wiz's mansion as they opened up to let the limo enter. The limo began to cruise down a long cobblestone driveway that wound past the front and to the back of the estate. Drako was impressed with the architecture of the 15,000 square foot ocean front property as they passed an eight port garage nearly packed with exotic toys.

Bringing the limo to a stop Drako's mouth had unconsciously dropped into his lap. The back of the mansion was lit up with bright lights. Huge blood burgundy bows were wrapped around the tall white columns. Long tables of white cloth covered platters of food sat in the huge open space. Music blared from high tech speakers and the lavish infinity pool was surrounded by model chicks.

"Damn." Drako exhaled in awe.

"Well, let's get inside." Damien was smiling again as the chauffeur opened the door.

"What the hell was that!" Wiz yelped, swatting at his nose. "God-damn, I can't feel my face!" He tugged his shirt over his head and tossed it aside as he yanked the glass doors leading to his patio open. "Ahh . . . yeah . . ." He exhaled as he stepped out and the scent of sea breeze swept across his face and whipped sensation back into his nostrils.

"The world is mine!" he yelled out with outstretched arms from his balcony that overlooked endless miles of ocean front property as a surge of intoxicated euphoria engulfed him. He looked down at his waterfall that cascaded into his vanishing edge pool and saw all of his guests partying it up. Just then he realized the music was playing so loud that no one could even hear him. Then he felt another tingling sensation as cool air whipped across his bare feet, causing him to look down. That's when he realized he was ass naked.

"Damn!" he hissed and shook himself back to reality. He trotted back through the doors and into his huge master suite, leaped his naked butt onto the chinchilla blanket draped across his oversized bed. "God-damn!" he cursed, feeling his heart palpitate. He felt like jumping back to his feet, streaking butt naked down his spiral mahogany staircase, and then through his grand foyer and out the back door so he could dive headfirst into his pool and come down off his high.

Wiz sucked in a deep gulp of air, exhaling slowly, and trying to simmer down his heart rate. He had no idea how long he'd been locked away in his room. All he knew was he'd been there ever since Damien's friend, Raoule had left him there.

Yes, tonight was the first night Wiz dabbled with the drug of choice for the rich and famous. Snorting lines of coke off a glass mirror seemed fitting after such a huge and unforgettable night, but after experiencing the roller coaster ride he just felt; he knew it was more powerful than he ever imagined. He also knew that once he got hold of himself this would be his last time.

Wiping the beads of sweat from his face after his heart rate returned to normal, he got out of bed and headed for his walk-in closet.

It had only taken Drako a few moments to locate Diamond as he stepped up to the white stone terrace and gazed through one of the tall wall windows. Diamond stood next to a ten-foot see-through fireplace.

"Dang, baby. This is nice." She complimented its marble finish. "This house has everything you could want!"

"No shit," Drako agreed, reaching for her hand. He led her back outside where they took a seat at a table placed close to the waterfall and took in the scene.

In no time Diamond was yapping about Wiz's lavish home theatre, then on about all the celebrities and up-and-coming artists who rounded out the list. Journalists, vixens, and groupies were all a part of the crowd. They saw Swirl, Jay-poon, and all the roster having a great time basking in the afterglow.

Drako watched as Damien and his friend mingled and networked the crowd. Drako had a good idea who'd be the man spewing the sex drug all over the party tonight. He spotted Wiz as he made his way out of the mansion and onto the terrace.

Wiz had changed into a comfortable pair of jeans and a fresh wife beater. His diamond chain hung from his neck and he toted a bottle of spades with him.

Too cool for his own good. Drako chuckled to himself looking at the dark millionaire frames Wiz wore across his eyes even though it was nighttime.

Both Drako and Diamond took hold of the scene for the next few hours. Everyone was having a grand time, but in Drako's eyes Wiz was having a little too much. It seemed as though the more the crowd thinned out the more Wiz tried to become the center of attention by acting sillier. The remarks he threw at his artists were much too harsh even in a joking manner. Wiz popped the cork on a fresh bottle and spewed champagne right at a group of glammed up women.

Drako was happy when Barz had finally led him back inside and into the entertainment room where Swirl and the rest of the camp had gathered.

Diamond had watched fake ass Myria along with White Chocolate mingle through the scene all night. It took a lot of resolve for Diamond to look the other way. It was apparent that after Myria won that award that her shit no longer stank! Her head was definitely way too big for her body and her attitude wanted every bitch in the house to know it.

Taking in enough of the scene Diamond told Drako to go and give Wiz their good-byes. Drako had had enough as well. He passed Damien and his friend on the way in. Drako didn't connect to Raoule's style at all. He had 'fleabag drug dealer' written all over him. It wasn't that Drako hated drug dealers; he just no longer respected the flamboyant ones.

Drako stuck his head in the entertainment room, but he didn't see Wiz. He was about to step the other way when Swirl yelled out to him, "Look across the hall, he's in the conference room with Barz." Swirl knew who Drako was looking for.

"'Preciate it." Drako threw Swirl a peace sign.

"Soo." Swirl tossed back.

As Drako approached the room he walked right into their ongoing conversation.

"Look man, I'm done wit' my songs. The shit ready to drop. I ain't tryin' to get into nothin' else. I want to—"

"Hold on, lil daddy," Wiz cut in with a slur. "Just pump your breaks a little, would ya? I got you, man. Just feel your way around the studio a lil more and do the things I'm asking you ta do. Then you can go out in the yard. I know you smart, but you just jumpin' off the porch wit' this here. Trust me, baby, I got a plan." Wiz hit him on the shoulder and turned up the bottle.

"Hmph!" Drako huffed. *This phony ass nigga spit the same shit at me.*

Wiz spun around and faced Drako with a shit-eating, phony ass grin on his face. "Oh, what up, Drako? I didn't know you were standin' there."

Drako took a good look at Wiz. He could tell he was spaced out, high, and had drunk way too much. "I know you didn't," he said without a mere smile.

"Well, I—"

"Look man, I just came to say me and Diamond are out." Drako shook his head at Wiz. "Say man, when you wake up tomorrow and look in the mirror I think you better start finding your old self before it gets out of hand."

Drako gave Jay-poon a scowl that caused him to drop his glare to the carpet. He turned back to Wiz. "And you best to get that plan together soon." He turned and walked away.

Jay-poon and Wiz watched him disappear down the hall and out the patio doors without looking back.

"What the hell is wrong with him?" Jay-poon turned to Wiz.

"Sst . . ." Wiz sucked at his grill. "Fuck him! You just spit that shit at Fatt Katt like the fuck I'm telling you and I guarantee you you'll have more paper than Swirl!" Wiz stepped off and left Jay-poon swimming in his own thoughts.

Drako didn't say a word to Diamond about what he'd heard when he grabbed her hand and led her back to their limo. His mind was already set. It was clear that Wiz was out for self. He had just slipped up and let Drako see just how grimy he could be. All those pre-rehearsed lines were merely skits that Wiz's scheming mind had conjured up for all Drako knew.

A Life for A Life

Drako masked his emotions as he always did best. There was no need to spin wheels over Wiz. No, Drako decided to tighten down on his game and set the wheels in motion for plan number three.

He looked over at the vanishing pool once again, but this time he imagined scheming ass Wiz floating face down in it with the water tinted crimson red. It wouldn't be a sensible move for him to do it now, but the way Wiz was handling things, it wouldn't surprise Drako if someone were to beat him to it.

"Don't trip over it, baby." Diamond leaned up and placed a soft kiss on Drako's lips as soon as the limo pulled away. "Just give him time. He's your friend. He's gone get it together."

Drako closed his eyes and relaxed his head back as Diamond leaned in close. *She might be the only reason this nigga ain't dead.* Drako's conscience echoed the thought once again.

"No Wiz! For the last time I'm not—"

"Pop!" He hopped up and slapped Myria across her face. "I'm tired of hearing you fuckin' whine!" He pointed a finger in her face and yanked her close to him with his free hand. "You go tell White Chocolate I'll snatch her ass off the screen just as fast as I put her on it! If you ungrateful bitches can't show me any appreciation then we need to get some bitches around here who can!" He shoved her toward the door.

"Get the fuck outta' here!" he yelled, not giving a damn about the tears streaming down her face.

He flopped back down on the bed, now feeling like a pimp. Dropping his chin back to his chest, he realized he had to be higher than Charlie Sheen. He was now taking his guilt out on anybody near him. He wasn't exactly sure why Drako looked the way he did, but the look that filtered through Drako's eyes made

Wiz feel like his sight almost disgusted him. He knew the combination of coke, pills, weed and alcohol had been too much. He wasn't even sure of what he'd done tonight. *Fuck it!* he thought of it all. *Tonight I just wanted to live my moment!* He lay back and closed his eyes. He felt comfortable. Damien had assured him he'd see everyone out and he'd secure the alarm system.

After Damien had seen all the guests safely off the estate, he took a seat and reclined on a comfortable chaise. Exhaustion had settled in and when Damien opened his eyes again it was past 6 A.M. Soft morning rays drifted through the tall glass patio doors and pierced his sleep. He quickly slipped on his alligator slides and made his way up the wide staircase to Wiz's room for good measure and safety's sake. But just before he reached Wiz's doorway his tracks were frozen.

The sound of sexual pleasure echoed from the room. He wanted to turn and trot back down the staircase, but curiosity gripped him like a pair of pliers. Inching up closer to the door, he squatted down and peeked around the corner.

What the? No fucking way! he thought, seeing Myria changing positions and White Chocolate getting comfortable spreading her legs before her. Myria had quickly bent over in the ramp position with the prettiest ass he'd ever seen by far now tooted in the air. Wiz raised up on both knees behind her and guided what looked like a tree trunk to Damien, straight into Myria from behind.

"Oh God, yes!" she gushed out as Wiz grabbed hold of her meaty ass cheeks and pushed himself all the way in.

"Unn . . . Fuck! Wiz, yess!" she squealed as Wiz began to pump faster and White Chocolate raised her pussy to meet Myria's lips.

"Hell yeah! That's it, taste her pussy, baby!" Wiz coaxed on, handling two of the prettiest black women at the same time that Damien had ever seen.

"Oh no!" Damien accidently gasped and pulled his head back at the sight of Wiz snatching back at least nine inches and burying it to the hilt again with the next plunge.

Myria screamed, wailed, and gushed with every stroke. Damien didn't even realize he'd stuffed his hand into his slacks and was masturbating the whole while until Myria's body began to twitch at the wake of her orgasm and he felt his own warm semen spew into his hand.

"Fuck!" he hissed sharply, mad at himself. But nevertheless, he jerked out the last few spurts and tiptoed back down the stairs and let himself out before he got caught wearing a pair of cum-stained Armani slacks.

Damn if only I had a dick that big, he thought to himself, opening the door to his SUV. *I could have all the black chicks going crazy over me, too!* He slammed the door, fighting with two harsh realities: he was jealous of brothers with big dicks and he was now officially into voyeurism.

Wiz fell asleep with an accomplished smile. *Run and tell that, you gum poppin' mothafucka!* he thought of Bless and the last rumors he'd spilled to Wendy Williams.

White Chocolate drifted off happily as well, knowing she'd finally fucked the big dick CEO without backstabbing her girl.

Myria fell asleep with tears in her eyes. Nobody knew if they were tears of joy or tears of pain. Neither did anybody seem to care.

Chapter Nineteen

Lewisburg U.S. Penitentiary

"That's my nigga right there!" Dub-D, who was Deuce's closest soldier, exclaimed as he pointed to the television.

"Be quiet so I can see!" Deuce angrily shot back.

"You can't see wit' yo' ears, fool!" Dub-D jokingly replied.

"Just shut the hell up anyway!" Deuce shouted.

"They gone show him again 'cause Red Rum 'bout to clean dis shit up!" shouted Dub-D, who was known for having diarrhea of the mouth.

It was now Tuesday night, and the common area was packed. The four small TVs sat up high on metal braces, and were only audible through battery-operated headsets. Everybody was waiting to see the once-a-year airing of the controversial Source Awards. One TV was on CNN and the other three were locked down on BET.

Deuce and his Bloods were there. Jet and his GDs were there, as well as many other gangs and gangstas. Then there was Toney Domacio. He sat quietly surrounded by his henchmen, but was probably the happiest man in the room, anticipating what Red Rum did and how Drako would carry it.

All the men were cleaned up in their prison best. They prepared the finest pastas from ramen noodle soups, and made

deep dish pan pizza crust out of Cheetos. They'd brewed the best wine from fermented oranges and grapefruit, and Toney had the weed and heavy narcotics running through the veins of all the users.

Although everyone was in a festive mood, every shot caller was still on point. They all smiled, but there were more concealed shanks available than there were muskets at the Civil War. This many gangstas in one place, some under the influence, could easily lead to trouble by merely saying the wrong words. Most gangs were geographically influenced, and wanted to see the East or West win it all, but Red Rum's music got love from every coast with its universal gangsta lyrics.

"Goddamn! I told you they was gonna win!" Dub-D shouted as he jumped up when Swirl and Wiz hit Collaboration of the Year.

"Sit down, fool!" Deuce argued for the fiftieth time.

"Dats' Drako, dats' Drako!" someone hollered.

"Oh shit, dat' fool cleaner than Usher tonight, ain't he?" Dub-D commented to anyone listening.

Toney Domacio smiled as he took notice of how Drako tried to turn his head away from the camera, but was still simultaneously caught at another angle from another camera.

"Fool 'bout to go onstage!" Dub-D spat as everyone momentarily waited in silence to see Drako stand up, but then quickly realized he wasn't.

"Dub-D, sit yo' ass down! You 'on know whatchu talkin' 'bout!" Deuce ranted.

Dub-D ignored him as he saw Diamond get up and walk on stage. "Oh shit! Oh shit! That's Drako's girl! She killin' Mariah and J-Lo put together!" Dub-D bragged.

"Oh, hell yeah!" a voice agreed.

"I know he hit dat' *every* night!" someone else shouted.

"She too pretty to fuck. I just wanna eat her and keep her," another voice yelled.

"That bitch in that baby blue phat, too," a familiar GD's voice shouted.

"Fool! That's Myria! I got pictures of her."

"Stop fakin', Dub-D!" someone inconspicuously yelled.

"Who dat'? What fool said Dub-D fakin'?" He stood in the middle of the floor with his arms spread wide in a 'come on' gesture, awaiting someone's challenge. He knew damn well nobody was gonna challenge him. He just wanted to prove he knew somebody almost famous.

"I thought so!" Dub-D angrily spat as he walked back over to Deuce. "Man, let me bust out on these fools!" he whispered. "Let me go get the flicks. I know it's Jet and them GDs; them fools think we fakin'! As soon as I said sumpin' 'bout Diamond, them marks hollered Myria!"

Deuce thought for a second. "You know Drako said keep that shit on the low. He said he 'on want Toney worried about him flossin' too much in them streets."

"Fool, fuck a macaroni Toney! This the Source Awards! Toney can see that Drako got his shit together. We need to get our shine on. Toney don't call our shots—you do!"

Deuce smiled, and that was all the booster cable he needed. "Go get da' flicks, fool!"

Jet watched as Dub-D left the common area. He turned to his man. "Watch that nigga," he said firmly.

"You think he goin' to get a knife?" his man questioned.

"Hell no! Dem' fools already strapped! Ain't no tellin' what dat' dummy might do." Jet moved a little closer to his man. "I ain't forgot what them niggaz did. One day Deuce gone be out the way and I'ma be the one to give it to Dub-D personally!"

They lightly smiled at the comment. Then someone yelled, "Swirl gone beat Fatt Katt!"

A few moments later, Swirl stole Breakthrough Artist of the Year. The ooh's and aah's filled the room as everybody saw how clean Swirl was and standing on each of his sides were Diamond and Myria.

All were gaping at Myria's revealing ensemble as the camera gave them a better view. "Man, I ain't had no pussy in eleven years! I'll make sure she love me when I get done."

"I bet Drako done fucked her!" another voice yelled.

Toney smiled to himself as he thought about how all the guys wondered what Drako was doing and who he might be brushing shoulders with. Toney's thoughts were broken, as well as everybody's lust for Myria and Diamond, when they heard Dub-D coming back into the common area.

He had taken off his tennis shoes and put on his steel-toe war boots. He held a large manila envelope high in the air. "Who said Dub-D fakin'?" he yelled as he walked to the table in the middle of the room and spilled the pictures from the envelope.

All the men quickly gathered around.

"That ain't her!" someone shouted.

Dub-D was five feet five inches with a short man complex and always felt he had to prove a point. "You fools 'bout to see what's real. Niggaz be gettin' at dem' Bloods!" Dub-D bragged as he pulled out a picture of Myria in a blood burgundy bikini, the same bikini she wore in the "Kill 'Em Slow" video. He sorted through the pictures. Some of them were of her on the video set and in the private trailer. He had some backstage pictures of Swirl's dancers, who had just been shown on TV, and he had pictures of Drako, only they were obscured views. Drako was turned sideways or backwards, but if you knew him, you could tell it was him.

Soon, Dub-D was getting pats on his shoulder and was now the man of the hour.

170

"How much you gonna charge me to sleep with a couple of those pictures tonight?" one of the inmates asked.

Dub-D smiled as he started putting the pictures away, in realization that he may have something of value. "Holla at me later—wit' dem' cigarettes. Can't ya see I'm busy right now?"

Deuce knew whatever Dub-D did reflected on him, and whatever Dub-D had, he had—and vice-versa.

As Toney listened to the jailhouse bickering, he was somewhat happy that the pictures made the tension in the room relax, yet he was somewhat unhappy that Drako would even send dudes like Deuce anything, because of this very reason. Toney knew that eventually they'd brag. He felt blacks were flamboyant and just couldn't keep their riches or accomplishments to themselves.

Jet stood back with his signature broom straw dangling from his mouth and a slight smirk on his face as he watched Dub-D. He'd hated his cocky ass ever since the day Deuce sent him with the message that they were standing behind Drako after squashing his beef with the GDs. Jet hoped for the day he caught Dub-D slippin'. *I hate dat' lil bastard! If I ever get my hands on dem pictures, he'll never see 'em again!* he thought to himself as the show returned from commercial break.

The last award of the night, Video Vixen of the Year, was up.

"Lyric gone win!"

"Nigga, iz you a fool? Dat' red bitch, Azzareya in dis' shit!" The men argued back and forth. Then—boom! All were stunned to see Myria take the show.

This time, they got a better look at her. "The only bitch to compete with her is Drako's girl!" a voice yelled.

"Well, since I can't fuck my man's girl, I'ma just fall in love wit' Myria," Dub-D shouted.

"Soon as you get back to yo' cell and get some Vaseline," Deuce joked out loud, making a few men laugh.

"Y'all fools laughing now, but ya better have them smokes when you come to borrow these flicks!" Dub-D shouted in his defense.

The inmates momentarily hushed their laughs as Myria delivered her speech. They got a good look at her pretty face as a few happy tears cascaded down. Then they watched her nail that sexy runway walk to exit the stage.

"Pretty bitch!"

"Look at dis' fine mothafucka here!"

"Somebody loan me a fiend book for tonight!" a man shouted, confirming that Myria had just started a fan club at Lewisburg Penitentiary.

Beaming with pride, Toney stood to his feet and headed back to his cell. Happy for Drako, he surely was. From the looks of things Red Rum was eating like no other. But with that and all the other things Drako had on his plate, Toney just hoped Drako wouldn't forget about him.

Toney quickly shook off the tingly feelings of doubt because at the end of this night, he, Deuce, Dub-D and the rest of the convicts would go to sleep happy. The Source Awards had been an unforgettable event, even for those who had to watch it from nineteen-inch shitty TVs at Lewisburg Pen.

Chapter Twenty

Drako

"I'm telling you, ma. I gotta bring you here. You're gonna love this place. The room service, the hospitality. I can't wait 'cause I know you gone make it special."

Diamond blushed. "You know I'ma hold you to your word."

"You know how it go with me, baby. If I say it, I mean it." He heard Diamond giggle before exhaling another happy sigh.

"But look, ma, get up and don't be late. My flight departs in just over an hour and I want you there on time . . . Oh yeah, be sure to dress comfortable. We gone cruise for a lil bit while I wrap some things up, so make sure you bring the laptop, my paperwork and that cell phone, feel me?"

"Gotcha. What else?"

"That's it, just be on time." Drako was about to end the call.

"Wait! Should I drive the Coupe?" Diamond asked sweetly.

"Fuck that goddamn car!" Drako barked a little harsher than he'd intended.

Diamond just held silent.

"My bad, ma. Real talk, I'm sorry, baby. I told you how I feel about that right now and besides, I don't think we need that kind of attention."

"I understand. I'll be there." Diamond tried to hide the hint of disappointment in her voice.

"We'll talk more when I see you."

"Love you."

"Love you more." Drako ended the call.

He knew Diamond was still hung up over the stunt Wiz had pulled just a few days ago. He'd called Diamond and told her and Drako to come outside, he was gonna stop by for a passing moment. Drako ignored the message, but when Diamond stepped onto the porch she didn't find Wiz; what she found in the driveway was a shiny black Bentley Coupe with a huge bright red bow wrapped around it. Diamond was ecstatic, she was in love with the car and completely taken by Wiz's sincere gesture.

However, Drako took it totally different. He knew it was Wiz's guilty conscience and getting rid of the Coupe didn't mean shit to Wiz with all the toys he had to play with.

Drako shook those thoughts away. This was no time to be spinning wheels over Wiz's bullshit. It would be plenty of time for that once he wrapped up the first step to his big money scheme. It had already been twenty-one days since he had been charging credit card numbers and billing them to his account. Nine days were left, and he had already charged over $1.3 million.

Drako looked around the humongous suite he had rented in the Waldorf Astoria. He made sure he left nothing behind. He zipped his full-length Louis Vuitton garment bag, which held the latest gray Cannali suit he'd just worn the day before to UBS Warburg Bank in Connecticut.

He had made the trip alone this time. He had successfully deposited six $9,000 cashier's checks totaling $54 G's into the account, posing as Mr. Scott Smith and further building his rapport with 'Charles' as he now referred to the bank manager on a first-name basis.

A Life for A Life

Drako picked up the hotel phone and informed guest services that he was checking out. He retrieved his bags, went downstairs, and the private chauffeur-driven Lincoln delivered him to La Guardia Airport to meet his flight.

A few hours later, Delta airlines nonstop flight landed Drako back down in Atlanta. He promptly made his way through the busy terminal and out the electric sliding doors.

As soon as he reached the taxi stand he saw Diamond pulling up in a sparkling white BMW, and stop at the curb right in front of him. He opened the back door, tossed his bags on the backseat, and then hopped up front with Diamond.

He looked over at the powder blue Juicy Couture seat pants that gripped her healthy thighs and then at the dark bubble frames on her face. "Damn, you look good." He leaned over her and pecked her pink glossed lips and let his eyes scan over her once again. *Damn . . . she know how much I like to fuck her when she put dat Juicy shit on,* he thought, feeling his dick twitch. But he quickly veered away from those thoughts, striking up casual conversation.

"I just knew you'd be late." He smiled, taking in the whiff of fresh vanilla aroma air freshener.

"Uh-huh, baby. I hopped right up, threw this on and stopped by the detail shop."

"Oh yeah? How you know to get vanilla aroma?"

Diamond giggled. "This short lil guy ran straight up to the car. He said 'Ay, shawty dis here Drako whip. I always clean his whip.'" She tried to impersonate his voice. "'He always get da vanilla,' he said next. So I let him do it. Then when he finished I tipped him a twenty. He said, 'Um, he always hit me wit' fiddy,

shawty.'" They both laughed. "Yeah, you can tell he straight from Bankhead," Diamond rambled on.

"A'ight, baby, that's all good. But did you bring my stuff?"

"Didn't I tell you I got you?" Diamond smacked her lips as she merged back onto the beltway. "Your laptop and the cell are underneath your seat. Your paperwork is in the glove compartment. Anything else?" Diamond inquired.

"Nah, baby, everything look like it's gone be all gravy," Drako said, feeling grateful to have a dependable woman like Diamond as he retrieved the laptop and started powering up.

"So where are we riding to?"

"It don't matter," Drako said, adjusting his seat. "It's a pretty day. Niggaz out cruising everywhere. Get off on Campbellton and cruise by Greenbriar Mall, then shoot down to Five Points and past Piedmont Park," he suggested.

Diamond lowered the stereo to a modest pitch, so Drako could concentrate and so they could chat.

She wrapped the beltway and cruised with the Sunday traffic for over two hours before Drako instructed her to pull over and park just as they approached Lennox Mall.

"You hungry, baby?" Drako asked.

"Not really. I just like to be out with you."

"Yeah, ma. Me too," Drako responded as he closed the laptop and turned the stereo volume down. "Baby, it's been twenty-one days. I done billed just over 1.7 mil' to the account and with the lil one hundred I started it with makes it a lil over 1.8. I 'on think I'ma wait any longer. I'ma go ahead and withdraw the 1.7 and leave the hundred behind."

"Why don't you take it all, baby?"

Drako sighed. "I thought about it. I mean, I'ma get it all, but I don't want any eyebrows raising from the bank with such a sudden withdrawal. I would still feel good if I only got away with the $1.7 mil'. Plus, I wanna see if and how long it takes this bank to transfer the funds to my offshore account in the Caymans."

"Drako, you ain't worried at all about that offshore account?"

"Nah, baby. Those accounts are just numbers. They don't go by name, and that doesn't even matter because the U.S. can't seize funds from there due to a treaty. See, once the funds are transferred there, then they're safe. All they can do is hunt the name down on the account I used to pull this shit off with, and good luck on that." Drako laughed at his cleverness.

Diamond paused, letting it sink in. "But what about the people's cards you hit? How do they get reimbursed?"

Drako laughed again. "Hell, I 'on know. I can't tell you nothin' about the victim. I just studied how to get the money and get away."

They both laughed.

"Okay, baby, tomorrow is Monday. I'ma withdraw the 1.7, and you'll be in your last week at Hertz. Don't even trip; they won't have a clue as to why the girl you're profiling doesn't show back up for work. I just need you to get a few more receipts this week 'cause I need to look for a few more scores like Scott Smith. Feel me?"

Drako looked over at Diamond as she nodded confidently.

"And the day you quit, I'ma get the other hundred. Wednesday will be day twenty-five. Later on I might try to get you on somewhere else, like the Marriott Marquise or the Hilton Hotel on Courtland."

"Drako, I hope that'll be a while. Shoot, I need a break!" Diamond complained, scrunching up her cute little nose.

"Stop it, girl, you ain't been workin' but a month!" Drako said jokingly, only to erase the phony smirk from her face. She grabbed his hand and whined.

"I know, baby, but I'm just tired of wearing all that makeup and that wig so much!"

Drako took her hand in both of his to calm her.

"I just hate working at them rinky-dink jobs, but forget all that! All this talk is making me hungry. Let's get some soul food," Diamond said.

"Let's go to Beautiful's over on Cascade."

"Say no more." Diamond cranked up the BMW. "Oh, but before I forget, I'm sorry about bringing up that car so much. I just thought it was nice of him."

"I understand, too." He laid a hand on her thigh. "That was exactly his point, baby. Wiz is so jacked up right now he don't think nobody, not even me, can see through his shit! He thought I was about to start pressing him for paper the other week and now he's throwing shit to keep me from asking. I'm telling you it's part of his guilty conscience, too." He squeezed her thigh firmer and watched her tuck her loose strands back.

"I mean, we'll keep it. We'll ride that lil shit till we get our own. I just don't want you to think it came from his heart. Let's just stay focused on what's in front of us now. It's time to see how our life and the other lives his bullshit affects are gonna go."

"We'll see." Diamond smiled again.

"Sooner than you think." Drako held a devious grin.

"Why you looking at me like that?"

Drako waited a moment. "What color panties you wearing under here?" His hand slid further up her thigh.

Diamond put the BMW in gear, smacking her lips. "None," she answered flirtatiously and pulled away.

Chapter Twenty One
Drako

Monday morning, Drako was back up and fully revived as he sat on the sink in his huge bathroom drinking coffee. He watched Diamond put the finishing touches on her makeup and replace her silky black hair with her blonde wig. "It won't be long now, baby." Drako encouraged her and carefully planted a good-bye kiss on Diamond's lips. He did his best not to smudge the makeup on her cheeks. He walked her to the car and lightly popped her ass as she got in. "White girl got back!" he joked.

"Just be on time to meet this white girl at Kinko's," Diamond replied.

"I got you, ma," he responded, closing the car door and watching Diamond exit the garage on her way to work.

Drako had come back in the house. He couldn't wait till 9 A.M. to call up the bank. He cooked eggs for breakfast and watched the news to kill time. Drako waited till about 9:45 A.M. to call Citibank in New York, where he also held the account for his fictitious business.

He instructed the bank manager to transfer $1,700,000 to his offshore account. The banker asked Drako a few questions; all the questions were drawn from information Drako had previously

used to open the account. The banker then requested a contact number. Drako gave him the cell phone number registered in the account holder's name.

The bank manager told Drako he'd return his call shortly. Drako hung up and waited patiently for a call back. Thirty minutes later, the banker called and confirmed everything was approved and the transaction would be complete within six hours.

Drako thanked the banker and hung up. Though ready to celebrate, he calmed himself. He never believed in hope, so he would only celebrate when he knew the transaction was complete. Drako lay down and awaited his next step.

At noon, Drako was pulling into Kinko's to meet Diamond. As soon as he pulled in, Diamond was exiting with a manila envelope in hand.

"You're late!" she said flatly as she approached the BMW.

"No, you're just early," Drako shot back defensively.

She smiled as she leaned over in the window. "You mad? You wanna spank the white girl for being naughty?" she teased as she saw Drako peeking down her cleavage.

Drako smiled. "Diamond, you know I 'on want no white girl. I think you just wanna role-play."

"It's okay, papi. Underneath all this makeup it'll still be Diamond workin' her magic."

"I'ma tear ya hot ass up!" Drako teased, then quickly caught himself. "Why we always flirtin' at Kinko's?"

"We flirt everywhere! We just be glad to see each other."

"Well, you gonna be glad to see me when you get home. Citibank said the transaction should be completed within six hours."

"Fa' real, baby?" Diamond was ecstatic. "Ooh, baby, that's so good. I'm so glad this is almost over."

"Me too. I can't wait for you to get home."

"As soon as I can, baby, as soon as I can." She blew him a kiss as she got back in her car.

They both cranked up and left. Diamond turned right, and Drako busted a left and drove straight back home.

When Drako returned home, he sat at the kitchen table and studied a few more receipts. He couldn't stop thinking about the 'free money.' As anticipation set in, Drako retrieved the number to his Cayman Island account holder. It was 3:15 P.M.; it had only been five hours, but Drako still dialed the number from his bogus cell.

He reached the automated service, listened to the instructions, and dialed the keypad to retrieve his account information. He then entered the number to his secret access code.

"Your current account balance is $1,800,000 and zero cents," the automated voice said, confirming that $1,700,000 had been added to the $100,000 that was already in the account. *Oh shit! I knew it could work!* Drako's body turned warm. A strong wave that felt like power surged through him. He was already feeling the stability and envisioning the thought of spoiling Diamond. He swatted a proud fist through the air and couldn't wait to share the moment with the woman who made it all possible.

When Diamond got home she waltzed straight into Drako's office where she knew he must've been.

"Well?" She stopped and placed her hands on her sides as soon as she saw Drako with his focus dropped to another pile of receipts as if nothing had happened.

He looked up and broke into a huge smile as he picked the cell phone up off the desk. "I'ma let you hear it for yourself," he said, punching in the digits as he strolled around the desk. As soon as the voice came on he put the phone to Diamond's ear.

He watched her glow and her eyebrows raise as the machine spit the account balance to her.

"Uh-huh. Ooh, baby, it worked!" She hugged Drako with excitement. Drako could tell how happy she was to share this moment and that they didn't get caught.

She pulled back and leered up at him. "So what now?"

Drako thought for a few seconds as he looked down at her now blue eyes, and then said, "Well for you, *Senator Palin* I think it's about time you take one for your country!"

"What?" Diamond said as Drako caught her with surprise.

"Take it or get dealt with!" He was already spinning her around and shoving her over his desk.

"You mean you're gonna take me right here in the oval office Mr. Big Black President?" Diamond fell into role.

"Right in the Oval Office," Drako huffed, staring Diamond in the eyes as she looked back over her shoulder. Drako had already hiked her skirt up over her ass and as soon as he tugged her panties halfway down her thighs, he planted nearly seven inches on his first rough intrusion.

"Aww fuck, Mr. President!" Diamond said.

Drako knocked her forward, causing her to spread her arms over the desk for leverage, sending his papers flying everywhere.

Her pussy farted and clamped down on Drako's dick like a glove. "Mm hm! Hold it right there!" Drako held her waist and nailed her hard again.

"Damn, Nigger!" Diamond yelped out and looked back again.

"So this is what it finally took to get you ta say it, huh?"

Drako clamped a hold that let her know she wasn't going anywhere. "Call me another one, you fuckin' tramp!"

"I–Oh–I'm su-sorry! Mr. Pre-president!" she yelled as Drako commenced to bang away.

"Oh yeah, Sarah!" He called her name and grudge fucked her till she came. Drako turned her around, lifted her up and plopped her back down on the ledge of the desk. He rammed his dick back inside, then satisfied his fantasy until her wig fell off and the black eyeliner streaked down her face like oil paint on a canvas.

"How you like that spanking? Huh, Sarah? Huh?" Drako pounded out the question through clenched teeth.

"Oh, please. I–stop. I loved–I–get that nigger dick outta me!" She panted in confusion as Drako bust his nut up in her. She clung onto him tightly as her body twitched out the last of her orgasm as well. Drako picked her up and carried her to the den where he had a quilt, a bottle of wine and some fruit all waiting in front of the fireplace.

They lay down, both still spent. They cuddled and talked, falling asleep almost $2 million richer in front of the cozy fireplace.

Chapter Twenty Two

Drako

Tuesday morning, Drako was startled by the sound of his cell phone ringing. He awoke to find himself lying alone on the quilt. Diamond was gone, the fireplace was turned off, and the tall grandfather clock was just about to strike 11 A.M.

"Whad up?" Drako angrily answered his cell phone.

"What you doin'?" Diamond's sweet voice chimed back.

"Where you at, girl?" Drako hostilely questioned.

"I'm at work in the staff bathroom sneaking to call yo' ass! Why ain't you up? It's eleven o'clock. You 'pose to be at Kinko's by noon."

"Damn, ma, I musta been out!"

"White girl put it on yo' ass, huh? Want some more?" Diamond playfully whispered.

"Hmph! I made a white girl confess that her ass was black, don't you mean?"

Diamond giggled. "Whoever came up with the saying 'once you go black, you never go back' sho' wasn't lyin'! Dang, you got my pussy sore."

"Girl, you crazy. Stop whining," Drako said lightly as he stood and stretched. "How could you leave me on the floor like that, ma? I meant to touch you up this morning."

"Stop it. I said I gotcha when I get home, but my pussy can't take no shit like last night. Dang, Drako, I won't be no good!"

"Don't trip, I got you too, ma."

"I'ma make sure I give you good, slow head tonight," she teased.

"That's all you do is call from that bathroom and play with me," Drako huffed. "Get back to work before they become suspicious. How can you be working if you always in that bathroom calling to check on me?"

"Shoot." Diamond sucked her teeth dismissively. "My work is done. I got the receipts already. Drako, don't you know how much traffic is in and out of here? Them people ain't thinking 'bout me!"

Diamond hesitated a moment, but Drako didn't respond. "I'm still gone give you head," she whispered.

"What?"

"As soon as I get home, you good dickin' mothalova!" Diamond could feel the smile that she'd just gained from Drako.

"Be careful wit' yo' crazy ass. I'm gettin' ready now. I'll be on time."

"Love you too, by the way. Bye."

Drako jumped up, took that five-minute shower and landed himself in a white Jordan sweatsuit and matching sneakers. He grabbed his classic Jay-Z "Reasonable Doubt" CD to add to his CD changer, then headed straight for the garage. He jumped in his 760, put the changer on "Dead Presidents," pushing his Li all the way to Kinko's.

Diamond tucked her cell phone back into her waistline and came out of the bathroom stall she'd been hiding in. She did a quick mirror check to make sure her makeup was still flawless.

A Life for A Life

She smiled to herself at how easily the pale toned base and eye shadow made her already light mulatto skin pass as a typical all-American Brittney Spears.

Diamond sighed at the thought of leaving her temporary solitude and returning back to the busy office on the other side of the door, but inevitably, she knew she had to keep pushing on. *Just a few more days,* she thought as she opened the door, only to be met with the loud sounds of turmoil from all the impatient customers.

She stood at the bathroom door and looked around the office before she advanced. Everything was normal, and Diamond began to move back into place. As she was approaching the service counter, she saw two clean-cut Caucasian men dressed in cheap blue suits. The taller man wore dark shades and the shorter man's eyes scanned the entire Hertz office space. But what made Diamond leery was that they were not in the service line. They were behind the counter, and the normally arrogant manager was now complying with their questioning.

She stepped aside and stood beside a vending machine in hopes of obscuring the roaming eyes of the short man. Diamond was clueless as to who these men were as she watched with caution.

As the taller man turned to follow the manager toward the back of the office, Diamond's premonition hit! She spotted the silver badge attached to his waist when he turned and his cheap suit coat opened. *This cannot be about me!* Her body turned warm.

The two men disappeared in the back; she reasoned to just stay calm. Diamond had almost reached the service desk when she noticed two more men dressed in the same fashion. They'd pulled up right at the front door in an unmarked car, and were about to enter as well.

Diamond's entire body instantly turned hot! She could feel her legs trembling beneath her. She still didn't know who they were or what they had come for, but her gut instinct told her something wasn't right. Diamond wasn't about to take the chance and wait and see. Her criminal instinct took over her thoughts and movements. *Get out of sight, girl,* she reasoned as she saw the next two men enter the building. Quickly, she stepped back into the bathroom unnoticed and closed the door and leaned against it.

What now? What could it be? It can't be nothin', Diamond thought. *Slow down, girl. Breathe slow, catch yo'self.*

She turned and peeked back out. Diamond barely cracked the bathroom door. She didn't have a good view, but she could see her work desk. The Hertz manager came into view, followed by the first two men. They went straight to her desk and started shuffling through the papers on top. *Oh God!* Diamond closed the door and nervously began to wave her hands in uncertainty. *It's me, it's me!"* Tears immediately welled in her eyes. Her first thought was Drako. Her next thought was a vision of the men handcuffing her and taking her back to federal prison.

"Oh God! Oh God! Please help me! I can't go back! I can't live like that!" she prayed aloud as she nervously fanned her hands and paced behind the door. Her mind raced faster as she looked around the bathroom. There were no windows to get out of.

"Hide, girl, hide," she said to herself as she opened the stall. She locked it behind her and sat on the toilet, then quickly changed positions. She stood on the lid and squatted so that if they looked inside, they wouldn't see her feet; it would appear as if nobody was inside.

Diamond tucked her head in between her knees and muffled her cries as best she could. She told herself she'd stay there as long as it took! She thought about Drako, and how hurt he was gonna be; then she thought of how good he felt and how much she'd miss him, how much she needed him, and how bad she wanted to hear his voice right now.

Squeezing her arms around her bended knees tighter, as she wished Drako could be her superhero and come save her once again.

"I'm sorry, Drako. I'm sorry, baby," Diamond panted between sobs. "Oh, God, don't take him away!"

She stopped suddenly. "What did Drako tell me?" She hushed her cries as her conscious began to speak aloud. "He said, 'Baby, if you gone fall, always do your best to fall forward—never fall backwards!'"

Diamond's feet hit the floor. *I gotta try to get outta here! They gone get me in here sooner or later!* She unlocked the stall and let herself out.

Her mind raced as she looked around the bathroom. *Stop crying, girl, and get your feet to moving!* She ran to the sink, quickly took off the glasses, and then removed the blue contact lenses. Diamond pushed the hand soap dispenser and filled her small hands with soap. Next, she quickly bent over and began to wash the makeup away from her face as best as she could, scrubbing hard and fast.

Hurry, girl! She rose to see her image in the mirror. The eye shadow and blush were gone, and even though her face was wet, a dark hue reflected through.

Snatching the wig off, she shook her black tresses down to her shoulders, and looked down at the image of her pantsuit. *What now?* She thought, spotting the reflection of a yellow raincoat hanging up in the staff bathroom. Turning around, she grabbed the coat, and her wig and her glasses out of the sink and ran back into the stall. Flushing the receipts, she threw the wig and glasses into the toilet and slipped the long yellow poncho over her head. The poncho hung down at least five inches below her knees. Diamond took another deep breath. "Get yo' self together, girl!"

She grabbed a newspaper out of the wastebasket then looked at her image in the mirror once more as she tried to straighten out her hair. *One more deep breath and Diamond gotta shine.*

Diamond opened the stained newspaper as if she were reading it as she opened the bathroom door and stepped out. Two Secret Service agents were passing by, exiting the office. Her peripheral vision caught the other two still hovering over her desk. Diamond kept her head down as if she were attentively reading the paper, as she walked right in behind the two agents. She kept her peripheral fixed on the other two until they were out of her view.

When the two men walking ahead of her reached the front door, Diamond was right on their heels. The first man held the door open for his partner, and then extended the same courtesy to the nice young lady that followed. With her face buried in the paper, Diamond almost bumped into the man. "Thank you," she said politely.

The agent poked out his chest with pride and said, "My pleasure." He held the door open a little wider than necessary as his gapped coat revealed his badge for her to see.

Diamond offered another shy smile, as she dropped her head back to the newspaper.

"It's a small burgundy compact car!" the agent shouted to the other as he opened up his umbrella. Diamond saw him watching her in her peripheral as she folded the newspaper underneath her arm and raised the poncho's hood over her hair.

She stepped off the sidewalk and moved toward the customer parking lot. The two agents went the other way to search the employee parking spaces. Diamond had left the keys to the car and was completely lost as far as direction.

The heavy rain started to fall harder as she walked away lost. Diamond looked back as she saw a cab pull up in front of Hertz. The patrons inside were paying the driver and about to get out. Diamond went back to the cab. As soon as the patrons got out, she rushed her way into the backseat.

"Oh God! Thank God you're here," she offered with a beautiful smile as she closed the door. "My mother is undergoing heart surgery right now, and these people don't even have my rental available for Christ's sake! Take me to Grady Hospital."

"I could get you there in no time, ma'am," the driver reassured.

"Well, please go. I'm already running late, handsome." Diamond was looking back as the cab pulled away. She saw the manager and the other two men step outside. They pointed in the direction where Diamond had parked, and when she looked over, they were opening the doors to the rental she drove.

Diamond turned back around and lay back on the seat. She let out a sigh of relief. "How long did you say, honey?" she asked.

"I'll have you there in twenty minutes, beautiful." Diamond gave him another fake smile.

As the cab made it out of Hertz and was passing Hartsville International, Diamond looked back and all the thoughts of when she and Drako had gotten busted resurfaced through her mind. The thoughts of her in prison and not with Drako flashed again. Then, the thought of how this could have happened lingered.

The moment the taxi reached I-85, Diamond relaxed her nerves. "Excuse me, honey. On second thought, I may have to stop downtown. Lemme make a quick call."

Meanwhile, Drako had been parked at Kinko's for over thirty minutes. *Where da fuck is she!* Drako had said to himself. *There*

she go thinkin' for me! Thinkin' I'ma be late, so she wanna be late.

When his cell rang, he knew it had to be her. "Where the hell you at?"

"Hey, girl, I finally made it. I'm sorry I took so long, but the rental car didn't work out."

This can't be real! Drako thought, feeling like a sharp blade cut him the moment Diamond addressed him with, "Hey, girl," which was their alert signal.

"What happened?"

"Oh, never mind me. I hailed a nice taxi. He's gonna take me to Grady Hospital."

"I'll meet you there."

"Harper's is fine. I'll ride with you from there." Diamond chose the spot and hung up. "My sister's gonna meet me at Harper's just off Peachtree Street," she said to the driver. "Could you get me there please?" She knew Drako was only a few blocks away and knew exactly what to do.

"No problem, ma'am."

Ten minutes later, Drako watched as the cab pulled right up in front of his BMW in Harper's parking lot. He jumped out of his car and trotted to the back door of the cab. "There's my brother," she lied as Drako got to the door.

"That'll be $21.80, ma'am."

"Pay him!" Diamond ordered Drako as she slipped out.

Drako quickly smashed a fifty into the driver's palm. "Keep the change, pahtna!"

The taxi driver pulled away with a smile as Drako and Diamond got in his BMW and pulled away. As soon as they hit Peachtree Street, the inevitable tears soaked Diamond's face. Drako squeezed her hand to console her as he steered the BMW with the other.

"Calm down, baby. Just tell me what happened."

A Life for A Life

Diamond did her best to control her sobs as she replayed to Drako the whole scene from the moment she stepped out of the bathroom.

Drako listened patiently. Once Diamond had vented, Drako squeezed her hand more firmly. He looked into her eyes when he stopped at the red light. "Diamond, don't worry, baby. The whole thing is you're here with me. I told you that they can't stop identity theft until after the crime has been committed. Baby, we got all the money! They can have the other hundred grand, we still 1.7 to the good!"

His response wasn't enough to pacify her. "What about me, Drako? They're looking for me! They got the damn car!"

"Baby, they ain't lookin' for you; they lookin' for the little valedictorian white girl from Oregon that you were actin' like! I told you, I can't feel for the victim. Them her problems; we ain't gotta feel none of that. And as for the car, it was reserved under a fake name. And you had no personal items in the car, right?" He began to rub her thigh in a comforting way as the light changed and he pulled away. "Baby, trust me, we straight. I'ma find out where we slipped so it don't happen again." Drako hoped he was right. His only twinge of fear was if they dusted the car for fingerprints which he thought was unlikely.

Diamond sat quietly and processed Drako's words. He leaned over and kissed her cheek. "It'll be all right. You shined, baby. I'm proud of you, and I love you more than I love myself right now."

Diamond instructed Drako to pull over in a McDonald's parking lot shortly before they reached Stone Mountain. When the car came to a stop, Diamond held Drako's hand with both of hers. She looked in his eyes. "Drako," she began softly, "you know that I love you with all my heart. My world really does revolve around you—everything about you. I live to satisfy your every need." She paused. "You know I got your back, and I

LIFE 193

support you at whatever you do. But honey, everything I love flashed before me today. God knows that I could never tell, but Drako, I couldn't bear the thought of not being with you, even if we're dead-ass broke! I can't imagine doing anything to risk losing you again."

She stopped again, thinking Drako would attempt to dissuade her decision, but he didn't. "I'm trying to say, I don't wanna do it like that anymore. Baby, just finish your other scheme. Something less risky will eventually surface." This time she knew he'd respond; she braced herself for his answer.

To Diamond's surprise, he leaned forward and planted a kiss on her lips. "I understand, ma. I love you too much to gamble you. You know I'ma find a way to weather this storm. It ain't 'bout what we need or don't need. I just feel like my brain is as complex as Toney's and Wiz's, and I'm just claiming what we deserve. We gone be a'ight, you feel me?"

Diamond stared at him with red, puffy eyes. "I know you gone make it right. You always do, baby."

Drako winked as he cranked up the BMW. He leaned over and pecked her lips again. "I'm glad you know me. Now, let's get home so I can reshine my Diamond."

She sniffled as she reclined her automatic seat back. Drako held her hand all the way home.

Chapter Twenty Three

Drako and Diamond

Drako pampered Diamond, fulfilling all her emotional and sexual needs for the rest of the week. He eventually consulted with Damien about what went down that caused agents to come after Diamond.

Damien told Drako that it had probably only taken one credit card company to flag a sporadic purchase, which could've triggered a probe of similar purchases on that account. Drako knew he'd charged several numbers more than once.

One week ago that same night, Drako got home and grabbed his hammer and called Diamond into the garage where she witnessed him smash his laptop and cell phone into a million pieces. He raked the pieces up into a garbage bag and kissed Diamond, who stood before him all cleaned up. She never said a word; she just stood there in her silk robe and the towel she had wrapped around her damp hair.

"I'll be back in fifteen minutes," Drako told her. He got in his BMW and drove to a nearby McDonald's and tossed the crushed parts into a dumpster that sat out back.

When he returned home, he and Diamond turned that page in their life. "No lookin' back, ma. It's too hard to move forward if we keep thinkin' 'bout the past."

"I'm still following, baby," Diamond chimed as they simply held each other the first night. No physical lovemaking; it was simply love of the minds.

It took several days before Drako had truly broken Diamond out of her funk. What had happened at Hertz had shaken Diamond more than he realized.

After about a week he started taking her out and enjoying lots of quality time with her. They pushed the Bentley, went to the movies, shopped and dined at Justin's and several other upscale restaurants, and they laid up all the time.

He traveled to Red Rum headquarters and took Diamond along with him on both occasions. Wiz was never there. Still basking in the label's success at the Source Awards, his life was so busy that he was making fewer public appearances and doing even less video cameos. But he was still constantly in the public's eye. Wiz was now monopolizing magazine interviews. His face was splashed on almost every industry publication. He was still creating more and more money-making beef, making him the foundation for hip-hop scandal. Drako hardly even checked on him, and when he did it was only by short text message.

Looking down at the few pictures scattered on the dresser, Drako realized that dealing with Diamond's dilemma made him reflect on all the things he valued most. He realized he'd been so caught up in achieving his own goal that he hadn't sent Toney any money in weeks. It made him feel like shit and he was hoping Toney would call soon; it would be good to hear the voice of the man who put him in a position to take care of himself in the first place.

He picked up the four pictures he'd taken back when he was in prison. Drako looked at him and Toney again, and then shuffled to a guy named Drip he'd also been cool with. He told himself he was gonna do better by Toney, and that it was time to reach out to Drip.

Drip had gotten released nearly two years before Drako and plan number three was churning at full speed in his head. Drip could be all he needed to bring it all together, just right.

"You okay, baby?" Diamond stepped in the room and spotted Drako gazing at the old pictures.

"Yeah, yeah, I'm good." He opened the drawer and dropped the pictures back inside. "I was just reminding myself to pick up those hip-hop weekly's for Deuce and drop Toney a few dollars." He watched Diamond adjust the baseball cap over her head smugly and letting the ponytail hang down her back.

"You ready to go?" She was still excited. Drako had surprised her and taken her car shopping.

"Let's get out of here." Drako popped her on her ass on his way past. He led them out the door.

✧ ✧ ✧ ✧ ✧

It seemed that Diamond couldn't have been happier. Of all the cars in the world, she simply wanted a candy apple red 430 Lexus Coupe convertible, which Drako purchased immediately. She insisted on driving when they returned home to Charlotte to see the Bobcats do their thing against the Atlanta Hawks.

Today, the convertible top was up as she zipped up I-85 North in pursuit of Bobcat Arena. She started out playing her Alicia Keys CD until they passed Greenville, South Carolina. Then she let Usher's whole CD burn its way past Gastonia. Drako had listened to her sing along on most songs and in between their chitchat.

As they passed the Billy Graham exit and reentered Charlotte, Drako pulled Usher out of the stereo. "A'ight, lemme get some Jay-Z or better yet, Drake."

"Why not Lil Wayne?" Diamond reasoned.

"It don't matter as long as it's Young Money."

"I know that's right, baby," Diamond agreed, letting out a small sigh. "Drako, I been thinkin' 'bout somethin', baby."

"What's that? Givin' me a son?"

"No, silly, but that would be cool, too," Diamond said with a giggle. "Seriously, I been thinkin' I wanna sing. I've written hundreds of songs—R&B, short raps, love ballads, all kinda stuff being wasted, just like my voice that you love so much."

"Ma, I 'on want you to miss what you like. I mean, I wanna see you happy and I wanna see you always shine—you know that. But I 'on want you subjected to all the bullshit in the industry tryin' to make it. I know ain't nobody gone sex ya, 'cause both y'all asses will be dead." Drako paused to emphasize his point. "But it ain't just that. This shit is a dirty game. Niggaz is schemin', using artists up and droppin' 'em when their light burns low."

"Drako, we ain't slow. We can read contracts. Maybe I oughta do some hooks and a few cameos with Swirl or some other Red Rum artists, just to get my voice and face out there."

"Well, hooks is cool, Diamond, but you ain't flashin' yo' ass all over Swirl and puttin' no bikini that could fit a Barbie doll on yo' ass!"

"I know that, baby! I'd just tell them tight short-shorts is the limit! Touch me wrong and they'll see how diamond shines." Drako smiled at her witty comment.

"You see Ashanti and Alicia don't get naked," she said. "All you gotta do is stick by your morals. You gotta make the industry respect you."

"I feel that. Listen, baby, we'll see about gettin' you on some hooks, but you won't be linked to nothin' no time soon. I may get my own independent label when this shit is all over. Feel me?"

"Ooh, Drako! That would be nice, and I'd be your label's first lady—and the CEO's *only* lady," Diamond emphasized.

"Oh yeah? We'll see. Now get off on 277 and let's go straight to the arena."

Diamond sucked her teeth. "Drako, don't be cuttin' me off with that *we'll see*! We'll see about what? Me, the CEO's only lady or see about the label?"

"Diamond, don't start this shit. You know I'm talkin' 'bout the label. Come on and enjoy Charlotte 'cause we out first thing tomorrow."

Diamond didn't argue; she knew damn well what Drako had meant anyway. She just silently thought about her next career move as they cruised over the 277 beltway and entered downtown Charlotte.

The couple were both in awe as they saw the new Charlotte skyline. The Bank of America stood majestically tall, and downtown's new building structures had given their old city a facelift.

Diamond steered into the heavy line of traffic just outside the arena. "Drako, you ever think about moving back to Charlotte?"

Drako thought for a moment. "Charlotte is nice—nice for a banker! It's a place to retire and have kids." He paused. "There is plenty of corporate legit money here, but we need to be around industry money, you know.

"We done been here and done this. I feel ATL suits us better. We got season tickets and great seats, so I think the only thing we'll be doing in Charlotte is visiting."

Diamond didn't argue; she just leaned over and kissed Drako's cheek, still following his lead.

They finally parked and headed into the arena. Dressed in twin orange and gray Bobcat jerseys and fitted caps, they walked down to their seats in the fourth row. They saw Nelly and Michael Jordan there to support their team as well as all the other dedicated Bobcat fans.

When the game was finally over, Diamond drove out to Bennigan's in South Park, where they ate and checked in a few blocks away at the South Park Hotel and Suites for the night.

Drako was happy to have Diamond back on track because he still had plans he'd started and one way or the other, he had to finish off his next caper and he had to do it soon.

Chapter Twenty Four
Wiz

Wiz felt as though he was hidden away from the entire world once the wrought iron gate was closed and he was safely nestled in the comfortable confines of his mansion.

Reclined back on a comfortable chaise on his terrace with a pair of Aviators splashed across his face, he was soaking in the late afternoon sunrays.

Wiz was doing his best to make his gossip hoarding buddy and columnist Joshua feel that he was paying him full attention. "Yeah, yeah, that'll be cool. That'll be cool," Wiz spat as his attention diverted back to his latest conquest, who removed her bikini top and stepped directly under the waterfall. She tilted her head back and let the water cascade over her face and down her breasts, bringing her nipples to full erection.

Wiz smiled at the sight, momentarily forgetting Joshua was even on the telephone, until Joshua's loud voice broke his trance. "Wiz, did you hear me?"

"Yeah, yeah, I heard," Wiz lied, quickly covering up the receiver with his hand. "Keisha …" He motioned her to come out of the hot tub.

Wiz then gave his full attention back to Joshua in an effort to end the call. "Look, Josh. You wanna know how I'm livin'?

Well, so does BET. MTV is gettin' at me hard for MTV cribs, but since you my man and I been wit' you since you was at *Source*, I'ma look out for ya."

"Good, good, Wiz. You know I just started at *Rides* magazine, and for me to book a shoot with you would really do wonders for me around here."

"I gotcha, whoadie. We'll do the interview over the phone, and then all you have to do is come out here and we'll complete the shoot."

"I'm sure I can get them to agree to that number."

"Good, good," Wiz replied as Keisha got out of the Jacuzzi and sauntered over to him. She grabbed the towel from the stand and dabbed the water from her face, but let the rest of the beading water glisten in the sun as it rolled down her body. "Josh, I'ma blow you up at *Rides* just like I do everybody. Swirl comin' next. Just get the check right then e-mail me. I gotta keep it movin'; I got other things that need my attention," Wiz bragged as Keisha straddled him cowgirl style and sat on his lap. "Get at me," Wiz said and ended the call.

Wiz laid the phone on the table then took hold of Keisha's moist ass cheeks. She leaned forward and pecked his lips. "Always business with Wiz," she chimed.

"Nah, baby girl, just business before pleasure," Wiz tossed back, causing her to smile.

Keisha's high cheekbones and chinky eyes gave her that look that Wiz had to have. "So is business over for today?" she asked.

"Can't you tell I'm ready to play?" Wiz replied as he guided her hand from his chest down to his semi-erect dick.

Keisha smiled wider. "Baby, I'm ready to roll."

He smacked her ass cheek firmly. "Go get Dame and bring a couple bottles of bubbly out." She hopped off Wiz's lap, grabbed her bikini top from the ledge of the Jacuzzi and sashayed back into the mansion with her orders.

A Life for A Life

Keisha had turned out to be 'that girl' for the moment, and was surely about to get some industry play if Wiz could help it. *Damn, she mad cool and don't ask no dumb ass questions,* Wiz thought to himself as she nailed what had to be the sexiest strut in the game.

He suddenly felt the vibration of his cell phone. He checked it, only to see another annoying message from Myria: *Wiz, call me soon. I miss you and I haven't been feeling well. XOXO.*

He briefly contemplated calling Myria back; he knew it was one of her silly ploys. It also dawned on him that once again, he had neglected her for the past month.

For about the last two weeks, Wiz had conducted all of his interviews over the phone from his mansion. He had been flying in an array of willing party girls to come entertain him and Damien and sometimes Swirl. Wiz had really begun to enjoy the X pills, and since Damien was trustworthy and had a steady supply, he became Wiz's best pal for the moment.

Wiz contemplated giving Myria another tired excuse to pacify her, but before he could he saw Damien and Toi—Keisha's friend, who was entertainment for the night, all walking toward him.

Keisha had two bottles of Spades, one in each hand. Damien had the large canister of ice, and Toi carried a tray of wine glasses. Everybody was all smiles and ready to party. Myria, on the other hand, hadn't wanted to indulge in any more X pills since the night of the after party. Those thoughts and the sight of Keisha made Wiz drop the phone back to the table. *Fuck it! Another day or so won't kill her!*

"Hey, Wiz." Toi approached first, greeting him with a flirtatious smile and her eyes dropping to his crotch area.

"What up, baby girl?" Wiz spoke like a gentleman, flashing his trademark diamond grill.

"You. I mean, Red Rum, that's what's up."

"You think so?" Wiz asked, shooting her a wink that made her blush.

He had never had any real talk with Toi, but body language and chemistry were clearly evident. He understood groupie love well, and his assessment told him that she was too fast for Damien, and had just come along for the ride and a free ticket into Red Rum. But Wiz didn't give a shit. He looked at her petite, firm frame as she sat the tray down beside him seconds before Keisha approached with her radiant smile.

Keisha sat the Spades down and straddled Wiz again. Damien sat in the next chair, and Toi immediately plopped onto his lap. "Life couldn't be better." He was already handing over the bag of pills.

"You got that right," Wiz replied as he pushed two pills into Keisha's giggling mouth.

"Uh-huh, let's get it poppin'," Keisha said, swallowing the pills.

In no time, the alcohol, weed, and X had everyone in a partying mood. The sun had set, and all the lights around the pool area illuminated, setting the tone as the girls danced to the loud music and splashed around topless in the Jacuzzi.

Wiz was lost in an intoxicated euphoria as he and Keisha passionately tongue kissed for minutes at a time. Damien was lost in the same state while he groped, played with and sucked Toi's breasts. Wiz was having all the fun his devious mind could conjure as he and Toi discreetly communicated through their eye contact. Wiz didn't stop until he faintly heard the ringing of his private line.

"Dammit!" he huffed with irritation.

"Don't worry about it, baby," Keisha cooed as she wrapped her legs around his waist, pulling him even closer and nibbling his ear. "I wanna go up to the pool and skinny dip."

Wiz liked the thought, but knew it could be an important call. "Hold up. That might be important." He pushed her away and climbed out of the Jacuzzi and got to the phone.

"Red Rum, holla at me."

"Yo, what up, son?" Bless' annoying voice spilled through.

"Yo, what up, playboy?" Wiz tried to act as if he was glad to hear from him.

"Yo, check it; I need to holla at you on some real official shit."

"Bless, I'm in the middle of some major shit. I'll hit you back later or first thing in the morning."

"Nah, son, I need you now. I'm going to Brazil to do a shoot tomorrow."

"They got phones in Brazil," Wiz offered jokingly, but meant exactly that.

"Look, man, niggaz done bootlegged my shit like crazy in New York!"

"For real, whoadie?" Wiz snapped with a voice full of concern. He turned to Damien and yelled, "I need to take this one inside."

Wiz stood back up as those sobering words forced his mind to speed. He wondered what Bless knew. "Just hold on, man," Wiz angrily said with even more of the phony genuine concern leading his voice, as he whipped up a way to pick Bless.

By the time Wiz stepped inside the mansion, he had already concocted a plan. "Now tell me what happened, partna?"

"Ay yo, son, I 'on know how these street vendors keep comin' up! They had my shit like two weeks before release! I got my peoples straight snatchin' 'em when they see 'em!"

What Bless had just mentioned was enough to slightly calm Wiz's nerves as he stopped at the kitchen counter and sat on the barstool where he could still see the pool area.

"Calm down, man. I'm glad you called me. I been going through the same shit. Why you think I fight so hard for the BET campaign to stop this shit?"

"I feel that, but losing money and—"

Wiz quickly cut him off. "Look, whoadie. I know it's fucked up, but we won't ever be able to stop that shit! It was before us and it's gone be here after us, feel me?"

"Hell, no, I can't—"

"Suck it up! All you gone do is have restless nights! You gotta do like me and everybody else and look at the flip side. That shit is just free promotion for yo' shit! Once your official shit drops, they don't get no more money! And wit' the units you moving, you ain't never even gone miss those lil chips! Trust me, I been there already."

Bless sat quietly for a few seconds. Wiz's nerves were on edge waiting for a reply.

"Wiz, where's the orange juice?"

He spun around to see Toi at the door. Toi's voice startled him. He had taken his eyes off the pool area for a moment and didn't even notice her come in.

"Look in the fridge," he whispered, covering the receiver while beckoning his head in that direction. She pranced over to the refrigerator and bent over much further than necessary, ignoring the orange juice that was right in her face and showcasing her G-string.

Wiz's attention was split between watching Toi and the pool area as he and Bless wrapped up the conversation. "I feel ya, Wiz, but—"

"Listen player, it's real. Watch how your units blow! How da fuck you think I pushed over eight hundred in my first week?"

It only took Bless a few seconds of Wiz's persuasion before Wiz could sense the assurance in Bless' voice. "Yeah, son, you always been official."

"Oh, fa' sho', whoadie," Wiz bragged, now confident that he had played his scheme all the way through without being caught. "I'm glad you see shit fa' what it is."

Taken with Toi's enticing gestures, Wiz covered up the phone again. "Come here, baby girl. Stay down so they can't see you."

Wiz had barely finished the sentence when she began crawling toward him on her hands and knees. He was wrestling with his shorts in an effort to free his dick. As soon it was out, Toi grabbed it and went to work, giving him a shameless blow job.

"Real talk, I'll hit you in a couple days when you get back, and soon, whoadie, we gone have to go to Brazil ourselves, ya heard? I'm out." He hung up, but held the phone to his ear and watched the pool area. He continued to speak, but his now vulgar words were being directed at Toi.

Toi had tugged Wiz's trunks all the way down to the floor and allowed him to step out of one leg. She had launched an oral assault on Wiz's dick. She slurped over the head while relaxing her jaws then shoved him all the way to the back of her throat. "Damn, you a head monster!" Wiz stated as he began to face fuck her. She stopped briefly to giggle at his remark, spit right on the head of his dick, and started right back up with an even more intense appetite to swallow him. "Shiit!" Wiz slurred, trying to hold his composure and keep a careful eye on Damien and Keisha back in the pool area.

A few moments later Wiz's hands held firmly to the back of Toi's head as he felt his balls begin to rumble.

"Oh, hell yeah! I'm 'bout to bust!" He looked down on her. "Swallow tha whole dick!" He clamped her face into his pubes.

"Oh fuck!" he grunted out. "Don't spill a drop!" He held her there and shot his load to the back of her throat.

"Mmm . . ." Toi moaned, draining every drop. She looked up at Wiz's contorted face as the phone slipped from his hand and

his knees buckled from the sensation. She held him in her mouth until his fat penis began to wane.

"Damn, lil mama. You'z a mothafuckin' beast!" he said through a set of tight grilled diamond teeth.

"Hmm . . . Just remember that." She looked at him with a confident smile and his dick still in her hand. "Make sure you make it happen again." She pumped his dick a few times then tongue kissed the head. "Or better yet lose Damien and tell Keisha you want us both."

Those scandalous thoughts seemed to ignite Wiz's fire all over again. "I dig you. You and Red Rum got a long way to go, baby girl. But right now gimme my dick back, grab the orange juice, and get on back out there."

She snickered and dropped the dick with a knowing smile. Raking her hair back in place, she crawled back to the refrigerator the same way she'd came.

This time she reached straight for the pitcher of juice and strolled right back out the door, only acknowledging Wiz with a wink and a lick of her sexy full lips.

Wiz sat back down on the barstool, still trying to gather himself. Things were happening so fast that he barely got a chance to wipe his brow as he told himself that was another close call with Bless. It made him reflect back to just days ago when he told himself that he really needed to sit down and reprioritize his life.

He'd been keeping up with how the news articles now regarded him. Wiz knew he was more than just a self-made mogul, he was now an icon.

He nodded at the thought. *But who in the hell would stop right now?* He stood up, readjusted his trunks and headed back out the door.

✧✧✧✧✧

A Life for A Life

Five minutes later Wiz stood over the pool, popped two more pills and chased them down with cold bubbly. Keisha's hand snaked under the water and when they emerged she tossed her bikini to the ledge.

"Come on, Wiz, we may as well skinny dip now."

Wiz glanced over at Damien as Toi straddled him. They were once again kissing passionately, yet her eyes were already locked on Wiz, ready to finish out their secret game of stare.

"Get in Wiz," Damien shouted obliviously. "The water feels great! We're just getting started."

Wiz caught Toi's wink just as his trunks dropped to the cement. *Damn, this gone be another long night,* he thought, lowering his nakedness into the water, with all hopes of pulling another successful trois before the night ended.

Mike Jefferies

Chapter Twenty Five

Drako

Drako sat patiently in the driver's seat of his rented DTS Cadillac outside of City Hall in Downtown Boston. He and Diamond had now been in Boston for two days.

She had given Drako a hard time when he had to explain to her that the only way he could finish out his next scheme was if she helped. She tried to hit the ceiling, but Drako kept his and her cool and he promised her that tomorrow would be the last day that she'd ever have to impersonate a white woman again.

He leaned over and picked up the folder from the seat where Diamond had sat moments before. He pulled the contents from the envelope to study once more. The papers inside were three certified copies of the last three tax returns for Mrs. Mary Williams. Just this morning, Diamond had walked into the IRS business office, showed her stolen identity and obtained three copies.

Diamond's last task was to simply go into City Hall posing as Mary Williams—the same woman she'd been posing as in Citibank in New York when she deposited money in the account—show the proper forms of ID, and obtain the deeds belonging to Mary's two apartment buildings.

He looked at his watch; it was 10:35 A.M. meaning she had been in City Hall for twenty-five minutes. Drako put the papers back in the folder and was preparing to go inside and check on Diamond. As soon as he placed his dark shades across his face and turned the ignition off, he saw her exiting City Hall. He could tell by her expression that she had once again been successful. He cranked the Caddy back up, and as soon as she got close, he reached over and pushed open the passenger side door.

Diamond got in the car and closed the door. As soon as Drako pulled away, she went into her pocket book, and handed the two documents to Drako. "Happy now?"

"Happy, but not as much as I am proud of you," he emphasized before leaning over and playfully pecking her sweet cheek. "I gotta get you to the hotel and get you cleaned up. Our flight leaves at 1 P.M. I'll tell you the rest when we get to New York."

By 8 P.M. they checked into a humongous suite at the Waldolf Astoria in Manhattan. Drako had lit some relaxing scented candles, and he and Diamond climbed into the hot tub so he could finish giving her the plans.

"You know this is important to me," he said. "We been depositing money and building a rapport with this bank for a good reason. The main reason is 'cause it's the only way to take money out."

"You wanna withdraw all the money, baby?"

"Nah, just listen. I told you I'ma teach you how to rob a bank without a gun." Drako could feel Diamond's body stiffen. "First, you gotta relax. I already told you I'm not gonna gamble you. You do have to go in the bank one more time, but all I need you to do this time is ask for a loan.

"Baby, you've built the rapport well enough, and the timing is right. All you have to do is tell them you own two apartment buildings and you'd like to take out a small equity against them. Those complexes are worth $17 million together, so asking for three million is nothing! You could simply get $1.5 on each property. With the small amount you're asking against such large collateral, it shouldn't be a problem."

"What if they want to see the deeds?"

"Then show them! Diamond, you gotta relax. Just remember what I told you; identity theft isn't recognizable until *after* the fact. The other woman you profiled at Hertz was a blonde. That's over with. And all you're doing is *asking,* you're not *taking.* And any information they ask for, you already have. It won't go any deeper than the last three tax returns, and you have copies."

Drako waited a few moments to let Diamond ponder the situation, and as always, she had another question. "They may want to see the property."

"Baby, that ain't even a problem. What makes this scheme so good is that the property is paid for. Citibank won't have to check with another bank about an outstanding mortgage on these properties. The most they may possibly do is send someone out to see if the buildings exist. I'm sure there would be no tenant there who even knows Mrs. Williams on a personal level."

"What if—"

Drako quickly cut her off. "Diamond, stop with the 'what ifs'! What if they say no? Then cool, we just withdraw all the money and keep it moving. What if they approve it? Then we get the money, transfer it to the offshore account, and then still make the first six payments back on the loan. After we've paid for six months, it'll take another three months for the bank to locate the real Mrs. Williams. Shit! With that kind of lapse it's almost impossible for them to figure this shit out!"

"So paying these payments are simply to protect me?" she asked after a few moments of thought.

"Now you feel me," Drako huffed with relief.

"You may end up giving back a couple hundred grand. Maybe, you are being too overprotective," Diamond said jokingly.

"Be quiet, ma. I told you I ain't gone gamble you. This is your last lick. I got other plans for you." He wrapped his arms around her waist and pulled her closer.

"What plans?" Diamond questioned as she craned her neck to look in his eyes.

"Plans to keep you forever."

"You never have to plan for that." Diamond turned around to face Drako before straddling her nakedness back down on his lap.

"All right, walk me through it one more time."

"Gotcha." Drako pecked her lips and started from the top.

At 8 A.M. Diamond was back up. She had replaced her natural tresses with the brunette-colored wig, and by 9 A.M. sharp Diamond was in full gear ready to enter Citibank.

It was approximately 9:30 A.M. when Drako watched Diamond enter Citibank. He had parked just a block away at Sloan Cattering Hospital, where he waited in the car.

Inside Citibank, Diamond waited patiently as her request for her personal banker—the manager—was granted. Mr. White came out, greeted Mrs. Williams, and escorted her to his office.

Diamond laid it all out. She needed money to refurbish a few rental properties. He asked Diamond a few questions, and she answered each one with ease. She then told him her properties were worth $17 million dollars and she was only seeking a three million dollar equity loan. The banker then asked Mrs. Williams how long it would take to obtain a copy of her property assessments. She went into her purse and produced the documents as she further informed him that they were paid for.

A large smile bloomed his face as he stood and politely asked Mrs. Williams to "wait here." He left the office and was back in less than two minutes. He came back with all the paperwork for her to sign in order to receive a loan. Diamond read them over and then signed the papers.

The bank manager assured her that he'd do his best to help. He further informed her that if she were approved, those funds would be available in fourteen to twenty-one days.

Diamond thanked the bank manager for his services. She then gave him her cell number and asked him to contact her there and that she'd be abroad in Europe in about seven days. He took the number with a smile and told her he'd contact her soon. He watched her walk out the door just as she did every other time.

After Diamond made it back to the car and told Drako how smooth the interview for more 'free money' had gone, Drako was both happy and hopeful. "You did good, ma." He leaned over and kissed her check. "You out the game, baby. It's time you kick back, relax, and enjoy what's coming your way." He laid a soothing hand on her thigh and told her he had made an extravagant dinner reservation and wanted to spend a night out on the town with his lady.

He took her shopping so she could put them in the proper attire for the night. She had chosen a nicely fit pant suit by Dolce and Gabbana and topped it off with a pair of sassy brown Vero

Cujo ankle boots. She picked out a beige Armani suit for Drako with a brown tie to match his chocolate Mauri gators and belt. Diamond knew the earth tones complemented his dark skin well.

Drako topped off the short spree when he tossed up twenty grand on a whisky mink that dropped right at her waist line.

By 8 P.M. Drako had shouted at the bathroom door at least three times. He was fully dressed and waiting on Diamond to appear. Once she finished her final touches and made her way out, she was so beautiful that Drako wanted everyone to see her.

She was looking forward to the dinner at the Shark Bar Drako lied about, but she soon found herself ecstatic when Drako handed her their VIP passes to club 40/40.

"Damn, Drako, I can't believe you made this happen!" Diamond hugged him tightly.

"Don't get too excited over nothin'. Wiz got us passes, and I knew it couldn't have been a better night at 40/40 than tonight."

"Baby, you're so sweet. I had forgot all about 40/40. I thought you just didn't wanna take me."

"Stop fakin', girl. You know damn well you ain't forgot. You just knew not to ask this weekend, 'cause gettin' in 40/40 was gone be hell!"

Diamond just smiled.

Jay-Z was having a virtually *industry-exclusive* night. The New Jersey Nets had just made the playoffs, and Kanye West had just dropped his album earlier in the week. Diamond locked her arm around Drako's. "Well, I'm just glad we're gonna be up in the mix."

"You're gone be the prettiest woman there," Drako replied as he kissed her cheek before they headed out the door.

A Life for A Life

The streets of Manhattan were busy with nightlife, and the line to enter club 40/40 was absurd, but everyone was waiting patiently in hopes of getting in.

Drako and Diamond had walked up to the VIP line. Drako gave the host the VIP passes, and like a magician, the security moved the red velvet rope for him and Diamond to gain entry.

The lavish club was packed inside. The state-of-the-art sound system was blasting Kanye's album, but then 50 Cent's club songs played, which fit the atmosphere perfectly.

Drako first led Diamond to the bar. They quickly found their reserved table, which Wiz had arranged for them. Diamond was starstruck as she saw how many famous people came out. Most labels had reserved tables for their camp. Diamond saw Queen Latifah, Busta, and cats from Violator were present and a host of New Jersey Net players were now dressed in designer suits and representing the Nets well.

Ya-Yo, Banks, and 50 were on their champagne campaign. The Wu Tang Clan and other rap stars and movie industry peeps were there enjoying the party. The baller chasers, groupies, and video vixens rounded out the guest list.

Diamond looked to her left and saw the Take Money camp perched at their table. Bless was pouring glass after glass for all the women that flocked. Diamond nudged Drako, leaned over, and then yelled over the loud music. "Look, Drako," she said as she pointed to their table. "Ain't that Gorilla Black with Bless?"

"Stop pointing!" Drako snapped as he observed the obese man in a huge black mink coat. He had his back turned at the moment and had a bottle of champagne in each hand.

Drako recognized the large man as soon as he turned around to get the attention of a beautiful girl that passed their table. "Hell naw, that's fakin' ass Fatt Katt!"

Diamond smiled again and turned the other way.

They drank and enjoyed the atmosphere for a little while. The alcohol effect and the excellent selections from the DJ had really put Diamond in a clubbing mood.

"Drako, let's dance."

Drako smirked. "You know I 'on dance."

"Come on, just once . . . for me," Diamond whined.

"Real gangstas don't dance—all they do is this," Drako said, reclining back comfortably after he picked his drink up.

"Well, Drako, I wanna dance, and you don't want me to dance with nobody else. If I dance alone, somebody's gonna ask."

"You know how to say no, don't ya?" Drako stated flatly. Diamond poked her lips out because she knew that dancing was not about to happen. She was disappointed, but deep down, she was still glad to get out and finally be at 40/40.

When Drako set his cup down, he looked at the disappointment on Diamond's face. He stood up. "You better enjoy this night—it won't happen again. We can dance at home." He was already smiling as he extended his hand out for Diamond to take. Diamond quickly took off the mink coat, and she and Drako went out to the dance floor.

The first song they danced to was the classic "Get Money" and the DJ kept on bringing it! He mixed old Biggie songs and Junior Mafia. Diamond loved Lil' Kim. He mixed the classic Jay-Z "Give It 2 Me," and everything else that made the Billboard charts as he took it way back.

Drako could dance enough to get by, but Diamond danced well, and she backed it up and put it on Drako until she found herself lightly sweating in the club's heated atmosphere.

Drako never would've thought he'd have that much fun, but the music and Diamond's sexy moves had kept him on the dance floor for an hour straight.

Finally, Drako pulled Diamond close. "Okay ma, that's it. I 'on like this shit from Camron, and these gators are tightening on my feet."

Diamond giggled. "Okay, baby, you done good. I ain't even realize my man could still dance like that."

"Don't try to flatter me; you put it all over me." He didn't give her time to respond as he grabbed her wrist and navigated their way back through the crowded dance floor all the way back to their table.

They had a few more drinks, caught their breath, and talked over the loud music. Diamond's eyes continuously swooped over the crowd looking for more stars. "Drako, you think Jay-Z and Beyoncé are here?"

"Coach Carter is definitely in the building; they're probably in a reserved booth upstairs. Just keep ya eyes open. We got about two to three more hours left. The night is still young."

Diamond looked back to her left. She saw Bless and Take Money still doing their thing. She saw Fatt Katt macking one of the girls sitting near him.

Diamond nudged Drako. "Look at Take Money's table." Fatt Katt stood up to let the girl out of the booth.

Drako looked and quickly recognized the girl—it was Myria! He then recognized Diamond's nostrils as they flared. "Diamond, mind ya business, and don't even think about gettin' close to her."

"I ain't thinkin' 'bout her," Diamond lied. "I need to go to the ladies' room."

Drako had seen exactly where Myria was headed. "Diamond, she ain't thinkin' 'bout you. Wiz ain't thinkin' 'bout her. I brought you out to enjoy the night, so enjoy it right!"

"Well, I'm just sayin'."

"Sayin' what?"

"She wit' Take Money. I guess her scandoulous ass will take *anybody's* dollars!"

Drako laughed. "Forget about her." He waved off the thought.

They hung out and drank for a couple more hours, and then Diamond finally told Drako she was ready to leave.

She stood and put on the mink coat before they left. She made sure they walked past the table Take Money occupied. Fatt Katt, Bless, and the rest of the camp were all unaware of who Drako was, as their attention was stolen by the lovely Diamond, who slowly walked past and was a few steps ahead of Drako. Diamond blatantly threw darts with her eyes at Myria.

For her part, Myria looked as if she'd seen a ghost, gasping at the sight of Diamond. Drako caught up and pushed Diamond on through the crowd and out the door. "I told you about being messy!" he huffed into her ear.

"Who the hell was that?" Fatt Katt asked.

"Nobody," White Chocolate answered. "Just another stuck up wanna-be."

"Wanna–be? Shiit, she shoulda made it!" Fatt Katt said as he craned his neck trying to get one last look as Diamond disappeared into the crowd.

"Let's go to the bathroom. Now," Myria said to White Chocolate. Her friend didn't want to move, as she was enjoying being a *public item* with Bless, but reluctantly went so she could calm Myria's paranoia.

When they got in the bathroom, Myria immediately started in. "Girl, I told you I shouldn't have come!"

"Myria, don't start that silly shit! Diamond ain't thinkin' 'bout you!"

"You 'on know! What if she tell Wiz?"

White Chocolate knew Wiz really wouldn't give a shit. "By the time she see Wiz, she'll be done forgot. Here, take these to calm down." White Chocolate offered Myria two X pills.

"No, I'm okay. Just forget it. Besides, Wiz ain't took me nowhere, and I needed some air."

"Uh–huh suit yourself, girl." White Chocolate popped a pill.

They went back out and White Chocolate finished playing the role of overnight celebrity at Take Money's reserved table. Myria, who had been brushing off Fatt Katt's advances all night, faked it for the next two hours, which felt like a week with his alcohol laced breath in her ear. Myria gazed at White Chocolate and Bless. *Damn, why can't Wiz have just a trace of do-right when it comes to me?* The thought lingered in her mind all night.

Chapter Twenty Six
Swirl

Life after post Source Award success only seemed to get better for Swirl. The hood legend continued to donate more money to help fund programs for youth all around his city. He often showed up at functions designed to help empower the community. And of course, all of his nicely compensated vixens were still products—straight from New Orleans.

The rapper was happy about his life and accomplishments at Red Rum, and all who saw him walk through the doors of the Q93 radio station could see just that.

Swirl wore a fresh pair of Dickies, white Reeboks, and a fresh white tank top to show off all of his hot tats. He sported his Red Rum chain. Humongous V.S. rocks twinkled from both of his pinky rings and his fresh diamond grill that lit the room up like Bling! Bling! Bling! Every time he spoke.

He had agreed to help the station promote its 'Stay in School' campaign. The Q93 staff were familiar with him, as he often visited them and appreciated the support of their heavy spins. For that, he was always glad to support them whenever possible.

He did his speech and recordings quickly, then left the studio so he and the Magnolia whoadies he brought with him could get ready to attend a local car show.

Swirl stepped out of the studio, and as usual, he was bombarded by fans. He had four of his blood burgundy whips parked out front and ready to compete in the 'Street Ballers' car show. All the spectators loved them.

"Swirl, can you sign my son's CD?" a fine ass hot girl asked as she approached with the CD extended.

"Fa' sho', lil mama. Swirl love the kids, too." He could see that the girl was clearly admiring everything about him, from his neatly braided hair to the expensive shades he had on, to the death-cold ice that he sported. "Here ya go, baby girl," Swirl said, smiling as he handed the signed CD back.

"Damn, Swirl, look at all that ice!" the girl said. "Why don't you have bodyguards like them guys on TV? You big time now, whoadie!"

"See these niggaz wit' me?" he asked, pointing to his three partners. "They all the help I ever need. I'm wearing ice, and ain't nobody gone take it off me, ya heard?"

"Mmm hmm, but you know how it go 'round here. People smilin' and plottin' at the same time."

"Fa' sho' dat, lil mama, but I ain't like them cats on TV. It's hood wit' me. It's just like my whoadie Juvie said, 'I'm a rapper, but I'm still a guerilla.'"

The girl just smiled at Swirl's comment. "You know what, lil mama, come by the car show tonight. You'll see the love New Orleans gives me."

"Oh, I'ma be there fa' sho'," she replied. Then she turned and walked away. Swirl watched her leave. He thought about her words as he subconsciously felt the 9 millimeter Ruger that held firmly on the side of his waistline. He wasn't fooled by the glamour, nor was he a studio gangsta. Street niggaz that knew

Swirl also knew he had an itchy trigger finger, and all he needed was an excuse to scratch it.

Swirl shook off those thoughts as he told his entourage composed of his childhood buddies, "Let's spin a few cuts. I wanna ride through Magnolia and uptown before we hit the car show." He didn't even comment as he looked into the gangsta faces of his true friends. They'd also heard every word, and they were always on the lookout for them wenches.

They loaded up with Swirl, pushing his Magnum wagon in the middle of their convoy as they cruised through the city streets of New Orleans.

Cobblestone streets and rows of nondescript buildings comprised a section of New York called the Village, home to one of the most controversial and most popular radio broadcasts on the East Coast. Inside one of the old structures, Hot 97 was hosting live guest appearances from some of the hottest MCs and industry moguls in the country. Today, Fatt Katt, his three bodyguards, and road manager accompanied him on air.

Fatt Katt too was happy about his accomplishments. He was once just a product of Brooklyn's Marcy projects, but now he was one of the hottest mainstream MCs in the nation. His albums were destined to become classics.

Other than constantly 'biggin' up' his borough and laying down the hottest Brooklyn summer anthem of the year, Fatt Katt hadn't given anything back to his community.

Fatt Katt was totally absorbed in the success of coming from nothing to a *whole* lot of something. He wanted to first off enjoy his riches alone. He'd purchased a nice hide-away home in Jersey, and was rumored to be in quest of purchasing a property in the Hamptons. Bless had marketed Fatt Katt in luxury. He

sported lavish minks, expensive suits, and the hottest urban apparel and custom Jacob jewels in all of his videos. Fatt Katt took the style and ran with it at top speed in his everyday life.

Fatt Katt was also smart; he possessed a New York state of mind when it came to getting money. He knew what to say, he knew what sold albums, and he focused on what the masses wanted to hear. The one thing he secretly understood best was beef! He knew whom to blast on in order to keep him controversial, and he knew who'd keep it on wax. He often made snide, subliminal remarks without Bless' consent, and his instinct always confirmed his choices to be right.

Fatt Katt reached for his bottle of vitamin water and reared back in his chair as he took a long swig. He sat the bottle back down and adjusted his headset as he sat across from the radio personality and listened to a caller's comment about Swirl's victory at the Source Awards.

Ready to snip the caller's air time, Fatt Katt leaned over to the microphone and yelled, "Fuck Swirl! The kid is bonkers as them wanksters from Yonkers!"

"You can't use those kinds of words on live air," the host reminded him for the third time.

"Yo, my bad again. I 'on know why I even waste air time on wack MCs whose careers I could end in less than ten bars."

"I'd hate to be one of the cats you're aiming at because right now, the whole East Coast is feeling you. Someone is calling and requesting your songs like every five minutes. You know they calling you *Big Cheese* now?"

"I hear it everywhere I go," Fatt Katt bragged.

The DJ hit Fatt Katt with as many questions as he could get in within the hour slot, and Fatt Katt arrogantly answered each one and promoted his album and living legacy with the best "mo' money, *no mo'* problems" attitude he could adopt.

A Life for A Life

"I ain't mad at them cats. They *want* hatin' on Fatt Katt to be a problem. I just want my official cats to understand that hatin' is just a way of life in the day of those wankstas while they deliberate over them ghostwritten bars!" Fatt Katt laughed at his last over-the-top comment just before the radio personality thanked him for coming as the show ended. Fatt Katt and his entourage quickly said their good-byes and left Hot 97 in an effort to make his next appointment.

They stepped outside onto Hudson Street to another beautiful promising day in the big city of dreams. The Peruvian flake-colored 4.6 Range Rover that Fatt Katt bragged about copping in his latest rhyme was parked right out front with his road manager's black 600 Mercedes Coupe right behind it.

The rapper and his entourage stopped to briefly discuss Fatt Katt's plans before he and his road manager temporarily parted ways.

"You're gonna *love* Brazil," the manager said. "You go ahead and join Bless. Y'all unwind for a week, and then when you get back, we'll start the 50-city tour right on schedule."

Fatt Katt gave his road manager a firm handshake to dismiss him and was about to jump in the driver's seat of his new Range Rover when he noticed a head rising from the slouched position from the driver's seat of a black Yukon parked about four cars behind their small entourage. The head was covered with a ski mask. *What the fuck?* His mind raced, sending Fatt Katt's adrenaline into top speed. His obese body moved at unbelievable speed as he reached out to grab his security guard's shoulder in an effort to alert him, so that he could do what he got paid top dollars to do best. Fatt Katt's dubious demeanor of a faker was no longer in question as he simultaneously ripped the chrome .40 cal from his waist before his bodyguards could react.

Fatt Katt was in shock. By the time he raised his gun two other masked, hooded gunmen had jumped out of the back door

of the Yukon. *Not today, mothafucka!* The MC immediately squeezed the trigger at the sight of the deadly automatic weapons the fast-moving men pointed in his direction. He got off two eardrum ringing shots, missing both of the gunmen, who immediately returned fire as they advanced.

Their first shots caught his road manager in the back, throwing his frail body to the asphalt. Fatt Katt continued to squeeze his trigger while he made a life-saving attempt to jump in the Rover. His security men reached for the guns in their shoulder holsters, but were too slow to prevail over the unexpected ambush.

All Fatt Katt could hear was the loud blasts that emitted and filled the air with death as the barrage of bullets struck and ripped through his first security guard's upper torso, knocking him to the pavement. "Hell no!" Fatt Katt finally screamed as he squeezed off another round to no avail. The lead gun shower rained down on Fatt Katt and his entourage. A bullet caught Fatt Katt in the shoulder. His obese body was twisted, and then tossed as his back banged against the truck. Fatt Katt still held the gun tight in his grip as he rose to take aim again. Suddenly, the whole world vanished into blackness; Fatt Katt's dome had just been pierced by a bullet. The last shots from the choppers dropped the other bodyguards' bodies to the ground.

The gunmen watched as Fatt Katt's lifeless body slumped down the door on the now bloody, bullet-ridden SUV. It lay mutilated in a puddle of blood with the rest of his entourage. The masked gunmen then jumped back into the Yukon just as fast as they'd jumped out. They sped away from the area with ease, leaving no trace or motive as to why the five senseless bodies were left behind.

Chapter Twenty Seven
Wiz

When Wiz awoke, his cell was flooded with messages of the terrible news. He turned the TV to BET, and in a matter of seconds, he saw a news anchor reporting the deadly blow the hip-hop community had suffered.

All the radio stations broadcasted theories of the account. Hip-hop heads all across the country were calling up the radio stations. New York, especially the borough of Brooklyn, was in a complete media frenzy and sulking over the untimely demise of one of Brooklyn's greatest MCs.

Wiz stared at the TV in complete shock. The news seemed surreal. After he had gotten off the telephone with Swirl, he quickly called Drako to see what he thought of the bad hand Fatt Katt had been dealt.

✧ ✧ ✧ ✧ ✧

Diamond was in an especially good mood. Drako had rolled over and sexed her good this morning. She was prancing around in housecoat and slippers, about to bring Drako's breakfast plate to bed.

Singing along to her Mariah Carey CD, she heard the phone ring. She started not to answer it, but she looked at the caller-ID and saw that it was Wiz attempting to break up her moment.

"Hey, Wiz," she greeted happily.

"Where's Drako?"

"Excuse me? What's up, how are you, or anything would be polite as a greeting to someone who's gonna be singing the hottest hooks on your label."

"Oh, my bad, lil sis. How you doin'? Shit just—"

"I'm good. Matter of fact, I'm great! My man took me shopping, bought me a phatt ass mink, and we killed 'em at 40/40—thanks for the tickets."

"No problem. Did y'all hear—"

"Yeah, everybody was there," she cut him off with excitement. "I saw the Take Money camp. Oh yeah, Myria was there too, and that girl . . . Chocolate somethin'. Looks like that skank will take anybody's money. Her nasty ass was sittin' next to Fatt Katt."

Wiz was stunned for a second at that even more surprising news, but for the moment, Fatt Katt was more important. "Fatt Katt is dead! Him and his whole entourage were gunned down this morning outside of Hot 97!"

What! How? No way! Diamond thought with a gasp, feeling instant sorrow and forgetting about the scandalous news she'd just waited to tell him. "Oh my God, Wiz! What happened? No, wait, lemme get Drako. He just got out of the shower." Diamond quickly left the plate where it was and went into the bedroom where Drako was getting dressed.

She announced to Drako that Wiz was on the phone and that Fatt Katt was dead. She put the phone in their bedroom on speakerphone as Wiz told them what he'd heard. Diamond and Drako hadn't played the TV or radio all morning. They were shocked. Diamond turned the TV to BET in hopes of catching an updated news brief as they all participated in a conference call in regard to the morning's tragic events.

Drako listened intently and commented on the shooting, but mostly let Diamond express her sympathy over the tragic event. Drako really didn't give a shit; he didn't know Fatt Katt personally, and he felt that nobody really knew the true motive that caused this to happen.

After Drako had gotten dressed and grown tired of listening to Wiz's sulking like a female, (in Drako's opinion) he put the phone back on private line and excused Diamond from the room. "Look, Wiz. That shit is over with. Ain't nothin' nobody can do to bring them people back!"

"I know that, Drako. I'm just saying—"

"Sayin' what? Wiz, you ain't even know that nigga! You best stop being so damn naive! You're a businessman, not a gangsta. That shit Fatt Katt was doing was real to some niggaz! You and him might be mutually faking, but everybody he been taking shots at may not be business like you. It is such things as *real* niggaz—gangsta niggaz, and them type of niggaz will die and kill for their respect. Just accept life for what it is."

"I'm just saying the man wasn't but twenty-five, and I was gonna get wit' him soon. We were all gonna do a lil thing in Brazil."

Drako had momentarily paused as he listened to the news anchor and the latest update:

> *Authorities have released a videotape of the three unidentified gunmen suspected in the brutal murders of Fatt Katt and his bodyguards. This surveillance tape filmed by cameras placed outside of Hot 97 caught the action. The*

footage displays the massacre vividly. Brian Miller, who authorities list as Fatt Katt's road manager, is reported to be in critical but stable condition at St. Vincent's Medical Center and is expected to recover. We'll have more on the tragedy as the investigation unfolds. I'm Kiesha Nashid, reporting for BET News.

Wiz told Drako that the local channels were reporting that the streets were applauding Fatt Katt for his attempted act of heroism before the final moments of his life.

"Looks like the only niggaz who should be worried is them niggaz in the Yukon—they left one breathin'," Drako said as the broadcast went off.

"Drako, I hope they get them niggaz fa' dat stupid ass shit!" Wiz angrily spat.

"It is what it is—reality."

"Man, why you so nonchalant?"

"Why not? I wasn't there, you wasn't there. Life gotta go on. I hope this makes yo' scary ass stop that fake beefin' shit."

"Aw, come on, whoadie."

"Look man, I gotta make a few runs," Drako said, sternly. "I'll holla at you later."

"Man, a'ight then," Wiz replied, not really wanting to go. "One!"

"One!" Drako responded, hanging up the phone.

A Life for A Life

From the moment Drako hung up the phone, life went on as usual. He continued on his path of hunger for overnight wealth as he met with a realtor in order to make the closing 'official' on a modest-sized building he'd discreetly purchased nearly two months ago right off Forsyth Street in Downtown ATL.

Wiz, on the other hand, didn't know how to purge the sorrow he felt. His heart went out to Fatt Katt, whom he felt truly had a tremendous amount of potential that the world would never know. Because of the fake beef, Wiz couldn't attend the funeral services, but he sent massive flower arrangements under a fake name with condolences to the families of the deceased. He also wrote a $50,000 check and secretly donated it to the charity fund for Fatt Katt's now fatherless four-year-old son. *Damn! Life can be so short.* The thought stung Wiz bad. He realized just how cold the game could be. Taking heed to the warning, he decided to chill with the fake beefs.

Mike Jefferies

Chapter Twenty Eight
Wiz

Wiz sat behind his keyboard in Red Rum headquarters expertly whipping all the right keys to make Diamond's octave-hurtling voice better as she sang the hook like a hummingbird over Swirl's latest hit.

Two weeks after Fatt Katt's death, the media began reporting about violence connected to hip-hop, which was at an all-time high. Wiz had taken a few days off, during which time Drako's words had finally sunk in—life goes on. All the records Swirl made dissing Fatt Katt were now selling at an alarming rate. And Fatt Katt's album was moving more units than when he was alive.

Wiz harbored a twinge of guilt, but his greedy mentality, coupled with his scheming marketing mind, had him trying to get Swirl's next album out as soon as possible, in an effort to ride on the highly profitable crest of despair.

He pushed the button on the keyboard to make his voice blare through the intercom on the other side of the booth's glass. "Swirl, I'ma turn your mic up. Diamond's voice is overpowering your lyrics every time I play it back." Swirl and Diamond both nodded their heads in agreement, and then took it from the top.

They were all working so hard, mainly to get Diamond's voice into mainstream circulation. Wiz had said that he felt Diamond was the component missing from R&B—that special voice heard when hip-hop and R&B meet. He even referred to her as the next Mary J. Blige. They'd all been staying long hours in the studio to get this project finished.

After seven hours, Wiz was finally satisfied. "That's a wrap for now. Come outta the booth. Camp closed."

The mogul and his star rapper retired to his third floor office and popped a bottle of bubbly, while Diamond went and called Drako.

Wiz was reclining in his oversized armchair with his bare feet kicked up on the large table as he observed Swirl, who was using his cell phone to arrange an assortment of female interests for him and Wiz to cap the night off with.

Wiz had just lit his large Cuban cigar of success when his cell phone rang. He checked the caller-ID and saw Bless' number pop up. "What up, dun?" Wiz answered jokingly.

"Dun!" Bless responded angrily. "You goddamn right yo' punk ass is done! You bitch-made, country-ass nigga! I can't believe you was da nigga behind them bootlegs, and I know you put da hit on Fatt Katt!"

Wiz was stunned at the false accusation. "Nigga, is you crazy? I ain't have shit to do wit' dat' shit!"

"Yo, save dat' shit for God! Yo' bitch ass gone need it. Yo' own peeps let it leak, bitch! And oh yeah, Brian conscious again, and the only thing he can remember is them blood burgundy hoodies and masks yo' dumb ass hit men wore!"

Wiz tried to interrupt, but to no avail.

"It's official, bitch! You best hope the Feds get you fo' I catch ya slippin'! Dis shit is off wax! I'ma let you country niggaz see how we do it up top!"

Before Wiz could respond, Bless abruptly hung up. Wiz sat there in shock at the bullshit hand someone had just tried to deal him.

Swirl, who'd heard Wiz on the phone and some of Bless' loud voice through the receiver, was calling Wiz's name repeatedly. "Wiz, what up?" Swirl's loud tone finally broke his trance.

"Whoadie, you ain't gone believe dis shit! That nigga Bless just accused Red Rum of puttin' a hit out on Fatt Katt!" His eyes were now locked into Swirl's. "Whoadie, dat' nigga even think I bootlegged his shit!"

"What you wanna do, whoadie?" Swirl asked, watching confusion flush Wiz's face.

"I 'on know; the nigga just threatened to kill me, Swirl!"

Fire dripped from Swirl's eyes. "Nigga, fuck dat cornball!" he shouted. "Dem niggaz don't want to see Red Rum. I wish he *would* bring dat' shit to New Orleans! Wiz, you got me! If he want it choppa style, New Orleans is the right place to find it!"

Wiz sat in silence and thought to himself as Swirl went on and on about what he'd do and what he thought they should do. Wiz thought about calling Drako, but he didn't want to hear lip, because Drako had warned him so many times about his bullshit antics. Wiz knew he'd started it, but also knew damn well that it wasn't him who'd offed Fatt Katt. The bootlegged units were sold and the profits were safely hid in the name of an undisclosed account that was untraceable.

"Should we tell Drako about this?" Wiz asked Swirl.

"For what? You my whoadie, too! Man, them niggaz ain't gone do shit! He probably just tryin' to run wit' this beef shit on his own, anyway."

Wiz sat and pondered Swirl's words and came to the conclusion that in a few days, when Bless calmed down and the

authorities proved his innocence, his slick gift of gab would once again prevail over Bless.

"A'ight, whoadie, keep this shit between us for a few weeks. We'll just beef up security when we travel out of New Orleans, and for now, we just gone stay tight and play it by ear."

Swirl smiled at the confidence Wiz had in him; he was willing to put his whole gangsta on the line for the man who made everything possible for him. They continued to chitchat about the turn of events when Wiz looked at the surveillance screen and saw Diamond getting off the elevator and approaching his office.

"Here comes Diamond. Just be cool," Wiz instructed.

When Diamond entered Wiz's office, she was still filled with the first stages of joy after entering the mainstream industry. She briefly chitchatted until security arrived to take her to the airport.

Wiz was smiling as he watched Diamond talk, but the sight of Diamond made his entire insides warm—seeing her and remembering her words: *Looks like that skank will take anybody's money!* Diamond had told Wiz she had seen Myria with the Take Money camp at club 40/40.

The 'what ifs' that Wiz never wanted to ponder were now confirmed. He knew that he'd left Bless' CD at Myria's house before the track was even released. She'd probably heard him and Damien on the telephone laughing about it, and he knew if she didn't tell him personally, it was still all the same for slipping it to White Chocolate.

Wiz knew how groupies worked, and was certain that Bless or someone in his camp had definitely sexed Myria—a thought that infuriated him.

Ain't no fucking way I'ma let this bitch get away! Wiz swore to himself. He was wracked with pain and disappointment. Never in a million years would he have thought that Myria had it in her to play him out in such a vicious way.

In Wiz's eyes she'd done the ultimate betrayal. She'd slept with the enemy and toyed with his pride. *Fuck that silly bitch! I'ma teach her who to play with,* he told himself as he fought to hide his emotions until Diamond and Swirl gathered their things and left the building.

As soon as they were gone, Wiz was back in his office. "Fuckin' slut! I knew it!" He pounded a fist onto the table as he got Damien on speakerphone.

Seconds later, he was on full blast telling Damien what had taken place. From Bless' threats, then on to Myria. After talking to Damien he now felt like Myria's actions had also threatened his reputation. He felt played, betrayed, and a silent, jealous revenge was definitely on it's way! The black ball card he threatened to use on White Chocolate was now being dealt to Myria.

"You make sure that bitch can't book a job advertising dog food! I 'on want to ever see her on the screen a-fuckin'-gain!" Wiz fumed with spittle in the corners of his mouth. "She ain't fit to wipe my ass. You make sure it's known that she's a tell-all, trash bitch!" He pounded the desk again, then flopped down in his armchair and reared back, telling himself from that day forward Myria no longer existed in his mind. She wouldn't get a chance to offer up a pathetic excuse, because every number she knew would be changed; only his private line would remain. *Run and tell that, you silly bitch!* he thought as he disconnected the call.

Wiz let out another huff as he leaned forward and opened his desk drawer. "Fuck it, let me try this shit again," he said with a mean scowl still on his face. He laid the mirror and the eight ball of coke Damien left him on his desk.

Chapter Twenty Nine
Wiz

In just a week after Bless' threat, Wiz's life seemed to have turned upside down! He'd once loved attention, camera flashes, headlines, and magazine covers. But now he was getting all the wrong kind.

It was now being speculated that he was connected to Fatt Katt's murder. Not only did Bless continue to threaten him, but now the hip-hop task force watched his every move.

Both he and Swirl noticed them everywhere. The media had received a statement from Fatt Katt's road manager, Brian Miller and were making a mockery of the news. They used the circumstantial evidence to scandalize Wiz and the face of Red Rum records. Every publication that reported stories of Red Rum being a label composed of thugs and gangsters who put out mob style hits flew from shelves.

The tweets went viral and online Wiz's reputation was a total disaster. *How in the fuck is this happening to me?* Wiz had asked himself many times with his face cupped in his hands. He hadn't experienced a rumor mill of this kind since the untimely death of Tupac Shakur and Biggie Smalls.

After his failed Tony Montana rendition in his office a week ago, Wiz had been too paranoid to get high any more. As the next weeks passed, he did his best to ignore the tabloid gossip. He refused to speak with any publications. Instead, he opted to focus all of his time and energy on finishing up and releasing Swirl's next album.

Other than his mansion, Wiz stayed hid behind the walls of his multi-million dollar studio.

Myria was a wreck. She worried about Wiz's well-being in the midst of all the gossip and rumors about Fatt Katt's death, but she couldn't reach him; all of his numbers had been changed. She knew he must've been hard at work with Swirl's next album, but he hadn't contacted her in weeks, and she couldn't understand why.

She took $600 of her depleting funds and caught a flight to Baton Rouge from Atlanta. She felt for sure she'd catch Wiz at the office.

When the cab pulled in front of Red Rum's headquarters, Myria quickly took notice of Swirl's souped up blood burgundy '96 Chevy Impala, Dianne's SUV, and a fleet of other cars clearly affirming that the studio was alive and jumping. She paid the cab driver and dismissed him. Happily, she went to the door and rang the bell only to get no answer.

After five minutes in the hot sun, she put her overnight Gucci luggage down and began to press the intercom switch. After five more minutes passed, she was pissed; she could feel beads of perspiration on her face and chest. Then she finally saw Swirl coming to the door.

She picked up her bags and put on her sassy diva persona. Swirl turned the keys and opened the door. Myria tried to quickly enter the air-conditioned climate, only to get a surprise shove from Swirl. She looked up to see the mean grit painted on his face.

"Bitch, you can't come in here!"

Confusion overcame her. "What do you mean? Wiz knows I'm coming!" she lied.

"You still lying, you funky gossipin' bitch! Wiz da one don't want yo' ass here! Trash ain't allowed in Red Rum!"

"Trash! Nigga, I *know* you ain't call me no trash! I'ma tell Wiz exactly what you said," Myria yelled as tears welled her eyes.

"Yeah? And he'll sho nuff be mad, 'cause trash is too good a word to describe you! Bitch, you ain't nothin' but weave-wearin' scum!"

Myria was shocked and heartbroken at the sound of Swirl's words as he maintained his sinister smirk. "Bitch, who we do and what we do at the Rum—stays at the Rum! Yo' gossipin' ass just spread your last rumor about this camp!"

"What the hell are you talkin' about? I haven't said a word about nothin', I swear!" Myria pleaded.

"Get the fuck off our property! Go stand in the street and wait on your cab, 'cause yo' triflin', street-walkin' ass ain't gettin' in here!" Swirl stated as he stepped toward Myria.

"No, no, I gotta talk to Wiz!" she shouted out of desperation as she tried to quickly weave past Swirl and get inside the door. He grabbed her small body by both arms. Myria tried to struggle free, causing Swirl to become even more aggressive. He finally shoved her to the hard pavement. "You think dis a game, bitch? Try it again and I'ma pimp slap yo' ho ass!"

Sitting on the ground she looked up in Swirl's face with tears streaming down her cheeks. She knew he meant good on his threat and that he could only be acting on orders.

"You think you cryin' now? You ain't seen shit! I hope you never work again! You ain't fit to work in the sleaziest shake joint!" He turned and went back inside.

Myria sat there and sobbed uncontrollably for at least twenty minutes before she partially regained her composure and called herself a cab.

She was still in shock as she reached the airport and purchased a ticket back to ATL. The next available flight wouldn't be in for a few hours, so Myria sat in the cafeteria of the busy terminal. Her eyes were puffy and red from crying when she was approached by two strange men, one black, one white.

The men introduced themselves as detectives and informed Myria that they'd watched the entire escapade at Red Rum. They asked if she wanted to press charges against Swirl. Myria promptly denied that Swirl had done anything. Then the two men began to ask her all sorts of questions about Red Rum and its CEO. They told her they'd pay her for any incriminating information and promised her anonymity. Myria not once wavered their way. She cursed obscenities and refused to cooperate with the authorities on any level about the things she claimed to have no knowledge of.

They offered Myria a contact card that she refused to take. She threatened to make a scene if they didn't stop badgering her. Annoyed, the agents finally just walked away. She watched them disappear into the thick crowd.

No matter what she and Wiz went through, Myria would never stoop so low as to help the authorities. She only prayed she and Wiz would soon work out their misunderstanding.

A few hours later, she finally caught her flight back home and officially began her life without Wiz.

244

A Life for A Life

A few weeks later, Myria was still distraught; she hadn't received a single call for work. Though she had been one of the most popular video models in the industry, she couldn't even land spots on videos shot on the lowest of budgets. And the $20,000 or so Wiz had given her last month was going fast.

She called White Chocolate, only to be dealt another blow.

"Myria, you my gurl and all, and I 'on know whatchu done went and did, but yo' name is shit out here. Right now ain't a good time. I ain't tryin' to get caught up in yo' mess."

"I ain't did—"

"Gurl, I'm pregnant with Bless' baby, okay? I need him right now. If you my gurl, you should understand. I'm tryna trap this money!"

"Well, what am I supposed to do?" Myria was still questioning White Chocolate like a child.

"I don't know, but right now, you gotta fix this on your own. I'll call when things calm down." White Chocolate abruptly hung up on Myria.

A few days later, Myria tried to call back, but White Chocolate's number was no longer in service. Her best friend had turned her back on her. Myria stood in the window, staring at the 'For Sale' sign Wiz's realtors had placed on her lawn, and tried to figure out how sugar had turned to shit so quickly!

Wiz reviewed the surveillance tape of Myria's encounter with Swirl. He smiled at his senseless act of revenge. He and Swirl smoked big weed and laughed at the footage over and over again as if it were shot for their entertainment.

He had everybody in the camp fooled into believing Myria was spreading industry rumors about Red Rum, and he used the tape as a warning: This was the fate reserved for traitors. Fuck

with Wiz and Red Rum, and you'll never work in the industry again.

Chapter Thirty

Drako

Several weeks had passed for Drako as well. However, he wasn't feeling the same effects of Wiz and all his troubles. In fact, he'd been purposely avoiding Wiz and everything that followed his immaturity. No, today he felt like he was at the top of his game! He felt he had the world in his hands. Well, at least half of it anyway, because with the success of his last scam Drako's offshore account now boasted a whopping balance of $4,800,000 which totaled three million on top of the 1.8 million that had already been deposited.

It had taken nineteen days, but just yesterday Diamond had received the call from Citibank telling her she'd been approved for the mortgage loan of three million dollars. Of course Diamond told them she was still abroad in Europe and asked that those funds be transferred to the number of her offshore account. Drako was so proud of Diamond as he opened the wall safe in his closet where he kept a small arsenal of handguns. He replaced a .40 caliber semi-automatic he'd just cleaned and picked up his briefcase and closed the closet as Diamond waltzed back into the room. As soon as he sat the briefcase down, she was snuggling up behind him.

"So what's the big surprise you wanna show me?" Her hands slinked around his waist. She peeked around his shoulder and into the briefcase he was pulling documents from.

"Don't worry, ma. We gone get to that in a little while. Right now I just wanted to show you that everything's comin' together just like I told you." He flipped a few pages and they were now both looking at the documents to obtain his legitimate businesses. "As you already know the construction company will do well, but the cement company is an even more stable investment." He scanned down the page, and then turned to the next. "The roofing company, I don't really like," he admitted, "But it won't cost much to buy into."

She rubbed her hands up and down his chiseled stomach. "I'm sure you and Dame have it all figured out. I never doubted that." Her voice was filled with assurance.

"I know that, but I'm not asking you to trust me. I'm giving you reason to keep believing in me." He craned his neck to look into her eyes. "Baby, the money in the account is gonna remain untouched. We still got money to live off of." He closed the briefcase and faced her. "Baby, I just wanted to tell you I'm proud of you, too. You did good. I will never gamble on you again. Why should I? I mean, real talk, we just put down two major moves. The credit card fraud got sticky, but we still made off with 1.7 and now this bank fraud got us another three million! We halfway there, baby. We worth almost five million that ain't nobody gone take!" His smile broadened as he gave his words time to sink in. Diamond didn't interrupt, she just listened attentively. "I got to play this last scheme out and this will be everything I promised, you baby. Everything." He held Diamond by her shoulders and began to caress her.

"Drako, I never asked you to promise me anything. I just chose to stand by you. I will continue to stand too, baby, but if you want to stop now just know that that is what I'm all for. I won't lie. In my opinion you've already won." She gazed up at him sincerely, but she knew Drako's mind had long ago been made.

"Ma, I know how you feel, but I'ma give it to you whether you want it or not. I ain't built this rapport and deposited all that paper in vain. All them trips to Connecticut gone soon pay off. This my biggest lick yet. It's gone get us past that ten mil' and you got my word, I'm outtie wit' the white collar shit after that."

Diamond saw the sincerity in his eyes, but she also saw something else within them. "So I hear you and I believe you. Now, I've gathered the pictures, magazines, and I have both money orders so we can stop by the post office on the way out." She was referring to sending Toney and Deuce the love he'd send almost every month. Diamond knew that when Drako had done good for some reason he still felt bad for Toney. He felt he owed the bulk of his success to Toney and he always wished he could do even more no matter how much he'd done.

"Nah, ma, I ain't trippin' on that." He kissed her forehead gently and nudged her toward the bed where she sat down. "I'm saying, ma, I been thinkin' a lot about you and this music thing and like I told you from the jump, I 'on really like you mixed up with no bunch of niggaz."

His thought took her by surprise. "Drako, where's all this co—"

"Let me finish, ma." The smile vanished from his face. "That tape you talkin' 'bout they playing wit' Myria and Swirl. That shit ain't cool. It don't sit well with me. He could've handled that better, ya know."

"Yeah, I agree. But what does that have to do with me? I know Wiz would never—"

"I know that, too!" he snapped forcefully. "But still, all them dudes gettin' besides themselves. I just think in the near future it'll be safer for all parties if I can get you away from all that." He squeezed her hand and looked into her eyes. "That's why I need you to trust me. I've already seen a lot in this industry. Through Red Rum I've seen the pitfalls and the perks. Back in prison I read all the books on the business. Tax law, incorporating, even branding. I mean everything. I feel in my heart with this kind of knowledge I just can't lose."

"So what exactly are you sayin', Drako?"

"I'm opening up my own label. I bought the building a few months back. Everything's nearly done."

"What? And you ain't tell me!" Diamond was stunned with joy as she bolted to her feet.

"I-I just wanted to do this on my own. No help from Wiz and only small shit from Dame. I'm using the funds from a legit account to do this and nobody knows really except the couple of guys I'ma be workin' with initially."

"You mean you got artists and all?" Her hand rested on her hip and all her weight seemed to shift to one leg.

"Well yeah . . . kinda sorta. I got two solid rappers and one guy who'd make a good front man. You know I'ma play the background on this."

"I can't believe this!" She shook her head happily. "You hid it from me, but I'm still proud of you." She planted a kiss on Drako's lips as soon as he stood up.

"I know." He popped her ass, then glanced at his watch. "Now gimme a minute to gather up a few things and we'll be ready to bounce." He watched Diamond strut back out of the room. After all the years she still looked so sexy to him as her hips bounced in another pair of Couture sweats. Losing her was not an option. He had plans for Diamond that even she would never see coming . . .

Meanwhile Wiz sat behind his desk looking over a fresh three album deal he'd just inked a new artist to. He'd gotten his grips on a hot new lyricist from Virginia Beach, known only by the sobriquet Thump! He was an imminent threat for all new artists, an underground mix tape monster and the anticipation of his mainstream album release was incredible. He'd successfully dropped Swirl's album on time and for anybody who looked at the mogul, he too seemed to have the world in his hands. But little did the world know, there was something totally different churning in Wiz's gut. The threats from Take Money Records now felt real. There were now no more courtesy calls in the late night hours from Bless after a radio show or tabloid dissed Red Rum. The tension the media was building was nothing like he'd ever felt and the absence of Drako was profoundly apparent. Diamond had made her way out to the studio several times to do her thing. He hadn't had a job that required full security service, but still he felt at times like this Drako would've naturally stuck his head in for a few days.

As hard as Wiz tried to deny it, anxiety was riding his back. He couldn't understand it himself. He knew most would be happy because regardless of whatever the media could throw his way, he'd soon be listed on that Forbes under 40 list. He knew he'd gotten away with tons of scandal. All the fake beefs he's sparked, buying units, and even the bootlegs were far behind him. This he was sure. Normally, he could manipulate the tabloids and other outlets to work in his favor, but now things were slipping past his own hands. Something was wrong. He felt there was something else breathing down his neck. He didn't feel safe, and he knew it was time to drop the farce and confide in his longtime friend, Drako. After putting away the contract Wiz wrapped things up. He sent everybody home and exhaled a deep breath. He flopped down in his armchair and dialed Drako.

Drako was broken from his thoughts as he slipped his foot into a fresh pair of Air Force One's. He'd heard his cell phone vibrating on the dresser. His watch read 6 P.M. and he was almost positive it was either Toney who'd call about every other week, or Deuce, whose body was in prison but his mind was partially still in the streets. Deuce tried to call every Saturday around this time so they could speak in their secret code and Deuce could be first to gather all the latest industry and celebrity gossip to circulate around prison. Drako made the few steps to the dresser and quickly glanced at the caller-ID and to his dismay it was from Red Rum's studio. For some strange reason agitation seemed to jolt through his body. He started to ignore the call altogether, but in the next moment instinct caused him to answer the call.

"What up?" he answered flatly.

Wiz was all smiles at the sound of Drako's voice. "I 'on know, homie, that's what I called to ask you. I ain't seen yo' ass in a month of Christmases it feels like. Diamond been out here doin' her thing, but you ain't even thought to stick ya head in on old boy."

"Seems like you ain't thought about me either."

Wiz laughed again. "Well, I'm callin' you now, ain't I?" he snapped. "Had to be thinkin' 'bout ya to call you, genius." He paused to chuckle at his own remark. "If Diamond can come, why can't you?"

"Diamond gettin' paid to come out there," Drako shot back.

"Ah fool, don't gimme dat, you 'on need no money, you ain't hurtin' for no paper!"

"Damn right I ain't hurtin'. And don't tell me what the fuck I need! It ain't 'bout what I need. It's about what I'm 'posed to have. What you need to do is rethink your drink and get me some mo' paper on the table!"

"Fuck is you trippin' on?" Wiz sat straight up totally stunned.

"You, nigga!" Drako remarked acidly. "I 'on see how a muthafucka who always braggin' about a Forbes list would even indulge in the silly shit you do." Drako was fuming. He'd broken his own code and let his feelings slip out under the weight of Wiz's bad judgment and the thought of him soon reaching the $10 million goal he'd set his sights on.

"Hold up, whoadie. My decisions are my decisions. That has nothing to do with your money. I told you a long time ago, anything you need, man, all you have to do is ask."

"See, that's what the fuck I'm talking about!" Drako grew even more aggressive. "What I need you to do is stop handling me like a chump! I'm a grown ass man; I ain't got no business asking another man for shit! All this goddamn money and you throw me a funky ass hundred grand or two." Drako was caught in a rage and his revelation cut straight through Wiz. Wiz's mind was in a state of disbelief. He'd forgotten all about confiding in Drako, as he never thought greed would have his long-term friend trying to shove his hands into pockets that were already welcoming. He surely felt the sting of the acid that leaked from Drako's words. He knew there was nothing he could say to try and fix things right now.

"Well," he spoke hesitantly, "I still need security."

Drako chuckled this time. "That's what you think I am. Security? Nigga, you gone need way more than that for me. Wiz, you so blind you can't see what's happening. Read the papers, player. Them Feds snoopin' all around your steps and you can't even see it! If you think this is a game, then keep playin'!"

"Fuck does that 'posed to mean?" Wiz made a weak effort to add base to his voice. Drako was about to go in on him even further when he looked up and saw Diamond standing in the doorway. Her expression said it all. She was shocked.

"Get at me when you get yo' mind right." Drako calmed his tone, glaring at Diamond once he realized Wiz had nothing to say. "And don't think I'ma be sittin' around waitin' on ya!" Drako hung up. He felt no sympathy for Wiz. Wiz needed a wakeup call and Drako felt Wiz should've done better by him. The feeling festering inside Drako had finally come to light.

"Drako? Baby? What just happened?" Diamond shuddered, stepping closer to him.

"Don't even trip over that shit, ma." Drako pulled his snow white Braves fitted cap on. "A closed mouth don't get fed. Trust me, he needed to hear that shit. Them pills, the fame—not just the money, got Wiz blind. I been trying to put a finger on why that nigga handled me like a chump, but I just can't."

"Well, stop over thinkin' it. The bottom line is we straight for now."

"Nah, ma, for always. I put that on everything! We both, in a way, laid down and gave that man a part of our lives at one time. We left him free and I sent him every contact he needed to make this shit possible. You don't repay niggaz like me or someone like you with what he gave us. You just don't." Drako nodded, unable to conceal the disgust in his eyes. "Now the Feds snoopin' and it's all his fault. I see the shit. Nobody has to tell me like they shouldn't have to tell him! We made this fortune on our own. And we keepin' it and I ain't going back to prison on the cause of them investigating or probing me behind his ass!"

"But maybe you oughta—"

"That's it, ma!" Drako's tone grew loud and forceful. "I 'on wanna hear nothing else about it! Wiz ain't helping me for real and this just the way it gotta be for now." He picked his keys up off the dresser and saw Diamond swallow the lump in her throat. "I'm sorry for cuttin' you off like that, but you know I got that thing in Connecticut, and I got something comin' up with Dame.

Something real important I need to see about. I got my word on this shit and it means a lot to me."

Diamond nodded. She knew when Drako meant business.

"You know I don't even want to discuss that with you. I can't afford to have unnecessary shit around me. Wiz ain't a good gamble for me right now. I said forever this time, ma. I'm responsible for you. Reality Records 'bout ta blow and you best believe I'ma keep playin' dat game raw as well! Fuck 'em!" He reached for her hand and led her out the door. Plan number three was in effect and sooner or later Wiz would feel the sting. Not only would it hurt his pride, but if done right, in time it would even hurt his pockets!

Wiz was still holding the phone in a daze. Today felt far too surreal. There was no way he could have ever foreseen the wedge that had slipped between him and Drako. He was now certain that the love of money is the root of all evil. On the inside he was wet with tears, but on the outside he knew he had to man up. He'd built Red Rum and he'd stand by it. Soon he'd get all the security he needed and then some. But for now he just couldn't stop replaying Drako's words.

When Diamond walked through the doors of Drako's building she immediately gasped in awe. Her hands covered her mouth and her eyes twinkled with excitement. From outside the building was just another modest-size cement structure void of windows. But now she was gazing up at a huge mural being tagged along the wall.

"Welcome to Reality Records." Drako hugged her tightly from behind. "This is gonna be my headquarters. It's gonna be a lot of work, but I promise you, ma, I'ma see this thing through." He leaned down and kissed her neck before leading her through a tour of the rest of the establishment. Soon, she saw both recording booths and the long mixing boards. There were headsets, various types of mics and all the extras. She trailed Drako up to the second level where they saw a full kitchen and several sleeping quarters to make even long stays comfy.

Finally, Drako led her to his office. Diamond was babbling about all she'd like to do and be at Reality Records the whole while.

"Chill ma, I need you to pipe down just a little," he told her calmly. "I mean, I know we got a ways to go. I want you to stay at Red Rum for now. Wiz does know how to market your talent. I want you to get the exposure. Then you gone step over to Reality Records and I can manage your career."

Diamond smiled wider, "I feel you, baby. Keep it under wraps, then we blow."

"That's my baby girl. Still following, huh?"

"You better know it," she chimed, pushing herself into his embrace. "Now, come on and let's break this place in." She was yearning for him as his hands roamed down her back and he squeezed her hips firmly.

"Oh, we definitely goin' there, but I got one more thing." He winked and led her over to the sofa and directed her to sit down. As soon as she did, he kneeled down right in front of her. In the same motion, he dug his hand in his pocket and came out with a small box he'd purchased at Harry Winston. Drako flipped it open with his thumb and turned the box for Diamond to see what was inside. When he looked up to see her face, Diamond's eyes were as wide as he'd ever seen them. She was fanning her hands frantically and it seemed as if she was fighting to catch her breath.

Heart stop. Heart beat. Slow down. Oh shit, it done stopped again. She knew she was looking at what had to be a nearly eight or nine carat diamond set in a platinum ring.

"Ma, I know it's real. Always has been, always will be, but today I want this to be official." She balled up her small fist and tried to contain herself from exploding with jitters. "I need to hear it; I need to know. Diamond will you marry me and be my Mrs. Forever?" He released a long overdue breath.

"Yes! Yes, baby. Of course I'll marry you." Diamond hugged Drako so hard this time as the rest of the tears erupted. He held her there and let her release all of her joy. Then he slipped the rock onto her finger. In less than a minute later, the ring was the only thing she wore. Drako made love to his soon to be wife inside of his long time dream—Reality Records.

The next few days had been a blur to Wiz. He'd called up Damien and had a few of the hottest NO chicks chartered to his mansion. Damien showed up with a sack of ecstasy pills and nearly a pound of exotic weed. He was laid up with an Indian-looking chick named Chilli and a Creole bombshell named Blondelle who was blazing up the video scene and several print ads. Normally, this erotic combination would lull any tension or problems on Wiz's mind. But after three days he still wasn't his old self. Chilli noticed his lackluster spirit.

"What's up, baby?" she asked, gently snuggling her naked body closer to his. "This ain't like you, you know we been cutting for years." She kept her tone to a soft whisper as she rose up on an elbow to see Blondelle still sound asleep on the other side of him. "Don't put no more of that stuff in your nose, baby.

All it does is keep your thing mushy." She began to massage between his legs. "Leave that shit for shorty," she said, referring to Damien. "He's experienced. That's his field. All you need is the feel-good tabs and us." She gently strummed a fresh manicured nail across his nose with her free hand. "And it's been a few days now. We need to get back to NO and you need to get back in the studio with Swirl. "Don't let me find out you losing that NO spirit? You know that ain't how we do it." She nudged him and smiled when she felt life blooming in his dick again.

"I got you, lil mama," the mogul snapped back, rolling over on top of Chilli. Normally, most females would come and go, but he and Chilli had a long history. She was considered a five star chick, well on top of her game. Every game. And she was all Wiz needed to remind him to stay on his. With that thought he proceeded to bone her good. By the time Blondelle woke up, his dick was on full brick! After Chilli came, she watched proudly as Wiz brought Blondelle to another intense orgasm before they both collapsed. Once they got back up, it was time for Damien and everybody to leave the mansion. He instructed Damien to clean house because he was definitely headed back to Louisiana to make sure Red Rum remained everything it was destined to be.

Chapter Thirty One

Vinny Pazo

Having just passed his seventy-second birthday and celebrating his thirtieth wedding anniversary, Vinny Pazo felt confident about the accomplishments and power he held at his disposal for so many years. He slowly rocked in his rocking chair in front of the cozy fireplace that warmed the confines of his neatly renovated log cabin nestled on the outskirts of Aspen, Colorado.

Vinny's muscular body had long ago reverted back to a childlike state. His large chest and arm muscles were deflated. His tight abdomen sagged from all the years of abusing fine pastas, cheeses, wines and pastries. He now used a cane to move around, and was confined to a dialysis machine for eight hours a day.

His fat cheeks sagged loosely from his dead-looking pop eyes, and underneath his expensive toupee was a bald, miserable man who was no more a bull than *Sammy the Bull*. He was sworn to Costra Nostra, but lived by a 'Costra-nono.'

His wife, who was twenty years younger and faithful to the fat bastard, no longer felt she was giving her love to a once strong

Brahma bull. She now felt like a caregiver looking after a patient in a retirement home.

"Time for bed, honey," she said curtly as she walked over and unhooked his dialysis machine. Vinny managed to smile as his wife stood up. She had dressed in a black and red Lady Marmalade showgirl's costume. It was similar to the one that she wore as a showgirl many years ago in Vegas when Vinny found her and proposed marriage one week later. All the tummy tucks, plastic surgery and frequent Botox shots made his wife appear ten years younger than she actually was.

"Take these." She handed him his glass of scotch on the rocks and two Viagra pills. Vinny quickly swallowed both pills and the double shot of scotch in one quick gulp. "Aah," he growled as the scotch warmed his chest. "I'm gonna make you feel just like the night I met you." He sat the glass down and used his cane to stand up. Vinny's wife helped him to the bedroom and laid him in bed where they rubbed and cuddled. She kissed him and undressed seductively, the way she used to on stage in front of cheering men.

It took another thirty minutes for the Viagra and scotch to take effect. As soon as they did, she climbed on top of Vinny in the only possible position left for them to have sex. She quickly took his pigtail-size dick and inserted it in her. Moving her hips up and down, she remained close in hopes that his small prick wouldn't slip out and go limp.

"Oh, Vinny . . . oh, honey, you make me feel so young!" she shouted, in hopes of making Vinny feel good and maintain his erection that she hadn't felt since this time last year.

"Uh . . . uh," Vinny grunted as he felt his balls tingle at the peak of premature ejaculation.

"Don't stop, Vinny, don't!" She was too late. Vinny's ugly eyes rolled in the back of his head as his fat face contorted with unfamiliar excitement. She no longer even hoped for the hopeless as she squeezed her vaginal muscles, milking Vinny dry. She wiggled her ass, savoring the final few seconds before Vinny's limpness slipped away. She leaned forward and kissed him. "That was great!" she lied as she rolled off her husband.

"I love you, Mrs. Pazo. Those pills are great!" Vinny said with a slight smile as he cuddled his wife closer.

"Uh-huh." She rested her head on his chest, saddened that she wasn't able to get off. They so rarely had sex. It seemed so unfair. And it wasn't as though she could cheat on him.

"Vinny baby, maybe we could do it once more before we leave?" she asked a couple of minutes later. Her question fell on deaf ears; Vinny's light snoring was getting louder and louder. Carla closed her eyes as she eased her fingers into herself and quietly finished Vinny's task. Vinny fell deeper into his comfortable slumber, knowing that this was the one place that no one knew about, the one place he could be alone with his wife— no guards, no interruptions, and no records of its existence. This was a safe house where Vinny could hide out and enjoy the lifestyle forever.

◊ ◊ ✧ ✧ ✧

After Wiz had cleaned himself up and shaved the stubble from his face, he was proud of the reflection he saw in the mirror. Chilli's words rang like an epiphany to him. All Wiz wanted was a clear head and to keep his empire intact.

When the charter jet landed in Baton Rouge, he was whisked directly to Red Rum headquarters. Swirl was right on his heels. It had been over five hours now and Wiz couldn't have ever felt better about what he had on his roster.

Today it was just him and Swirl as he watched him putting it down in the booth. Over and over Wiz would drop a new track to see Swirl bouncing on his toes like a boxer. A few seconds later,

he'd find himself hyped for the track, his focus trained to the floor as he nodded in tune with the beat. After the next few beats, he stepped up to an open mic and went in! Freestyle after freestyle his energy was so high that he dripped sweat from his shirtless body. He was covered in tattoos and it was clear to see that they, just like his lyrics, were a true part of him.

Wiz listened as he banged out a track they both loved for about the third take. "I'ma play it back once more." He spoke through the intercom as he signaled to Swirl that he was stepping away from the keyboard momentarily. Swirl tossed up the peace sign and nodded his head from the top all over again. Wiz and everybody knew Swirl was a true hearted booth rat.

Wiz had bounced up the stairs and into his office. He flopped down in his armchair and let out a sigh of relief. He reached for a cigar as he felt a sense of accomplishment again, but he quickly had a second thought and dropped the cigar back into the open case that sat on his desk. He'd closed his eyes and reclined back to catch a quick moment of relaxation, but in the next instant he thought he heard commotion in the distance. His eyes popped open and he spun his chair around to peek at his surveillance screens. "What tha—!" he snapped, sitting straight up. He swatted at the monitor in confusion. He thought he had to be dreaming. The screen showed like a gangster flick. There were at least forty agents running up and surrounding the perimeter of Red Rum headquarters. Panic was the first action to move him as he tried to stand up and run to the door, but tripped over his own feet. He recovered even faster and made it to the intercom that went straight to the booth downstairs.

"Swirl! Swirl!" he yelled several times over the loud music.

"What up, whoadie? You a'ight up there?" he finally responded once he saw the intercom's light.

"Hell no! Get yo' ass up here. The Feds all over this shit!"

"Oh shit!" Swirl's final response came fading through as he dashed away from the speaker.

A few miles away from the Pazo's cabin on the 15th Fairway, near Aspen's ski runs, Damien and Drako were preparing for work in an elegant stone cottage. For the last few weeks, Damien's rented home had served as their headquarters to plan for the task ahead of them. Drako was thoroughly impressed as he looked around the room. Lying on the floor were thick insulated white camouflage snowsuits with light shades of gray. They even had snow boots to match.

The large dining table had a host of ammunition, two Ruger Mini-14s, two Glock .40s, six revolvers ranging from .38s, .44 Bulldogs, and .357 Magnums. There were bulletproof vests, silencers, night vision goggles, hunting knives in different sizes, and there were small chunks of C-4 explosives along with detonator switches. There were handcuffs, rope, and even duct tape.

The elegant limestone wall was now used as a blackboard; it had an enlarged aerial photograph of the cabin and five different blueprints showing how the interior of the cabin was possibly built. Drako smiled as he thought how this could easily pass as a secret CIA command post.

As Drako picked up the vest and put it on, Damien walked over and handed him a photo. "What the fuck is this?" Drako asked.

"It's the generator located here in the rear of the cabin," Damien replied as he pointed to its location on the aerial photo. "This is the switch to kill the power."

"You are very thorough, Dame; I like it," Drako said, finally giving Damien an open smile. Damien smiled back. "I don't get

it. If you got this shit so down pat, why haven't you cleaned up this trash a long time ago?"

Damien's smile quickly vanished. "Drako, don't misunderstand me. I want Pazo more than Bush wanted the oil in Iraq. Had it been up to me, I would have hired someone to waste this bastard years ago! But that could be sloppy. Whoever kills Vinny, I would have to kill them as well. Vinny is a powerful man and loved by many people who don't really know him for what he truly is. Toney and I never had anyone to trust with such a secret until you came along. Toney knows that I have the brains to do this, as you can see, but Drako, I'm not a killer; I don't have the heart to give Pazo the death that he deserves." Damien looked straight in Drako's eyes. "This shit is personal for Toney, and you and I are the only people who he truly trusts to pull this shit through, so I hope you understand."

"I understand clearly. I lived with Toney for almost eight years, and I understand exactly how the fuck he feels, and I understand the pain he wants Vinny to feel. Dame, as long as you have me, you got heart. You just get me there and I'ma make that fat pizza eatin' Pazo feel this shit!"

Damien grinned. Drako kept poring over the details.

"This shit looks like a CIA invasion. This man is eighty somethin' years old! Just get me in, and I'ma let 'em know this is a wedding anniversary present from an old friend—Toney Domacio. Pop two in his fat ass and I'm out!"

Damien quickly turned to Drako with wide eyes. "Drako, please don't dare to underestimate him! He's an old man now, but he's murdered his way to the top. If he senses you coming, he knows it's his life or yours. He will not hesitate to kill you, and I'm sure he's armed. A black conscience like his makes him sleep with a pistol; it doesn't matter how comfortable he thinks he is."

A Life for A Life

Drako read the petrified expression on Damien's face, and knew exactly how serious he took Pazo, and Pazo's demise. "I feel ya. Now let's walk through this shit again."

Damien's face began to relax as he went back over the plans with Drako. The plan was for him to drive Drako about a quarter mile away; Drako would hike the rest of the way to avoid being heard. Since Vinny would already be sleeping, he wouldn't even realize that Drako's first move would be to disconnect the generator. Damien knew there were at least three locks on the door, and possibly a wood plank, so kicking the door in or shooting off the locks wasn't an option. The second move was to place the C-4 explosive on the door, get fifty-feet away, then hit the detonator switch. Damien told Drako that with the house being dark only to Vinny and his wife, his advantage with the night vision goggles should make it easy for him to gain control of the situation. Once those steps were taken, he could communicate back to Damien through headsets to keep him informed of what's going on.

"Toney said I'll never lose with the shit you use," Drako said.

"Toney told you right!" Damien glanced at his watch. "We have approximately two hours and it'll be 4 A.M. We both agreed that should be the best time for the element of surprise."

"It's time for Red Rum!" Drako shouted as he began looking over the weapons. "I'ma be on top of that fat, spaghetti-eatin' bastard like a Navy Seal!"

In less than a minute Swirl had leapt his way up the stairs and he and Wiz were staring at the screens as the Feds beat away at the front glass door.

"What we gone do?" Swirl spoke first, shattering the shock they were caught in.

"Man, they're here now. We gotta let 'em in before they tear this shit up! We ain't got nothing to hide and they ain't got nothing on us. Just let me talk and this shit'll be over before it starts."

Wiz hit his lawyer's number on speed dial and handed the phone to Swirl. "Tell 'im what's happening and tell him I 'on give a fuck what's on the table, he best to get here now or lose his best paying client!"

Wiz went downstairs and let the Feds enter Red Rum's camp.

They roughly pushed past him after the first agent stopped and shoved a few copies of paper in his face. "We've got a search warrant for these premises," he announced, smiling.

"Fuck you! Search what? For what?" Wiz argued as the other agents ignored him and fanned throughout the building.

"Where are the weapons?" he pressed on.

"Ain't no fuckin weapons here!"

"Drugs, money, maybe there's even a body here."

The head agent ordered Wiz to sit down. A few moments later, another agent was bringing Swirl down the stairs where he sat him beside Wiz.

"Are we under arrest?" Wiz growled.

"Not unless we find the wrong thing."

"Well why the fuck are you holding me?"

"I can detain you with probable cause."

Wiz and Swirl sat and watched as the agents turned Red Rum upside down. They searched through files with a fine-toothed comb, logging onto computers, and checking every crevice thoroughly and still came up empty.

It took almost an hour for Dale Cissaro, Wiz's high-powered attorney, to arrive. Wiz stood up as Dale walked straight over to the agent and introduced himself. He peeked over the search warrant which made it perfectly clear that it rendered no authority to hold Wiz.

"Nah Dale, I'ma stay," Wiz said cockily, with his lawyer now present.

"I advise you to leave. Even if they don't find anything they could still alert the media and you'd be bombarded with lots of questions."

"He right, Wiz," Swirl quickly agreed, gesturing his head toward the door.

"Wiz, I'm your representative. I can wrap things up here. I'll make sure your building is secured," Dale added.

Wiz gave in and he and Swirl prepared to leave.

"Bingo!" an agent yelled out. "Hold them, and don't let them go anywhere!" He was stalking his way over to the head agent holding up two large Ziploc bags filled with weed.

"You're under arrest for possession of marijuana. Please turn around and place your hands behind your back." The agent flashed an annoying smile. "I knew you were hiding something! This is just the beginning."

Wiz dropped his head in disappointment, but slowly turned around and complied with the officers. "Y'all know this is a bullshit rap!" he hissed as the agent stepped forward, pulling his cuffs, then proceeded to cuff Wiz.

"Wait!" Swirl shouted. "That shit is mine. I brought it here and I'ma man-up to that shit!"

"Wiz owns this place, and he's going to jail for at least tonight," the agent fired back.

"My client will do no such thing!" Dale started. "This man has claimed those narcotics; a verbal sworn statement that I and at least twenty of your agents can attest to."

"I don't give a shit what he says."

"Sir, this isn't a place for you to harbor your personal vendettas. You've been clearly unprofessional, and I'm sure a few notations of your excessive harassment would look nice on your superior's desk. I'm sure he'd love to hear from the NAACP."

The agent studied Dale's face for a moment, and concluded that he looked like a man who had Al Sharpton on speed dial. He thumped the butt of his cheap brand cigarette to the ground and left it smoldering on the elegant hardwood floor.

"Take him away!" he barked in Swirl's direction.

Swirl placed his hands behind his back and was taken into custody.

"I got you, whoadie," Wiz said as they led Swirl out the door.

"Shit ain't nothing new. I can lay a few hours, ya dig?" Swirl said.

"Dale, I want him out! Follow them to the jail!" Wiz fumed.

"I thought you wanted me here?" Dale questioned.

"Nah, I got this. I ain't got nothing to hide from these corny muthafuckas, ya heard?"

"But I—" Dale started.

"Can they arrest me?"

"Not if it's clean," confirmed Dale.

"Good, then go get Swirl. Fuck the media! I built this shit, and I'ma be sittin' in my armchair till the day this muthafucka fall, ya heard!"

"You're the boss," the lawyer stated just before he shot the agent a promising glare that had piles of lawsuits written all over it. He then turned and headed out the door.

Wiz sat back down and watched as the agents concluded the bullshit search. The agent who'd been playing the role of good cop strolled calmly over to him.

"Wiz, you look like a really smart kid," he began, "Hell, you have to be to have all of this."

Wiz ignored the agent as he leaned over and picked up a cigar off the table and lit it.

"You may not want to talk to me now, but these people hope to indict you. They're building a case now. They've gotten tips about Fatt Katt's murder, leads that point directly back here. The road manager told us the killers wore your blood burgundy colors. We've even deciphered the lyrics to Swirl's song, 'Kill' 'Em Slow'." He stopped for a moment as Wiz laughed hysterically.

"You may think it's a joke," the agent went on, "but the lyrics depict a recount of exactly what happened outside of Hot 97."

"You goddamn dummy!" Wiz laughed even harder in his face. "This is entertainment. I'ma business man; I say what people pay to hear."

"The FBI thinks you hire for murder, or may be a murderer yourself. The driver of that Yukon was the same height and weight as you."

"How you know? Y'ull weighed the tape?" Wiz chuckled and exhaled a cloud of smoke in the agent's direction.

The agent fanned smoke. "I don't think you pulled the trigger. But I do believe you know who did. If they acted out of revenge, then you should come forward. Save yourself and all you've built here. I'm trying to help you. If you work with us—"

Wiz dropped his cigar and balled over in laughter. "Get yo' cheese-serving ass off my property. I ain't no rat and you ain't gone find no rats around here to feed either. I'm glad we got rat traps all over Louisiana. Tell 'em to get some in New York, too!" Wiz was confident they'd never tie him to Fatt Katt's murder.

The agent looked over Wiz's expression, disappointment was obvious. "All right, guys, let's go," the head agent yelled out.

It was then that the 'good cop' dropped his mask and showed his true colors. "You know you're a smart mouthed little midget fucker! One day that fancy lawyer won't be enough to save you. You're goin' down and I'ma watch you drown!" He stormed out the door behind the others.

Wiz flopped back down on the sofa gazing out the glass front door watching all the Feds disperse. "Fuck!" He pounded his fist into the sofa. No matter how hard he tried, no matter how innocent he was, he still felt like someone was purposely throwing rocks his way. He'd just spoken so greasy to the agents and held his ground, but inside he knew that 2nd degree murder was a serious offense. If somehow they could pin that rap on him it could easily cost him his life. That thought washed a hard reality over him.

For over a week now Wiz had launched a relentless search for anybody with motives to tarnish Red Rum's name. The underground buzz was hot! It surged through groupies, video chicks, and die hard Red Rum fans alike. He was probing at every outlet he could think of. He decided to pick up the phone and call Damien, who had especially been on top of things around New York for him. Damien's people kept a close eye on Take Money Records and all of Bless' major moves. As soon as Damien picked up, Wiz told him what had just went down. He then consulted with Damien about possibly arranging a new security team.

Just as Wiz had ordered, Dale followed the agents down to the precinct. Swirl was booked on possession of marijuana and a measly $10,000 bail was set. Dale paid before the ink could hardly dry on the charge and Swirl was released almost immediately. The media had a ball. They snapped pictures of Swirl being released and published articles questioning Red Rum's legitimacy.

A Life for A Life

An undisclosed amount of marijuana was seized by FBI agents while conducting a search at Red Rum's headquarters. The FBI has confirmed that the agency is conducting a criminal investigation into the record label, but declined to provide any further details.

Wiz nodded his head in disgust at the news article. The media masses were the biggest scammers of all. They'd blown the few pounds way out of proportion and made a payday while doing so. Dale was staunchly defending his empire, but the media and by extension, the public, had already made up their minds, it seemed.

Now with the Feds trying so harshly to pin anything on him, Wiz was beginning to fear losing his image and all he'd worked for.

Chapter Thirty Two

Drako

Other than Damien's voice coming through the earpiece, the sound of two-foot-deep snow crushing under the weight of Drako's snow boots was all that he could hear. It had started to snow heavily, and even with night vision goggles, Drako could only see clearly a few yards ahead of him.

The heavy vest and white camouflage backpack made the quarter mile hike feel like a Mount Everest slope. The wind chill factor didn't help either; it felt like the strong winds were cutting through the snowsuit more and more with each step. But Drako, dressed like a soldier in a special ops unit, pushed all the negative thoughts to the back of his mind. He wanted to get Pazo as bad as Toney wanted Pazo.

"I got a visual on the spot," Drako said through the earpiece headset to Damien, who was waiting back in the SUV.

"Good, good. Stay with me until you disconnect the generator."

"I gotcha, I gotcha," Drako responded, huffing. He fought through the dark in as close as he'd ever been to an arctic climate for about fifty more yards as he ran up on the small shed that housed the generator. "Okay, I'm here, Dame," Drako's tired voice whispered through the headset as he caught his breath.

"Make your move," Damien replied flatly.

Drako had already taken off the backpack as he stooped beside the small shed, using the utmost precaution to stay camouflaged. He took out the bolt cutters and severed the chain that held the lock. As soon as it snapped, he opened the door and went straight to the switch.

"Step one complete," Drako announced as he continued to move along as if he'd been trained by the military. He stayed low as he slowly crept up to the back door of the cabin and pressed the putty explosive up against the door.

He ran back behind the shed and squat down. "Dame, this is it. Everything's in place. The next time I call you, I'll be on my way out." He didn't wait for a response; he pressed the detonator switch, and then heard an explosion. Drako was back on his feet. The Mini-14 with the silencer that once hung from his shoulder strap was now held firmly in his hands as he quickly leapt the three short steps with one bound. He got down low as he gained entry of the back door and put his back up against the wall as he heard the horrific screams of a woman.

Just one second earlier, Vinny choked with fear as he woke to the unfathomable. His confused mind raced quickly. He never could have imagined this day. Vinny had no idea if it was the police or if one of the families had tried to overtake him. The only thing he knew for certain was that death was on its way. He quickly shoved his wife out of bed. "Shh! Stay down!" he whispered as he grabbed the pistol from the nightstand. The last of Vinny's adrenaline shot through his body in an effort to save his life as he got to his feet. He didn't need a cane to move this time. Vinny steadily held the gun in front of him as he approached the room door.

Drako moved in a crouched down position in the direction of the screaming. He saw images in shades of green through the goggles. He also saw Vinny as he eased up to the bedroom door. Vinny had his back against the wall as he reached his arm out and tried to switch on the light.

Drako stayed quiet as he realized that Pazo was really at a disadvantage and couldn't see a thing! Squatting behind a couch, Drako crept closer to the door. Vinny's hand continued to search the wall until he found the switch. Click, click, click, click. Vinny flicked it up and down, but nothing happened.

"Shit!" Vinny exclaimed, retreating his hand. Drako quickly tossed a vase across the room and it crashed against the far wall.

Pazo sprang from the door, firing round after round in that direction. "Die, you bastard!" Vinny yelled in a heavy Italian twang.

As soon as Drako got a safe enough visual, he eased the .40 caliber from his thigh holster, leaped forward and swung the heavy butt of the Glock, crashing Vinny on the side of his skull. The brute force knocked Vinny's obese body straight down to the floor as the gun dropped from his hand. Drako moved fast, picking up the gun and stepping over Vinny's unconscious body.

Drako heard the sobs grow louder and louder as he approached the room with caution. The Mini-14 hung from his shoulder and the .40 caliber extended firmly in front of him. He heard the sobs continue, and they were quickly affirmed when he saw the old lady crouched on the floor. Her hands roamed the dark floor in front of her as she searched for something.

Leaping over, he snatched her up, and then swung his Glock, crushing it right into the center of Mrs. Pazo's skull. Warm blood splurted from the gaping hole onto his face. Her nearly lifeless body crumbled to the floor. Spitting the nasty taste of blood from his lips, he quickly cuffed her naked body, and ran straight back to Vinny and cuffed him.

Drako then searched the rest of the house and made sure they were alone. Once he was sure, he ran back outside and turned the generator back on.

Drako spoke through the headset as he reentered the cabin. "Dame! Yo, Dame."

"I hear you. Is everything good?" Damien questioned.

"The perimeter is secure and I got power. Gimme a few minutes with this pig!"

"Stay in touch and make it fast!"

Drako entered the cabin and found the light switch that Pazo had been reaching for. He turned it on and brought light back into the cabin. Mrs. Pazo's naked body lay still as blood from the large contusion puddled onto the wooden floor beneath her.

Drako picked up the wife's body first, and sat her in the rocking chair. He struggled to lift Vinny's 300-pound body and sit him in a chair that he moved from the dining room table. Drako removed his backpack and grabbed the duct tape. He first began to tightly tape Vinny's legs and realized that Vinny was regaining consciousness. Drako sped up as he finished his legs, then duct taped his entire upper torso to the chair, starting from his shoulder.

"Who are you?" Vinny questioned. "Who sent you here? What do you want?" Drako ignored his every word as he completed his task. Leaving Vinny in ignorance made the anticipation worse.

Drako quickly duct taped Mrs. Pazo in the same fashion. As soon as Mrs. Pazo regained consciousness, she began to cry uncontrollably. "Please Vinny, do something!"

Her pathetic cries were annoying as Drako slapped her across her bloody cheek as hard as he'd ever slapped any man.

"Shut the fuck up, you walkin' dead bitch!" he yelled with anger.

"Please no, please don't hurt her! It's me you came for!" Vinny pleaded before Drako could turn around and slap Vinny even harder. Blood instantly gushed out of Vinny's nose and ran down into his mouth.

"Wait, no! Please don't let her see me die."

Drako glared at the once mass murderer turned rat.

"Who are you? Who sent you?" Vinny asked again.

"I'm reality, bitch! And it's time you met me!" Drako said in a death-promised tone.

Vinny thought fast. He realized that this was the voice of a Negro. He knew the mob would never send a black man after him. Not him. *Who could he be working for?* he thought. *Maybe a friend of somebody I whacked?*

"Listen, I don't know what you came for, but if its money you're after, I'll get it for you. Whatever you need," Vinny pleaded as Drako silently watched the pitiful bastard cry. "I don't know you and I don't know who sent you. Just tell me what you want and I'll deliver."

Drako turned and punched Mrs. Pazo directly in her face as hard as he could. The loud thump knocked her and the rocking chair over on its side.

"Jesus! Please don't! Listen, son, just listen! I don't know you. I have no idea who you are; this can all be over. Please just listen! Whoever sent you or told you about me could never give you what I have to offer you! There is money close by." Drako's silence encouraged him. "Trust me, whatever they've offered you is *nothing* compared to what I can give you! Just name it!"

The mention of money sparked Drako's interest.

"Take the money, son. You can disappear. I will not look for you. I won't ask about you. You can just go. You'll be a very rich man." Vinny watched the masked intruder as he stood silently

276

still. Vinny knew the mind of a criminal, and knew that he was contemplating those thoughts.

Drako thought for a moment before replying. "How far do we have to go to get this money?"

Vinny's heart raced with hope. "Not far at all. It's easy as pie."

"How far?" Drako asked again, calmly. He glanced over at Mrs. Pazo, who was coming to. He walked over and up righted the chair with her in it.

He then kneeled in front of Vinny. "All I came for was the money, and I was told that the owner of this cabin had it. I understand you don't want your wife to see you die. I don't wish to kill you; I just don't want repercussions, either."

Vinny couldn't believe his ears. "Oh, God! There will be none! Just take the money and call someone to come untie us after you're away. Nobody's gonna hurt you, I swear on my mother."

"Where is the money?" Drako asked as if he agreed.

"Move the dresser against the wall, then move the rug it sits on."

Drako moved the chest of drawers as Vinny and Mrs. Pazo prayed for this nightmare to end. After Drako scooted the heavy oak dresser aside, he lifted the rug, but all he saw were planks of chestnut wood that matched the rest of the floors throughout the cabin. "Now what?"

"Get the axe from the shed out back. The money's in the floor," Vinny quickly responded.

Drako jogged to the shed to retrieve the axe. On his way out, he spoke through the headset. "Dame."

"I hear you, are you en route?"

"No, gimme a few more minutes."

"Drako, hurry the fuck up! Don't trust Vinny until he's dead!" Damien sternly replied.

"I gotcha. I'm in control of this," Drako stated before he reentered the cabin with the axe over his shoulder.

He went straight to the spot and began chopping the axe into the floorboards. Chunks and shards of wood began to fly from the floor with each lick of the heavy axe. The Pazo's watched him silently.

A few minutes later, the profusely sweating Drako had beaten the planks away, revealing a large wood panel covering a hole in the floor.

"Now remove the wood," Vinny ordered.

Drako lifted up the board and revealed two large military cache boxes. They were both chained and locked.

"The key is in a safe deposit box. Just shoot the lock off."

Drako went to his backpack, got the bolt cutters, and broke the shackles. Drako opened the boxes, and to his surprise, there were four huge army duffle bags inside. Drako reached in to retrieve the first bag; it was much heavier than Drako would have ever imagined, as he dragged it out with both hands.

"There's $750,000 in each of those bags," Vinny stated.

Drako nodded as he retrieved all four bags and dragged them to the middle of the floor near Vinny and his wife.

Drako could hear Mrs. Pazo still weeping as she prayed for an end.

"Now you have it. So please take the money and leave. It can all be so simple. My wife has nothing to do with this, and I don't want her to suffer in my sight any longer."

"Sir, you are absolutely right; it *could* be this simple, and I wouldn't want your wife to see you die senselessly either," Drako calmly stated as he heard Mrs. Pazo's cries stop. Then he watched Vinny's fat bludgeoned face relax at the thought of buying his way out of something else. "You know why?" Drako asked, not giving Pazo time to respond. "'Cause that would not be enough punishment for a cheese-eating rat like you!" Drako snatched the ski mask from off his face. Vinny's eyes widened in terror.

Before Vinny could make a sound, Drako slapped him so hard that all Vinny could see was white specks; his ears rang loudly like a siren, and Mrs. Pazo yelled out as she saw the blood and saliva fly from her husband's swollen face.

"Shut the fuck up! You need to feel the pain you've put people through, you snitchin' mothafucka!" Drako slapped him again. "I'ma make sure she see you die *slow!*"

Drako snatched up his backpack and pulled out a ten-inch stainless steel hunting knife. Mrs. Pazo's cries filled the room, but still fell upon deaf ears. Drako looked at Vinny in complete disgust. Vinny had been in Drako's shoes too many times in his life; he knew that his life ended here. Vinny yelled not another word; his eyes only stared at his wife. She was going to be the last image he saw as he prepared himself to die.

Drako knew that Vinny had accepted his fate, and there was nothing else Vinny wanted more than to end this anticipation. Drako laughed. "Nah, Vinny, she ain't gonna see you die. You gonna see her die!"

Drako dropped the knife as he approached the screaming terrified woman. Drako punched her in the head as hard as he could. The very first punch knocked the old woman out cold. He then grabbed a handful of her hair and lifted her head up.

He took his right-gloved fist and began to beat Mrs. Pazo's face in. He viciously punched her over and over again. The sound of the heavy blows filled the room until the bones crushed in her skull and her swollen face turned blue. "You feel that, Vinny? You feel that? You sorry piece of shit!" Drako cursed after every blow.

Drako's heart went out for Toney. He was in a blind rage. Damien's voice coming through the headset was inaudible to Drako. He made Vinny watch him beat the life out of her until he

was completely out of breath. Drako then stomped her in her bare chest, knocking the nasty sight of her swollen head back to the floor.

Drako turned around and smiled at Vinny as his chest heaved up and down. "Happy now, you sorry mothafucka?" Drako laughed as he picked up his knife. He waited a few seconds to catch his breath, but realized Damien's voice was blaring through the headset.

"Damien?" Drako said through the mouthpiece.

"Drako, what's going on?"

"Come in, drive up. It's okay. Vinny has a gift for us."

"Drako, don't trust—"

"He's gone! Now come on!" Drako sat in silence as he stared at Vinny. Inside, Vinny really had already died. Vinny was once a true gangster, and it reflected as he said no more words to save his life. He still had no idea who Drako was or what his motive was, nor did it seem to matter anymore. He stared blankly over at his wife's corpse as tears streamed down his face.

Damien was in shock when he entered the cabin. Drako was sitting on the couch much too calmly for this situation. He was no longer wearing a mask, and nearly covered in blood.

Inspecting further he saw the blank look on Pazo's bloody, swollen face and realized that he was still alive. Just then Damien caught hold of what Vinny stared at. With one glance at Mrs. Pazo he vomited immediately. "Oh, God!" he screamed as he held his stomach and turned away from the ghastly sight. Mrs. Pazo's head had swollen up as large as a pumpkin. Every part of her head that wasn't covered in blood was now turned blue-black. Feces and piss ran down her legs, and her chest area was badly bruised. She appeared inhuman, like a circus sideshow freak, and Damien knew that only a madman could inflict this kind of pain.

"Goddamn it, Drako! What the fuck did you do?" Damien yelled as he looked at the blood splattered everywhere.

"What needed to be done," Drako calmly replied. "Vinny's not even dead, Drako!"

Drako stood up. "Oh, yes he is," he said calmly. "He's already dead; his soul died long ago."

"Why didn't you just—"

"Shut up, Damien! I couldn't! I wanted you to see so you can tell Toney exactly the way a pig squeals right before he dies! I always told Toney he'd see."

Damien knew this shit was personal for Drako. He said no words as Drako moved forward with the knife.

Drako slapped Vinny's cheek lightly. "Vinny, ain't nothin' left but to give you your anniversary gift. From an old friend— Toney Domacio!" Vinny's eyes came back alive in shock. He no longer felt fear, just pure disbelief.

"Domacio!" Pazo's voice dripped with disgust, "That double-crossin' son—"

"Pop!" Drako froze his word with another sharp slap to his fat face.

"Damn right! *Toney Domacio!* And this is *your* reality! I came to take your life, too!" Drako thrashed a clean line straight across his bare chest causing him to wince in pain.

"Argh!" Vinny screamed pitifully as pools of blood gushed from his body.

"Squeal, pig!" Drako yelled as he grabbed Vinny by the head. He poked the tip of the knife right under Vinny's right earlobe, then with one swift, steady motion, he shoved the knife in deeper and from there sliced straight through to Vinny's throat all the way to his other earlobe. Blood gushed out uncontrollably. Vinny's eyes never closed, but his screaming squeals came to an abrupt stop.

Drako let the back of Vinny's head go as he turned to Damien, still smirking. "Did you hear that?"

"Hear what?"

"The pig's last squeal!"

Damien looked at Drako's smirk and couldn't believe how serious he was about that question. "Oh sure, oh sure," Damien replied as he thought it best to affirm.

"Good! Spare Toney none!"

"Let's get out of here, Drako. They'll never find these bodies—at least not before the wolves eat 'em."

"Yeah, you're right. But first, look at what I got out of Vinny." Drako pointed to the bags.

Damien looked inside and couldn't believe his eyes. He quickly gathered his thoughts as he looked at Drako. "You deserve *every* penny of this."

Drako smiled. "Good, now help me load up and let's blow this spot." Damien nodded.

Drako gathered the bags and moved around the corpses as if they were never there. Then he went back and got his backpack. He stepped over Vinny's corpse, and then looked at Mrs. Pazo's corpse. The horrific stench of piss and shit was evidence of her death, but not enough for Drako, as he slammed the knife into her chest, leaving it embedded in her lifeless corpse.

"Aahh! What the hell did you do that for?" Damien grimaced.

"Just wanna be sure. Vinny claimed his death—she didn't. I don't wanna be the cause of no miracles," Drako stated as he dragged the last bag to load it in the SUV.

The hit had been a success and Damien pulled away feeling like he was the true wise guy of the whole situation.

He was now certain about the type of wings Drako wore. He was more than ready to tell Toney and deliver the good news.

Drako soaked in the feelings of final redemption. He'd finally made good on his word to Toney, and had a newfound fortune that would be even more reinforcement behind Reality Records. Drako wished more than anything to see the look on Toney's face when he got the news.

Chapter Thirty Three
Wiz

Dale Cissaro had given Wiz the disturbing news. At this time the Feds could not come up with enough evidence to close Red Rum's doors. However, Wiz was the main suspect in Fatt Katt's murder. The government had now officially launched a full investigation and if they could gather the information they hoped for, Wiz would be facing a life sentence behind bars.

It had now been two weeks since the raid at Red Rum and Swirl's release. Wiz and Swirl were now making an unsuspected trip to Atlanta. In most instances they'd be rushing off to a set compiled of video props and green screens, or perhaps to another coveted industry event. But today's visit wouldn't take nearly as long. Wiz had received lots of feedback from the searches he'd sparked several weeks earlier. There had been one peculiar source that had gained Wiz's attention. The source had texted several anonymous messages. All the one line messages were simple and to the point. The final text received read:

If you're searching for a motive, here's a start.

Attached to the message was an address. The text had come through on one of Wiz's old numbers, but still it was a private line which made him feel as though it had to have come from someone who is or was once close to his camp. It was killing him

to know who'd sent the text. He was still trying to make sense of it all. Glancing in Swirl's direction, he heard him jack the hammer back on the .40 Taurus. Swirl watched a single bullet slip into the chamber, then flipped on the safety with a smooth thumb motion.

"Man, you think this could be a set up?" Wiz said, not feeling much confidence.

"Hell naw!" Swirl spoke up fast. "Don't nobody think we'd move on that lil shit and they'd never recognize us coming." Swirl sounded sure of himself. "Don't matter anyway, right now we just checkin' shit out. But I'm telling you, if a nigga ever bring any harm our way, whoadie, I 'on give a fuck who it is! You know how I'ma bring it. Soo-woo till I die!" Swirl's voice cracked with certainty. "And behind this Red Rum . . . man, I'm tellin' you I'ma deal wit' it!" Swirl nodded his head, emphasizing his point.

Wiz nodded, agreeing as the navigation system finally steered them down the right street.

"Just drive by like normal," Swirl first instructed. He sat up straight as they cruised by unnoticed behind the dark tints of the black Lincoln Town Car they'd rented.

After cruising by the address twice, which seemed to be another dead end, Swirl's mouth was twisted into an irritated scowl.

"Pull in!" he barked, "Man, this can't be shit. We gotta be in the wrong place."

Wiz whipped right up in front of the building. Swirl stuffed the gun in his waist and hopped out the car, telling Wiz to follow him. As soon as they stepped up to the glass front door, a clean cut man dressed in urban apparel and looking to be maybe in his late twenties was right there to meet them. He recognized their faces and opened the door immediately.

A Life for A Life

The moment Wiz stepped into the foyer, his eyes traveled to a massive mural that swallowed up the entire right wall. The huge wall paid homage to all the fallen soldiers of hip-hop. The burners had tagged everyone. Aaliyah and Lisa "Left-Eye" Lopez were the prettiest angels ever tagged. Big Pun, Jam Master Jay, Biggie and Tupac stood side by side at what appeared to be heaven's gates. From Old Dirty Bastard to Soldier Slim, all the way down to Pimp-C, none of the greats were forgotten.

"Whad up, fellaz? I'm Drip. What can I do for y'all?" the man who seemed a bit starstruck asked easily.

As soon as Wiz's eyes left the mural, he grilled the man up and down. "What is this place?" he asked, holding his nasty smirk after sizing him up.

Drip caught the glare and looked at Wiz like he was from another planet. "Huh?" he held his arms open and smirked right back. "Sheeit, this Reality Records, shawty. I thought you knew."

Reality Records? What the fuck? Who . . . Hell naw! The sound of the name rang loud through Wiz's ear. He felt the imaginary gut punch, and then the first sting to Drako's ultimate plan rocked him dizzy.

To be continued.....

**A Life for A Life
Part 2: The Ultimate Reality!**

LIFE 285

A Life for A Life
Part 2: The Ultimate Reality!

Introduction

"Reality Records!" Wiz mean mugged the man standing in the foyer of a building that an anonymous tip had led him to.

"Yeah, Reality Records," the man repeated himself and tightened up the scowl on his face, realizing Wiz obviously wasn't appeased with the politeness he'd offered at first.

Wiz sucked at his platinum teeth, never taking his eyes off the man who'd introduced himself as Drip. Without turning his head he reached out and patted Swirl, who shot the man an even colder glare. "Let's get up outta here." Wiz turned and stalked back out the door.

"Reality Records, ha?" Swirl capped hotly. "We'll meet again." He brushed over his waistline and nodded on his way out the door.

Drip made a step closer to the door and stood there stunned as he asked himself what in the hell had just happened? In the next flash he watched two of the hottest celebs in the industry jump back into a black Lincoln Town Car and nearly burn rubber getting back onto Forsyth Street.

Before Wiz could make it out the parking lot his whole body had turned warm. The moment he flopped behind the driver's wheel he happened to glance to his right, and when he did his gut instinct was confirmed. The sound of Reality Records still reverberated through his mental. But staring over at Diamond's red Lexus Coupe he knew that Drako was somehow behind this label.

"Fuck!" He slammed his fist into the dashboard and pressed the accelerator even harder. "This some underhanded bitch-ass shit! I knew something was up with Drako! I can't believe he sided with some other niggaz on me!" He smacked an open palm to his forehead. "Man, I should'a seen it comin'! He, out of the blue, kept trying to press me for more paper!" Wiz nodded his head in disgust. "After all I done for him! Man, I tossed that nigga hundreds of grands when he hit the bricks! Put him in a house, copped the 760, and whoadie, you know I ain't stop there!" Wiz was fuming more heat with every word. "I gave this nigga toys! He pushing a Bentley Coupe and all! Man, it was first class everythang! You know that shit, whoadie!" Wiz snapped, watching Swirl nod agreeingly. "Enough just ain't never enough for some, ha? And now this man want to step outside and be my competition! I 'on get this shit, whoadie. I just don't get it!" His thoughts were scattered into a million pieces.

Swirl sucked at his platinum teeth with a knowing smirk. "Whoadie, I been saw the malice in that man's eyes," he decided to speak up. "But them yo' people, like way before my time, so I saw best to mind my own, ya dig?"

"Yeah, yeah, I feel ya," Wiz said, easily trying to calm his rage. "That was my friend. Man, this shit ain't all about no money when it's between us." Wiz's voice cracked. "I guess he got his reasons." Wiz seemed to curb his attitude a bit as he merged back onto the beltway.

"You think . . ." Swirl said hesitantly, "he had somethin' to do wit' dem folks stomping through our doors?"

Wiz glanced at Swirl sideways and gazed off in the distance. He thought a moment before answering, "Hell naw, man. That

shit ain't nowhere in 'im. This 'bout something else. I can't figure him out. It's like to me he developed some type of control issues in the pen after all them years. I don't think he can accept me being the boss. So maybe he wanna be his own. But that other shit ain't him. I know it ain't. That's in my heart, whoadie." Wiz went silent again as they cruised on.

"Well, how you gone handle up?" Swirl asked the inevitable.

"It's business, that's all, whoadie. If he want to get in the waters with me I'ma just crush that shit! We gone keep making good music and keep this shit on lock! Just business."

Swirl sat for a moment before he gave his final thought. "A'ight, I hear you and I respect you bein' in charge of this business. I respect you leadin' this camp. On the business level, I'm wit' it, we'll crush everythang. But when or if it gets personal, Drako's *your* friend. I ain't finna' be the nigga to keep handin' out passes and bags of respect. I done had enough from er'body and like I said I want to be clear wit' you, whoadie. I 'on give a fuck who it is . . . It's soo-woo if he brang it!"

Swirl's face told it all. He meant every word he said before he laid the pistol on the floorboard, reclined his seat back and closed his eyes. Neither one spoke a word until they reached their final destination.

✧ ✧ ✧ ✧ ✧

"Now isn't this better?" Diamond asked as soon as she positioned the tall indoor plant in the corner of Drako's office.

"It's cool, ma. Whatever you think," he said, not even glancing up from the papers strewn about his desk.

"Well, if you gonna be spending time here this place needs life. It needs to breathe." She stepped over and flopped her behind up on the ledge of his wide desk. Just as she was about to lean over and steal his attention something else stole hers.

"Look, baby!" She pointed to the six monitors on the wall

behind him. When Drako glanced up to see Diamond's eyes looking like those of a deer caught in a set of headlights he immediately spun his chair around to survey his security screens.

"What the fuck!" He was taken by suprise as he leaned his face closer to the monitor. "Damn! How . . ." he stammered in confusion, but got to his feet even quicker at the sight of Wiz and Swirl standing in the lobby of Reality Records.

"Dang, how the—"

"I 'on know and I 'on give a fuck!"

Diamond slid off the desk and rushed to Drako's side. She saw that defiant look in his eyes. "And I ain't 'bout to tip-toe around these niggaz, either!" He pushed past Diamond and headed for the door.

"What are you gonna do? Where—"

"Whatever I have to!" he said with his tight jawbones jutting from beneath his dark skin. "Just stay here!" he bellowed, not allowing Diamond another word as she vanished out the door.

By the time Drako trotted down the steps and rounded the corner, Drip was standing near the door, gazing at the parking lot. "Where did they go?" Drako shouted, making quick steps toward him.

"Man, I-I 'on know?" Drip turned to meet Drako's loud voice with a baffled expression.

"Shit!" Drako huffed with anguish looking out the door himself. He rubbed his hand over his baldhead as Drip noticed his chest heaving up and down. "Fuck did they want?" Drako didn't attempt to hide the anger on his face.

"He just asked what was this place," Drip said, still lost. "Sheeit, I told him this Reality Records, shawty! Hell, I thought he knew," Drip said honestly.

Drako nodded and gave thought as Drip turned to lock the front door. Drako saw the butt of his .45 still tucked safely in the back of his pants.

"I shoulda' moved faster; I saw that shit Swirl was giving you."

"Yeah, I peeped that shit, too," Drip admitted. "Is everything okay? That nigga Swirl was packing some heavy heat!"

"How you know?" Drako's brows furrowed.

"Man, you know a nigga conscience gone always make him check to see if he holdin' up tight. The first time he grazed his waist I ain't trip, but he did it again so I knew he had somethin' heavy, Feel me?"

"Oh yeah?" Drako shook his head as his mouth twisted up into a gritt. "You mean to tell me that nigga came up in my shit packin'!"

"Sheeit!" Drip slurred his trademark curse. "I whatn't even trippin' over that 'cause if that wide-eyed fool woulda' reached for that pipe it woulda' been the last thing he remembered!"

Drako shook his head. He knew Drip was street savvy and short-fused, but a thinker just like him.

"We beefin' already or what?" Drip asked as he stepped over to the counter, pulled the pistol from his back and laid it on the countertop.

"I 'on do no beefin' and I ain't wit' none of that paper gangsta shit! If I speak the shit I'ma live it—simple."

"I know that, but I'm sayin' from the look of thangs I thought you'd be telling me somethin' I *don't* know. Swirl poppin' slick and—"

"Look, whatever fall between me and Wiz, just make sure you stay out of it!"

Drip gave a cool nod to Drako's unbroken glare. "Well, what about—"

"That nigga Swirl has gotten beside himself lately. I used to respect him as a man, but he just received a pass. If he step outta line again I'ma see 'bout 'im," Drako assured.

Drip nodded again, further letting Drako know he was with it.

A Life for A Life

"I ain't mean to catch up with my old camp this way or so fast, but fuck it, we here now. Reality Records 'bout to blow and ain't nothin' gone take our focus." Drako said, knowing it was gonna come down to this eventually. "I'ma play the back on this like we been talkin' 'bout, but I want you to keep these booths busy. And from this day forward I want you to tighten up on this door. Reality Records ain't no revolving door or no hangout spot for nobody. No exceptions! Let everybody know we puttin' in work around here. They come here to utilize studio time. We gone run a business first and foremost. See, at Red Rum they eat and shit from the same pot, that's why the whole world stay in his business."

Drako turned his head to see Diamond approaching. He turned back to Drip, lowering his tone. "I 'on see how they found us so fast."

"Man, are you serious?" Drip leaned his back against the bar and shrugged his thin shoulders. "You done signed two of the hardest rappers in Atlanta. Them young cats is proud! They tellin' er'body! Sheeit, and if we gone be out here tryin' to eat off the same plates as Gucci, them Brick Squad niggaz, and Jeezy, we best ta get behind 'em!" His revelation sank like water through dirt. Drako knew Drip was about getting paper!

"The door's open," Drako said confidently as he stepped away and led Diamond back up the stairs.

Drako sat back down in his chair shortly after he sent Diamond home. He picked up his remote control and replayed the tape once more. He watched the black Lincoln whip up to his building. Then he watched Wiz and Swirl enter his establishment. Drako was seething inside. Not necessarily at Wiz. He knew Wiz was often silly, but never stupid! He was mad at himself for not keeping the lid tighter for just a few more months or at least until he could pull off the lick he'd been priming for months in Connecticut.

He told himself with the cat now out of the bag it didn't matter. He felt he needed to disassociate himself from Red Rum for now. He needed his mind right to finally avenge his first and only true mentor, Toney Domacio. Wiz and Red Rum's negative attention wasn't about to stand in the way of his plans. He still felt sour as to Wiz only tossing him pennies, but now was no time to fiddle over his motives. In time, he and Wiz would cross paths again, but for the moment Drako couldn't shake the thought of the four hefty, Army duffel bags that contained three million unexpected dollars in cash thanks to Vinny Pazo. Pazo's blood was the only blood he'd gotten on his hands since he'd been released from prison. It felt good. Just like the money, the freedom and the thought of soon surpassing the ten million dollar goal he'd set his sights on.

Yep, Drako was feeling himself. He felt stability, not remorse, and he planned to keep it just that way. Turning off the three minute event after watching the Lincoln bolt from the screen, he set the remote on the desk and stood to his feet. His mind was made up: Anybody that crossed his path or tried to stop him would be the next blood spilled on his hands. He cut off his office lights on his way out, hoping that for Swirl's own sake he'd choose to stay in his place.

Group Discussion Questions

1. Do you think Wiz should've treated Drako any better financially when he got home?
2. Did you think Drako would've waited Wiz out a little while longer before reverting to his darker self?
3. Would you say Wiz's drug use is typical for a celebrity in his predicament or do you see it leading to disaster?
4. Do you think Myria could've told Wiz's business, and do you feel she was just like all the other groupies, except she'd just found her way in?
5. Do you think Wiz possibly should've treated Myria better from the start? And was Diamond wrong for even telling Wiz she'd seen Myria at Club 40/40?
6. What do you think of Drako and Diamond's relationship?
7. Do you think Damien gets enough credit?
8. Who do you think killed Fatt Katt?
9. Did Wiz deserve it when Drako finally blasted out on him and parted ways? And do you think Drako is capable of running a relevant label?

10. Do you believe Reality Records could possibly compete with Red Rum and would you like to see it?

11. Were you surprised at the way Drako carried out final redemption for Toney against Vinny Pazo?

12. What did you think of Drako's schemes?

13. What did you think of Wiz's scandals? And of the two, Wiz and Drako, do you consider one to be the good guy while the other is the bad? If so, who is who?

14. Which character or characters would you like to see more of in the sequel?

15. On a scale of one to ten, what did you think of this book?